Blood Will Out

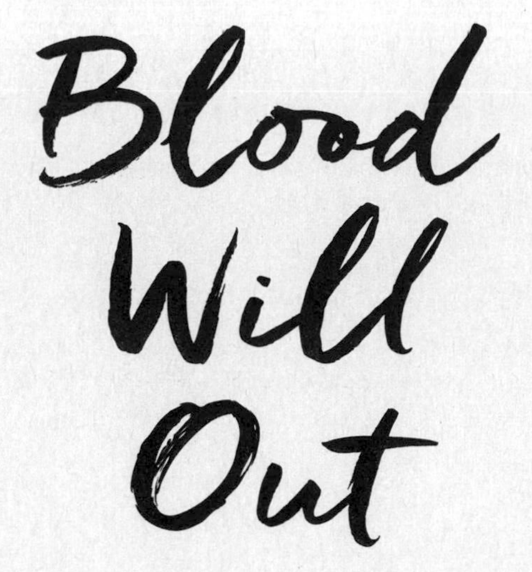

Jo Treggiari

PENGUIN TEEN

an imprint of Penguin Random House Canada Young Readers,
a Penguin Random House Company

First published 2018

1 2 3 4 5 6 7 8 9 10 (RRD)

Jacket design: Leah Springate
Jacket image: Moment Open/Getty Images

Manufactured in the U.S.A.

Library and Archives Canada Cataloguing in Publication

Treggiari, Jo, 1965-, author
Blood will out / Jo Treggiari.

Issued in print and electronic formats.
ISBN 978-0-7352-6295-9 (hardcover). —ISBN 978-0-7352-6296-6 (EPUB)

I. Title.

PS8639.R433B56 2018 jC813'.6 C2017-904341-2
C2017-904342-0

Library of Congress Control Number: 2017945564

www.penguinrandomhouse.ca

Penguin
Random House
PENGUIN TEEN CANADA

For my father, Arnaldo,
who encouraged me to read all the books.

You will be hollow.
We shall squeeze you empty, and then
We shall fill you with ourselves.

GEORGE ORWELL, *1984*

CHAPTER ONE

Someone seemed to be shouting her name from far away—"Ari Sullivan!" She sat up and was instantly rocked by a wave of nausea and an excruciating pain that knifed through her head. She clutched her stomach and moaned. She was breathing too rapidly and she felt as if she were about to pass out. She forced herself to take deep breaths, counting between inhalations. Gradually the pain subsided to a throbbing ache and she peered around in shock. She could see nothing. Was she blind? She blinked rapidly but there was no difference.

It was dead quiet except for the thrum of blood in her ears. Pushing herself onto her knees, she crawled forward a few inches. She could feel earth under her fingers, smell the dank rooty cool of it. She ran shaking hands over her body. She was wearing jeans, a T-shirt, a sweatshirt and running shoes. She ached all over but nothing seemed broken, except for maybe her head. There was a lump at the back of her skull, but the worst injury originated just above her ear. She probed that area and felt a mushy spot. How had she hit her temple? She moved her head gingerly, half-afraid it might detach from her neck. Another crescendo of pain battered at her and she breathed through her nose, imagining that she was at the cool blue bottom of the pool. Take stock, she told herself, remembering the guidelines she'd learned in lifeguarding. Assess the injury. Her neck muscles were stiff but her spine was all right; her fingers wiggled, and she could feel her toes even though she couldn't see them.

Okay, so she'd live, probably. Now, where was she? Her brain cried in agony, as if all her nerve endings were centered in her skull, but she struggled to focus. Clearly she'd had an accident, fallen down the stairs to the cellar. But not her cellar, she decided, trying to pin down the muddied swirl of her thoughts. Her cellar was concrete-floored and brightly lit and smelled of laundry detergent and fabric softener. Not rotted leaves and swamp water. She was somewhere unknown.

"Mom, Dad?" she breathed, as if the sound of her voice might summon something terrible from the pitch black. All the horror movies she and Lynn had giggled over came back to her in a flood.

The darkness pressed down, a physical weight as if she were pinned under two tons of water. She held her eyelids open with her fingers and still there was nothing—not a flicker of light. This must be what it felt like to be buried alive. And with that thought, it seemed suddenly as if there were not enough air. She gulped, choked, desperate to fill her lungs, and felt the hysteria swell until it burst from her.

"Help! Help! Please!" Over and over until, propelled by rising panic, she was on her feet, unsteady and swaying, her voice ripping out of her throat. "Anyone!"

CHAPTER TWO

I am remembering the very first time. I am nine. My eyes follow Ma Cosloy's finger from the pigs to the knife as she tells me, "You tend to them. You tend to this too." Her work-rough hands are on her wide hips. She looks ten feet tall and not a hair straggles from the tight bun she wears from early morning to night. If I were to sketch her, it would be as something carved from granite, not flesh. She is unyielding. One couldn't call her expression kind, but it is not without compassion. Even so, I wouldn't dream of arguing.

The chosen piglet comes snuffling around my feet. He knows me. I bottle-raised him and his siblings and now, at near three months, he is the biggest. His rubbery snout prods, greedy and insistent. He is looking for acorns in my pockets. "None today, Ferdinand," I murmur, fondling his soft, pink ears, looking into his bright, curious eyes with their white lashes. Pigs are only slightly less intelligent than dolphins and apes. No one wants to hear that though, because we like to eat bacon so much. I named him after the gentle bull in the storybook: the one who wouldn't fight even when provoked. I scratch along his spine, feeling the stiff hairs. He leans and pushes against my side, his trotters scrabbling in the hay. I gather him up in my arms. He is a good weight but not impossible for me to lift for a short time. His whiskers brush my cheek in wet kisses. His breath smells sweet from the breakfast of hot bran mash and potato peelings he's just had. I put him down again and he frisks, puppy-like.

He trusts me and wants to be near. Even when I move over to the other end of the barn, with the big iron pot full of water bubbling over the fire pit, the knotted ropes and pulleys hanging from the blackened rafters like a simplified web, the razor-sharp knife lying ready on the table. Old stains spatter the floor; bluebottle flies buzz. He follows me there, making those grunting sounds that mean pure happiness. Smart as he is, he has no idea what is coming until he is hoisted into the air by his hind legs, and by then it is too late.

Later, when I have been scoured clean with the bristle brush and a bar of Ma Cosloy's gritty rosemary soap, which never lathers no matter how much you try, and my skin is sore and tingling, and I am alone again in the shed, I sit with my knees tucked close to my chest. My heart gallops. Ferdinand's squeals still ring in my ears; his blood is a cold slick of metal in my throat. The bath is an iron pot, similar to the one in the barn, and at first the water was scalding but now it has cooled, though it is still warmer than the frigid air around. I can see my breath and the small window is beaded with moisture, and my fingers and toes have pruned, but still I sit in the dirty water replaying it all in my mind. I barely recognize the emotion rushing through me. Exhilaration? Excitement?

My best shoes are cleaned and polished; my new clothes are folded neatly on the bench next to the rough towel. Ma Cosloy only finished sewing them last night. I know they will fit well, but the seams will scratch and the fresh-dyed cloth will feel stiff against my neck. My old clothes have been taken away to be soaked and scrubbed with lye, though I think the stains will never come out. I think about the colors I have just seen. So vivid and unlike the browns and grays and solemn blacks I am usually surrounded by, those I am clothed in.

It's as if Ma and Pa Cosloy and I live in an old photograph—monochromatic and yellowed, the house and barn timbers bleached by the sun, and the earth stripped of nutrients and turned to ashy dust. On occasion I look at my adoptive parents and wonder if their hearts are as shriveled and hard as the dry old potatoes I find sometimes after the fields have been plowed. My heart, though, feels as if it is swelling—plump, juicy, like a split ripe plum. It's as if I was blind before and now the colors are so bright in my mind that they hurt my eyes and fill my entire rib cage with wonder. That was life that spilled thickly over my hands. I can still smell it on me: rich as beef broth.

I think of a line from my favorite tale, "Black as Ebony, White as Snow, Red as Blood," and I trace an outline of Ferdinand on the glass, his body limp, his neck articulated, the new lines I made with the knife. I can't wait to capture it in my sketchbook.

CHAPTER THREE

"Help," she yelled, over and over again. "Someone? Please, help me!"

She blinked hard against tears, but they splashed forth as she continued to shout. And then somewhere along the way the words turned to screams until her throat was raw and her ribs hurt and her head threatened to explode into a thousand shards. Blackness washed over her as if she'd taken a dive into a vat of ink, and then nothing.

Minutes? Seconds? Hours? Ari had no idea how long she'd been passed out, but she came to still curled up on the dirt, arms hugged around her cramped body. The truth crept like cold snow into her heart: no one could hear her.

And no one—not her mom or her dad or Lynn or Coach—was coming.

Where was she? Her mind was dull. She couldn't think past the pain pulsing near her right eye. Putting her fingers to her head, she investigated the pulp of matted hair and the congealed mass of blood. It made her fingers tacky, and the metallic tang caused her stomach to heave again.

Was she concussed? Or worse? A traumatic head wound?

Was that why she was unable to see? She felt for her tiger's-eye bracelet, the beads warm from her body heat. Tiger's eye for bravery. Lynn had one too, and Ari almost seemed to hear her friend's voice. *For fuck's sake, grow a pair, sweetie!* Which was basically what she'd said when Ari had hemmed and hawed about trying out for first string on the swim team. And you know what? She'd made it. So . . .

When they were young, before they'd conceived of the signal-flag-out-the-window idea, she and Lynn had been convinced they could communicate telepathically. They felt the same way about so many things—from Oreos to Iceland to *The Little Prince*—that they often finished each other's sentences.

Come find me, Lynn, she prayed.

The tears were gone, sucked up by the desperation that gripped her now. What if she were never found? Where could she be? How had she gotten here?

Think, Ari.

Okay, start with what you know. She took a deep, calming breath. She knew her name. "Ariadne Isabel Sullivan," she said into the black. *What else?* "Seventeen years old, five foot seven inches tall. 132 Fox Street, Dempsey Hollow, 453-8678. Best friends with Lynn Lubnick. Likes swimming, mushroom pizza and glitter nail polish. Dislikes centipedes, turnips and mean people." Her voice sounded so thin, so weak. She straightened her spine and spoke louder. "Absolutely hates what chlorine does to my hair."

She reached into her back pocket. No phone. Where the hell was her phone? Had it slipped out when she fell? She patted the ground all around her but found nothing. She felt the feathery slither of a many-legged insect as it scuttled over her hand. Centipedes liked damp, dark places. She'd seen one crawl out of the basement sink drain once. She leapt to her feet but lost her balance as another wave of dizziness assailed her. *Fuck fuck fuck!* Crashing forward, she connected with something solid. Pressing her hands and then her forehead against the rough, slimy coldness until the white flecks stopped their frenzied dance before her eyes, Ari felt her head clear a little. The surface felt like a wall and was slightly curved under her palms. She detected the indentation of bricks. She tried to hook her fingers in but they slid free; no way to climb, then. She stood on her tiptoes and stretched her hands up; it extended beyond her reach. She crouched down and felt along the bottom until she touched the gritty soil. There was no door or opening. A bitter draft blew from somewhere up above, carrying the autumn scent of decaying leaves. She crumbled a pinch of dirt between her fingers. It was slightly damp, though whether from rain or ground moisture she didn't know.

She realized she could just make out the shadowy shape of her limbs. She placed her palm against the wall and walked. It was circular. She pushed off from it and inched forward, hands held defensively in front of her, counting steps under her breath. Her shoes were almost silent on the hard-packed earth. Eight paces toe to heel, roughly eight or nine feet in diameter, before she hit the bricks on the other side. Walls surrounding her, stretching up who knew how high. A childhood memory sparked. Summer in the country. Her grandmother warning her to "stay away from the cistern where the old barn used to be. The cover is all rotted away." She hadn't listened of course, but spent hours on her tummy throwing rocks and sticks into the deep water. And once there had been a desperate rat swimming around and around in circles, unable to find a way out. A cistern. Like a big well buried below ground. She was at the bottom of a big fucking well! She made a circuit, clawing at the bricks, feeling like the rat. Perhaps there was a ladder bolted to the side? A rope with a bucket?

A flicker of hope rose in her and was extinguished just as quickly. No escape. The rat had just stopped swimming at some point, even though Ari had thrown down the biggest chunk of wood she could find, thinking it could use it as a raft. It had just given up.

She turned around and sank down on her butt as her legs gave way beneath her. Turning her face up, she squinted, trying to see to the top of the wall, but it seemed miles away and still too dark. No silhouettes of trees, no stars. A well with a cover over it, then.

She yelled again, caught up in the terror, even knowing it was no use. Cisterns weren't located in the middle of town. They were on private land, out on the country back roads where town water couldn't be piped in, far from anywhere.

How had she even gotten here? Had she driven herself in her dad's VW? Had she come with someone else who even now might be going for help? Lynn? Lynn didn't have a car either but maybe. . . . She grabbed onto that slim hope and tried to calm herself.

The pitch blackness continued to weigh down on her like some tangible thing occupying all the space. Was enough air getting in? Her brain was a lump of unresponsive flesh. It was hard to follow the broken trail of her thoughts.

"The well cover is on," she said out loud. Saying the words helped her think. It reminded her of struggling her way through algebra with Lynn. "It's a series of logical steps," Lynn would say. "You go from here to here until you get to the answer."

"Therefore, someone must have placed it there." She squinted upward again.

Someone *is coming back for me.*

But who? She saw a figure, silhouetted, face in shadow, a mouth moving with words she could no longer recall. The last thing she remembered was—*what*? Her brain fuzzed, the headache back again, pounding with a furious intensity.

Big blocks of time seemed to be missing.

Shopping. She remembered shopping. She tried to hold on to the thought as she felt her consciousness rush in and out, scrambling for the fleeting image of clothing racks, and Lynn's familiar smirk. She hooked into the memory, desperate.

It was Friday, after school, and they had been looking for dresses for the big fall dance at the end of October.

"What do you think?" Lynn asked, holding up a short, tight red number with tiers of net flounces, and spaghetti straps.

"Sure, if you want to look like an eighties reject."

"Like early New York, Madonna cool? Or Kajagoogoo groupie?"

Ari whistled a few notes of "Too Shy."

Lynn's face fell. "Really, poppet?"

Ari shrugged.

They'd recently scored a crate of record albums from the Goodwill junk shop. All eighties New Wave, pretty-boy bands with bleached-out hair and tons of eyeliner. Luckily Ari's dad was a hoarder and still owned a turntable and a pair of gigantic speakers. It was funny how big all the electronics were back then; those boat-like boom boxes, the headphones that covered half your head.

Lynn put the dress back, an exaggerated pout on her lips.

Ari skimmed along the next row, passing pastel dress after pastel dress. Mint green seemed very unpopular, judging by the number left on the rack. She sighed. "Movie? Cherry licorice? My treat."

Lynn didn't even look up. "We're on a mission. Victory or death!"

"Does it matter? Really? In the bigger scope of things?"

"Of course it does. It's the little things that count the most. Like a rite of passage."

"I'd rather be spending the night in a haunted house, or hunting a polar bear with a fork," Ari grumbled. "And my feet are killing me."

"That's because you have no arch support in those cute flats. And you can't kill a polar bear with a fork. You're a girl, for Pete's sake. You're supposed to live for shopping."

"I'm not that kind of girl."

"Oh really? What kind of girl are you then?"

"The boring kind who's boring."

Lynn shushed her, intent on something in her hand.

"This," she said on a slow exhalation, holding up a draped bodice, one-shouldered, off-white dress with a pearly sheen to the material and a dramatic slit up the side.

"You'll have to wear some super high heels with it," Ari said. Lynn was curvy but petite. "Or you'll look like a scoop of whipped cream." She swallowed a snort of laughter.

"Not for me, twit, for you."

Ari opened her mouth to argue but Lynn cut her off. "Remember the jeans? You thought they'd make you look doughy."

"Dowdy."

"Same difference."

"Not really. Are you saying they *did* make me look dowdy?"

Lynn made an exasperated noise. "No. What I am saying is, aren't you glad you listened to me?"

Ari nodded. They *had* looked pretty good: not too flared, not too straight, and they'd done wonders for her non-ass. She'd picked up a gorgeous linen blouse with delicate lace panels and cap sleeves to go with them. Her arms, toned from swimming, were about the only part of her body she liked. Well, her upper arms. Her lower arms were too downy with hair.

"It looks so . . . grown-up," she said.

"Hello, we're seventeen. In some cultures we'd be considered spinsters already."

"Oh yes, where'd you read that? Wikipedia?"

"Wikipedia rules, ducks. You'll look smashing in it." Kajagoogoo and the rest of the British New Wave invasion had given Lynn a thirst for British slang.

"I—" Ari began and then couldn't go on. She was no match for Lynn's energy when it came to shopping, or her skill in arguing. They'd already been to all six of Dempsey Hollow's upper-tier stores, and the so-called secondhand alley, and now they were on to what Lynn had named Attack Phase II. It was easier just to give in.

They walked toward the changing rooms, Ari examining

the dress more closely and trying to figure out what kind of material it was made of. *Silk?* she wondered, walking into the back of Lynn, who had stopped abruptly.

"Well, lookee lookee," said a smarmy voice. "Teen dykes on a shopping spree."

"What the hell are you doing here?" Lynn said. "Following us again?"

She turned to face Ari, her lips pressed into a thin line, and grabbed her by the arm.

"Let's go this way."

They moved to the left, slipping between the narrow racks of clothing. Jack Rourke cut across and stood in the middle of the aisle with his arms folded over his wide chest. He eyed Ari's dress. "So you're the woman," he said with exaggerated emphasis, "which means that you"—he moved toward Lynn—"must be the man." His voice dropped in register. "Do you feel like a man, Lubnick? Under those clothes do you look like a man?" He rubbed his hand suggestively over his crotch. "Want me to break you in? She can watch."

"Go away, Jack," Ari said, wishing her voice sounded more assertive.

Jack flicked his flat eyes over her briefly and then lasered in on Lynn again.

"You don't know what you're missing."

Ari could feel the anger shimmering off Lynn. Jack Rourke constantly dropped innuendos. "For fuck's sake, Jack. Do you have to be such a pig?" Lynn snapped.

He stared at her for a moment, guffawed, and then started squealing. The sound followed them all the way to the dressing room.

"I hate that guy," Lynn said. "If I could get away with it, I'd set fire to his car. Stupid entitled wanker."

Ari pressed her arm.

"I'm okay, I'm okay. I just get so sick of it." She forced a smile. "C'mon, forget that asswipe and his microscopic penis. Let's see gorgeous you in that fabulous dress."

Ari submitted to being hustled into an available cubicle. Lynn pushed her toward the chair, twitched the curtain closed behind her and stood with her arms crossed over her chest.

"Strip."

"Aren't you going to try anything on?"

"I'm going back for that tight kimono deal."

Ari tried to remember which one that was exactly. Lynn had modeled dozens, most of them with accessories, bags and shoes. *Go big or go home* was one of her mantras.

"The turquoise in the vintage shop?" She kicked off her flats and then slipped out of her shorts and T-shirt, wishing she'd put on something other than her grimy sports bra today. She should have remembered these oh-so-attractive walls of mirrors, which showed side and back views as well as front, all bathed in lovely fluorescent lighting. They brought out all the shades of dingy yellow in her sagging white cotton underwear. She folded her clothes carefully and put them on the chair, stalling for time.

"It was teal," said Lynn, snapping her fingers to hurry Ari along. The vibrant color had been spectacular against Lynn's creamy skin and dark hair. And the wrap bodice had accentuated her boobs.

"It won't fit," Ari muttered, more to herself than to Lynn. She was crap at picking out the right clothes for her body, and was therefore always disappointed. "Or if it does it'll look like a potato sack."

"I picked it out, remember?" Lynn said.

"It doesn't matter. My shoulders are too broad, my calves are too muscular." She broke off, having caught sight of the back of her head. The humidity was doing something outrageous to her split ends. She smoothed them down and then reached for the dress.

"Five . . . four . . . three . . . two . . . ," Lynn counted down. Ari knew she was perfectly capable of throwing open the curtain so that everyone would see Ari standing there in her underwear.

The material was silky under her fingers—without that stiff polyester feel that set her teeth on edge—but it didn't look like lingerie. This was probably way out of her price range. She tried to read the tag and became aware of Lynn's tapping foot. Her friend was practically vibrating with impatience.

"I could move with even more agonizing slowness," Ari remarked.

"I could loudly comment on that saggy bra of yours. Then the sales lady will come in with her tape measure and insist on measuring you in front of everyone and their mother."

"That's so mean. You know how scarred I was by that experience."

"I survived it."

"That's because she let everyone within a two-mile radius know that you are a perfect C cup. Not"—she dropped her voice—"barely a B. She said I had a 'measly bust-line.'"

"You're still growing. Just trust me."

Sighing, Ari tugged the dress over her head. The material rustled as it fell toward the floor, ending just below her anklebone. In the mirror behind her she saw Lynn's eyes widen, and then her friend jumped up and down, clapping her hands. "I knew it!" She grabbed Ari's thick reddish-brown hair and gave it a quick twist, holding it against the back of Ari's head with one hand and achieving a casual-though-elegant style that Ari had never mastered. Ari turned slowly, looking at every angle. Somehow the dress, with its draped neckline, narrowed her shoulders and gave her the illusion of a waist. No, not just a waist—a figure with hips and everything. It hung in soft folds, hugging the slight curves of her body, shimmering with a pearly light that brought out the tawny color of her skin and added depth to her pale green eyes.

"Oh," Ari said.

"Yes, 'oh' and 'wow' and 'I told you so.' I understand women's bodies." She sounded so smug, Ari choked on a giggle.

"You can borrow those strappy red satin shoes I have," Lynn continued, batting away Ari's hand as she once again tried to see the price tag. "So that'll save you a wodge of money."

"Wodge? You going to keep that up?"

"As long as I possibly can, love."

"Listen, I know I can't afford it, so this is torture," Ari said. She'd scrounged and saved her tips from the café and had done extra yard work around the neighborhood to augment the allowance her parents gave her, but still—there was no way. "And it's not like I'm wearing it for anyone."

"Yes, you are going with me, and, yes, I appreciate it since the lack of teen lesbians in this town is outrageous. But don't pretend that you're not going to be staring at Stroud Bellows the whole time, hoping and praying . . ."

Ari tried to think of a snappy rejoinder. Stroud Bellows was new to the school, but given his natural gifts and abilities, he had shot straight to the top of the social ladder. He was on the swim team and played water polo and had the most amazing upper body, just the right amount of chest hair, and dimples. He smelled like the pool, which, as it turned out, worked like an aphrodisiac on Ari. Her eyes were continuously drawn to him even when she was supposed to be practicing her strokes. *Inhale, stroke, Stroud; stroke, exhale, Stroud.* He had seriously messed up her rhythm to the point that Coach Jenkins had asked her what the hell was going on and whether it was "a female thing." Coach never spoke below a shout, so pretty much everyone in school had heard. Ari had sunk beneath the surface until the cold water cooled her cheeks and then crept the walk of shame all the way back to the changing rooms. The thing with Stroud was entering its seventh month, having lasted all through the summer, and had she said anything to him besides, "You dropped your towel," in a voice too mouse-like to be audible? No, she had not.

"He just bettered his time in the butterfly," Ari said.

"Yup, he's one stellar dude, all right." Lynn's voice positively oozed sarcasm. Ari raised her eyebrows, but her friend had turned away.

"Anyhow, why don't you give him something to look at besides you in that drab Speedo?" Lynn said, kneeling to flare the skirt of the dress out to check the hem length and peeping up at her with a serious expression in her eyes.

"I'm going with *you*," Ari said firmly. It would fuel the lesbian-duo rumors but she didn't care. She would do this one thing even if deep down inside she harboured the wish that Stroud would ask her to be his date.

Lynn sat back on her heels.

"Yeah, but I don't think I'm going to give you the action you're looking for. And, by the way, ditto. I just want to dance and make out with a cute girl who likes me. Is that too much to ask?"

"Maybe there'll be some kids from Center and United."

Their high school, Parkview, was small, so dances were open to other students from the surrounding areas.

"Have you heard of a sudden influx of gay kids?" Lynn got up and gripped her arm in mock excitement. "Did I miss an explosive article in the *Bulletin*?"

The *Bulletin* was the local newspaper Ari's father edited.

"Sorry." Reaching out to hug Lynn, she said, "If I was ever going to crush on a girl, it would be you."

"That's sweet, ducks. And also what all the straight girls say. But none of you ever put out." She softened the words with a hug back. For a moment they stood together looking at their reflections in the mirror. Ari could still see the two little kids they'd been. She half-wished they'd never had to grow up. Everything felt complicated, and she yearned for simple.

"Does it suck so bad?" she asked, pushing the dark curls off Lynn's face.

"I feel like I'm stuck in a box with a black-and-yellow caution label on the outside. 'The Lesbian.' Next September can't come fast enough for me. I'll finally be treated like an adult. An individual."

Ari moved from side to side listening to the swish of material against her legs. She didn't share Lynn's excitement for college. Lynn had six younger brothers and sisters and lived in a small house with her mother, who also happened to be their high school principal; she couldn't wait to break out. To Ari, the Hollow was familiar and comfortable. She knew who she was here: squarely in the middle, academically and athletically. Coach and her parents might as well have been different species, but one point they agreed on was that the only thing holding her back was herself. "Reach, goddammit—be a shark, not a tadpole!" was how Coach so eloquently put it. Her parents just wanted her to dream bigger. "The Hollow will always be here for you, Ari. It doesn't change," her mother said. "It's not as if you can't come back."

But Ari didn't want to come back, because she didn't want to leave.

Next year, Stroud was probably going to be playing water polo at the tiny local community college. It was stupid to not be able to see further into her future than some boy who had never even looked at her apart from checking out her form during laps, but she couldn't help it.

Was she stuck in a box? She didn't believe so. It felt like a nest, safe and warm and lined with soft feathers, but the idea of Lynn thinking less of her was unbearable.

"I want to make all my own mistakes," Lynn said. "Hundreds of them!"

She smiled, but then caught sight of Ari's face in the mirror. Her beautifully thick eyebrows rose.

"Nothing," Ari said, avoiding Lynn's gaze. With a groan she continued, trying to inject some backbone into her voice. "It's not that I'm scared or anything. I just want . . ."

How to word it? *Familiarity* made her sound like the most boring person on earth. What was that expression? Familiarity breeds contempt? Other synonyms? The *expected*. *Routine*.

Rote. Rut. Oh god! It was just like when she'd tried to explain why she preferred swimming in a pool to open water. Because there, sitting at the bottom, looking up at the swimmers above and the four walls around her, she felt completely in her element, in control of everything from her breathing to her calm, collected thoughts. Finally she said, "Anything could happen out there."

"Exactly." Lynn did a little pirouette. "Anything. Everything! God, the thought of it makes me feel as if I have never been able to take a deep breath." She smoothed her hands over her ribs. "As if I've been trapped inside myself. Don't you feel like that?"

"No. But I like it here, remember?" It was hard not to be transported by Lynn's enthusiasm. She felt the corners of her mouth turn up.

"Fair enough. So—two-point-four kids, two-car garage, Stroud in the master bedroom?" She paused and looked closely at Ari. "My god, you're obsessed. You should see your face right now."

Ari stopped smiling. "What's your deal with him? He's never done anything to you, has he?"

"Not directly. He's one of those people who gets other people to be mean for him, like his good buddy Jack Rourke out there. And he pretends to be less smart than he is. Why would someone do that?"

"No. That's not him." Ari thought of his eyes. They sparkled like pool water. They had to be a window to a soul that was deep and pristine.

"Yes, yes it is. Seriously, is that all you want?"

"Not *all* I want. . . . Swimming, college, I can do that stuff here."

"But there's so much more. Things you haven't even imagined yet. Roads you haven't taken. People who will completely change your world."

Ari stared at her reflection. Her gooseberry eyes looked back at her, all watery and without spark, as usual. She thought about the animation in every line of Lynn's face, the way she carried herself as if she were six foot three as opposed to five foot three, and straightened her shoulders out of their customary slump. Maybe if she looked the part, she could act the part.

ɞ

Ari drifted in and out of consciousness, the blood singing loud in her ears, agony worming around her body. Half her world was made up of the dark unknown, the other half a series of bright snapshots awash in artificial light: Lynn's face; the changing room; storefronts; people, fuzzy and indistinct. With an effort, she struggled to think. Her head hurt so badly, the dizziness was so intense, that she felt trapped in a chaos of thoughts and images, like a fever dream. Slowly her prefrontal lobe threaded the memories together. What had happened next?

She'd bought the dress, though the number on the cash register window had made her gasp. Lynn's hand on her arm had gripped and then tightened until Ari released her death hold on her dad's credit card and handed it to the cashier. It would take at least two more months of extra jobs to pay her father back.

"Take a walk on the wild side," Lynn said.

Afterward, they'd returned to the vintage shop, where Lynn found an only slightly flea-bitten antique fur muff to go with the teal kimono dress.

"Look, it's granny's dachshund," she said, making it leap at Ari's giggling face, and then they'd bought ice cream cones —raspberry for her and chocolate-chunk hazelnut for Lynn— and ambled in the direction of home, reveling in the end-of-September smell of bonfires and the tiny maelstroms of falling leaves, talking about the importance of accessories.

Autumn was Lynn's favorite season. She couldn't pass a heap of leaves without jumping in it. It was right at the end of the tourist crush and residents were tidying up their yards, the summer people locking up for the winter. They'd spotted a mountainous pile just across the road on the back lawn of the big hotel and run toward it, hands linked.

The squeal of brakes was earsplitting. A camouflage-painted pickup truck swerved, fishtailing over the road as the driver spun the wheel and plowed into a metal garbage can, coming to a screeching stop in a flurry of broken glass and flying trash.

A great hulking shape wearing green khakis hurled itself from the truck's cab. Lynn and Ari skipped backward to the sidewalk. Ari almost tripped on the curb.

"Oh shit," she said. "Sourmash." So called because he distilled his own whiskey.

"What the hell do you think you're doing?" Sorkin Sigurson yelled. He pointed a filthy finger at the traffic lights. "That light was red, you stupid bitches."

Ari felt Lynn tense up beside her. She threw her arm out to hold her friend back and watched as her pink scoop of ice cream toppled and fell.

"Fucking redneck alcoholic hillbilly meth-head freak," Lynn muttered, foregoing her nouveau British slang. "How dare he call *us* stupid!"

"Just keep walking," said Ari, but Sorkin was blocking their path. He looked back at his truck, idling at an angle half on the sidewalk, at the road now littered with refuse and glittering chunks of glass.

"My headlights!" he roared, running over to check the front end. "My freaking BMW adaptive frigging headlights!" His swarthy face had turned purple, his eyes bulged. "Twenty-five hundred apiece," he moaned. "Rocky, you're my witness, right? These bitches ran out in front of me."

Ari's heart dropped like a stone.

Until then, she hadn't noticed the other man in the truck, even though he was only a few feet away. He was slumped low in the seat, one arm dangling from the open window, his greasy head lolling. Sourmash's bellow made him jerk like a marionette and then shrink down even further.

"Rocky, get your sorry ass out here and help me wrangle these girls!"

Ari had seen Rocky around, a skinny, shaky man who followed Sourmash like a whipped dog. He shook his head and mumbled something incomprehensible. Ari could see his Adam's apple going up and down like an elevator, and he picked a crusty sore on his lip. Drunk or high, she thought.

"I'll fucking get you, you *kusser*!" Sourmash yelled, pounding on the hood of the truck. From the venom in his voice, Ari guessed that was some kind of Scandinavian insult. She was glad she didn't understand it.

Lynn shook with anger. "I told Mom she should have let me order the pepper spray," she said. "I'd use the whole can on him."

His head whipped around and he fixed them both with a beady eye. And then he was suddenly within arm's length.

Gunk was spattered all over his shirt and pants. His fingernails were caked with something black and he smelled really bad, as if he'd been sleeping outside all week.

"I'll report you to the cops. I'll sue your parents. It was red. You were walking on red," he yelled.

"It was about to change," Ari blurted out. "You weren't even near the intersection and you were speeding." *Shit, what's wrong with me!* She pressed her lips shut.

Sourmash made a sound like a wounded bull and some spit flew out of his mouth.

"Cell phone?" Lynn said quietly.

"Recharging at home. Yours?"

"Nelly hid it 'cause Mom won't get her one."

"Shit."

"You! Girl!" With horror, Ari saw that Sourmash was pointing a stubby forefinger at her. "How much do you have in your purse?"

"Not five thousand dollars," she said, staring at his hands. They were huge. She thought one of them could encapsulate her head, or wrap all the way around her throat and break her neck like a pencil.

"I'll take what you've got," he snarled. "You can owe me the rest."

She was frozen in place, skewered by his finger like a bug mounted on a board. Out of the corner of her eye she saw Lynn edge sideways a few inches, bristling with an energy that meant she was seconds away from breaking into a full-on panicked run.

Good plan, but Ari couldn't will her legs to move.

Lynn bolted.

She stopped a dozen yards past the truck and looked back. Ari had no trouble reading her lips. "Ari! What the f—"

Ari shook her head; still her feet remained glued to the ground, as if she were in a nightmare. The air grew thick while Sourmash circled around her like a shark.

"Give me that!" he roared, grabbing at her shopping bag. "You owe me." She tried to hold on to it but he ripped it loose, inspected the contents with a sneer and then tossed it in the back of the truck. Could she elude him? Grab the dress and run? It was just out of reach. Three hundred dollars down the drain. Rocky was apparently passed out with his trucker cap pulled down over half his face. Not that he'd be any kind of help.

Suddenly, she was possessed by a white-hot fury. How dare he do this? How dare he take from her?

Go for the eyes—and the balls—if he comes any nearer. She was wearing soft, broken-in ballet flats with no toe protection. Could she get her keys out of her purse before he was on her? Use them as a weapon? She fumbled at the clasp with stiff fingers.

"Ari, I'm calling the police," Lynn yelled. "The po-lice!"

"What are you going to do about my lights?" Sourmash demanded, ignoring Lynn, who was pretending she had a cell phone. His finger stabbed at her again, and Ari jerked back and dodged to the left, finally shocked out of immobility. She got the truck between them, feeling instantly safer. She could evade him all day if she had to. Taking the opportunity, she hooked the shopping bag with one finger, hitching it over her shoulder.

A tarp draped on top of a hulking mass in the back lifted in a gust of wind and slipped to the side. Staring back at her was the bulbous eye of a deer, the head hewn from the body. Its skin had been removed in a neat segment from the neck down to the hooves, and the belly cavity was split wide open. Broken ribs gleamed like the bleached planks of an old boat, and there was a warm, rich smell that reminded her of raw hamburger. Her stomach churned. And then a hand clamped tight on her arm. She jumped, feeling her stomach ricochet into her throat.

"Ari," Lynn yelled in her ear. "Run, goddammit!"

CHAPTER FOUR

At first I couldn't see the path, but now it is clear to me when the transformation began. It began the first time I held a knife and knew it was for cutting.

I'm not a fan of all that psychological Freudian mumbo jumbo: blaming my parents; blaming my trouble with toilet training; blaming the world. Sure, my teenage mother had some drug and alcohol problems and some issues with anger, and Ma and Pa Cosloy weren't ones for hugging and kissing, but they clothed me, they fed me, they sheltered me.

I can't picture my birth mother, though I was told we share the same intense expression, the same bold eyes, which first pierce and then slide away when our gaze is met. Shifty-eyed, Pa Cosloy used to say. I was also told that when I was brought to the hospital, not yet five years old, deep-bruised and suffering from a dislocated arm and various broken bones, I did not go home again. I went straight into care and then one year later to the Cosloys for fostering. Not so much because they longed for a child but because they needed an extra pair of hands around the farm. My mother went to jail.

These people do not get the blame.

Nor do they get the credit for what I am becoming now.

I practiced on the chickens, wanting to see how all their parts fit together. They weren't as smart as Ferdinand but there were lots of them. It was simple enough at first to blame foxes when Pa or Ma found a hen's head in the trough or a clutch of feathers in the yard. I was young though, and I didn't have the smarts to hide my tracks for long, not then. It didn't occur to me there was anything wrong with it. It is the way of the world. The dragon devours the maiden; the knight kills the dragon. The wolf eats the pigs; the woodcutter slays the wolf.

The chickens were disappointing anyway. They didn't fight. They went limp almost as soon as I picked them up, squawking in a way that begged me to wring their necks, and their fluid was thin and watery, drying to mud-brown. Nor was there enough of it. I wanted something that would stain a surface with dull crimson, like the bull's blood they used to mix into linseed oil and paint the barns with. Unfortunately, we had no cows.

I was beaten for it, of course, but I didn't care. I could cast my mind out from my body like a lure from an unspooling fishing line, think of other things, fixate on a burst of color beyond the gray shed or the rough bark of the stump I leaned over with my pants down around my ankles.

Pa had a system to his beatings. First being, he sent me out to cut a willow or birch stick.

"Bring me back one about yay big," he'd say, pointing to his thumb, two inches thick, "and make sure it's got plenty of spring in it." That's where they got the phrase "rule of thumb," did you know? Used to be law a man couldn't beat his wife or children with a stick that was thicker than his own thumb.

Pa methodically counted out twenty-four lashes of the stick; three blows for each dead hen. I could feel the trickles running down my calves. My buttocks throbbed with a pulse like a heart. Pa waited for me to haul up my pants and gestured that I sit down. It was uncomfortable *to do so but I didn't question him and I managed not to wince as my weight settled into the deep cuts cross-hatched on my skin. I watched him fill his pipe, the slow, measured motions of his hands as he tapped out the golden flakes of tobacco, and waited for him to speak.*

There were no questions about my well-being, no concern. I had done a bad thing; he had meted out punishment; justice had been served. That was the way his world ran.

He understood me not at all. Bodily pain was nothing to me. By that point I had been beaten many, many times. Being locked in the slaughter shed for four nights without food or blankets and only the pig water trough to drink from was nothing. I was made of nothing. I observed; I considered; I went to the dark, safe place in my head and I burrowed there like an animal.

"I thought you understood. I can't abide waste," Pa said. "Your Ma neither."

The chickens were going to be killed anyway, I thought. Who cared when?

I waited. Usually once I'd had my beating, the matter was done and not spoken of again. We might go to church twice that Sunday if it was necessary; I might have to empty the outhouse buckets, haul a ton of clean earth and lime, or clear rocks from the south field until my muscles were so weary I couldn't hold a fork. But he clearly had more to say. I looked at his fingers, the hard yellow calluses like cheese rinds, the white marks from squeezing the whipping stick so tightly. My fate lay in those broad hands with thick black hair matting at the wrists. I tried to predict my future. I was like a baby bird resting on his palm. Would he let me go or would he close his fingers around me and crush my fragile bones?

"Go in the shed there and fetch me the gun on the wall," Pa said, rubbing his hand over the top of his balding head and then replacing his cap.

I admit that a flicker of fear, sharp yet thrilling, ran through me, but I did as he asked. The shed held stacked logs, tarpaulins and small garden tools, broken furniture in need of fixing, traps for winter hunting and, set on hooks above a small window, a rifle. I lifted it down carefully—Pa used to say an unloaded gun was as good as no gun at all—and brought it to him.

"This was my first firearm," he said. "Given to me when I was about your age." He looked directly at me, which was rare. "Had more sense than you do." His eyes fluttered away again as if he couldn't bear the sight. "This here's the safety."

He popped the cartridge out and showed me the bullets arranged like small golden eggs inside. "You've got a round of five in here." He clicked it back in and drew the bolt back. "Safety's still on," he said, thumbing it. I nodded to show I understood. Hot excitement flooded my veins. He handed me a heavy box with more bullets and I tucked them into my pocket.

"You can shoot anything wild." His eyes found mine again and I forced myself to meet his gaze, though I hated being looked at. "Try to kill it with one, maybe two shots. Keep your gun clean and dry; come to me when you need more ammunition."

And then he handed it over.

I had never felt such power.

CHAPTER FIVE

Forty-seven times she'd stumbled around the circumference of the cistern, using a rough, wet, crumbling patch on the wall to mark the beginning of her route. Although her legs were trembling, she couldn't stop herself from moving. Sitting down felt like giving up; walking and counting gave her sluggish brain something to focus on. Plus, she hoped it meant she wouldn't pass out again; that had seemed too much like drowning. Twenty-five toe-to-heel paces from start to finish. Roughly twenty-five feet in circumference. It felt smaller, cramped, this round space, as if the walls were pushing in, as if sooner or later she would be crushed between the bricks. Forty-seven times twenty-five was what? She couldn't begin to remember how to do multiplication.

"And who the fuck cares anyway, Ari!" she yelled, kicking aside the flurry of dead leaves in her path. She should worry about the things she did know. The cold, hard facts.

It had gotten no lighter. The pain in her head was gone but her eyes were still bothering her. Vision fuzzed, sparks like a lightning storm behind her lids when she closed them. She'd bashed into the wall a couple of times, scraped the skin from her shoulder and knuckles.

She was pretty sure she had a concussion.

No one could hear her. She'd yelled *help, fire, rape* over and over again, scrabbled on the ground for rocks or something heavy enough to dislodge the cover at the top. There was nothing with any kind of heft, even if she'd possessed the strength and been able to avoid being brained when it fell back down to earth.

There were physical needs she had to address. Finally, after stalling for as long as she could, she had picked a place to pee and now the sour scent mixed with the earthy smells. It made her feel like an animal, as if she were losing herself in tiny increments. If she died here, would she smell like the mouse that died behind the kitchen wall? A sweet gassy odor that had lingered for days.

Which would kill her first? The concussion? Probably not, since she was still upright and ambulatory. Starvation? She could go a couple of weeks probably before she had to eat her fingers. But thirst? "Oh yeah, dehydration," she said. "That'll take me out in a few days." A crazed laugh escaped her lips. How long had she been down here already? She was parched. She licked a brick. It tasted like moldy cheese. She could drink her own urine—she knew it was sterile from some survivor TV show—but she had nothing to collect it in.

Her head wound had stopped seeping, and the ooze of blood glued her hair against her scalp just above her ear. She scratched at it. The lump on the back of her head had already shrunk down. Pressing it felt like a bad bruise, like something she might sustain from falling on hard ground. But the serious deep wound by her ear? How had that happened?

Something clicked into place like a key in a well-oiled lock. She'd been lying on her back when she came to. The ground beneath had been cold, very cold, all her body heat leached away into the soil. So she'd been lying there for a long time. And now she remembered hearing a voice, low-pitched, the words a distorted buzz, and seeing a thick length of metal, a pair of smooth black hands—gloves? leather? rubber?—then a shock of excruciating pain in her skull, a sharp shove against her chest, and she'd been falling. She recalled the silhouette getting smaller and smaller and then the dull thud as she hit the ground. She must have fallen boneless, close to unconsciousness before she even landed.

She blindly felt for the wall and sank down against it. The terror came howling back, wiping her mind of everything but one question: Who? She was suddenly breathless; her heartbeat juddered in her ears. Her hands were lumps of ice.

Who would do that to her? Who was crazy enough?

Sourmash. *You owe me*, he'd yelled. There'd been a look in his eyes, something hard and predatory that had made her think she was one step away from ending up like the deer in the back of his pickup.

She knew one thing: he'd be coming back for her if he wanted her to pay. He wouldn't leave her here to starve, would he? He'd want her to know that it was he who put her here, and then he'd exact retribution of some kind. Did he just want her to beg him for her life? In his sick mind she deserved to be punished, but how far would he take it? He was a hunter. He was a drunk. He'd hurt her. She wanted to kill him. She furiously blinked away the tears, scrubbed at her face with her hands and straightened her back, realizing that her eyes had adjusted. She could see the dirt grimed into her knuckles, the bricks, a giant drift of dead leaves in the middle of the shaft like a pile Lynn would make. Far above her was a sliver of something that could be the moonlit sky. The cover must not be on all the way.

She looked at her sneakers extended in front of her. Then, at the opposite wall. She scooted forward, reaching for the bricks with her toes and pressing her hands against the wall behind her. It was too far. For a moment she'd thought that maybe she could brace herself on either side and scootch her way up, but she couldn't span the distance with her body. A pro basketball player couldn't have done it.

Something white-hot broke open inside her and filled her veins with adrenaline. She had to get out of here. She had to try something. Anything! She stood up and slammed her shoulder into the wall as if she could break it down. The impact knocked her back to her knees. The image of a bird beating itself to death against a window blazed in her mind but, clenching her jaw, she pushed it away. She stood up again and took a run at the wall, trying to defy gravity and force her body up toward freedom. Her fingers slipped from the bricks. But she did it over and over, possessed by fury and fear. Eventually, battered, shaking, her head splitting again, she sank down on the ground. Three fingernails had broken off at the quick. She stuffed her fingers into her mouth to ease the sting, tasted iron. She gathered an armful of dead leaves, mounding them around her in an attempt to comfort herself. There was a rank smell that reminded her of roadkill. She felt something heavy in the pile and lifted it out. A bone! She hurled it away in disgust. An animal that had fallen down and then starved to death? One of Sourmash's kills? Would bones be all her parents ever found of her?

Her shoulders were deeply bruised but she welcomed the hurt. It reminded her that she was alive and still fighting.

When Sourmash came back, he'd have to climb down to her. Could she hide beneath the leaves? Leap on him and brain him with the bone? She crawled over to where she'd thrown it. It was big, about the length of her forearm, with a bulbous lump at one end. She stowed it nearby.

She rubbed her freezing fingers together and blew on them, then tucked them into her armpits to warm up. How had she gotten here? There was no way she'd go anywhere willingly with Sourmash. Had he kidnapped her? Roofied her? How much time had elapsed between her last memory and now? How long had she been unconscious? And what about Lynn? They'd been together, so where was she now? Going for help? She was still missing a huge chunk in the interval between shopping and waking up at the bottom of the cistern. There was a key, lost somewhere in the depths of her brain, that might unlock everything. What had happened after the shopping trip?

Lynn. She summoned up her friend's face, using it as an anchor to situate herself in the past—to fan hope and find courage.

She remembered standing by the truck, holding her dress bag, willing her legs to move. Lynn had come back, pinched her sharply just below her elbow and yelled, "Ari, run, goddammit."

Ari slid her moist hand into Lynn's and they didn't stop running until they were safely at the far corner. Just before they rounded it, Ari looked back. Sourmash was yelling at Rocky through the truck window. His hands twisted in the air as if he had Ari's neck between his fingers.

She followed Lynn onto the next block, which was filled with pedestrians and cars and shoppers. *Here* was where everyone was. Someone elbowed her as they went past but she stayed where she was in the middle of the sidewalk, Lynn pressed against her side, and let the calm settle around her like a cuddly sweater.

It seemed as if her heart had stopped beating for those long minutes and now it was scrambling to remember a regular rhythm.

"Did you see the dead deer?" Ari said.

"Yeah, I caught a glimpse." Lynn's lips turned down in distaste. "He just rocketed up to the top of my shit list."

"Wow," Ari said, feeling how dry her mouth was. She clutched her purse to her chest; the dress bag swung from her shoulder. "I totally stood up to that psycho. I thought he was going to kill me. Or eat me." Adrenaline was surging. It felt like lightning in her veins.

They left the main street and walked along the chain-link fence that bordered the park, a familiar route their feet took automatically. Little kids were playing in the sandbox and on the slides. Their happy laughter wafted in the air. Eventually Ari's pulse slowed. The whole scene had taken on an unreal aspect, as if it had been a bad dream. A car with a gunning engine made them both jump, but it was just a boy in a souped-up Corolla.

"My lights!" Lynn yelled suddenly, flinging out her arms like an overzealous actor.

Terror dissolved into giggles.

"You don't think he's going to call the cops, do you?" Ari asked, clutching her aching stomach, when she had breath again for speech.

"Never going to happen," Lynn said with faux confidence. "What about the still? What about the meth factory? You noticed his junkie buddy in the car?"

"Those are just rumors though." Her heart lurched as she flashed on the deer. "He does like to butcher his own meat. Shades of *Texas Chainsaw Massacre*."

"He kind of reminded me of Horace—sound and fury signifying nothing."

"The Roman poet or the L.H.?" They'd done a poetry course in their final quarter, starting from the dawn of time and working their way up to present day.

"The Little Horror, of course." Lynn's three youngest siblings were Horace, the Little Horror; Meryn, aka the Little Monster; and Ben, aka the Little Bother. The others were the triplets: Mark, Nelly and Christina, now aged ten, and known collectively as the Shits. Lynn's mom had had them all two years apart, except for Lynn, who was seven years older than the triplets, ensuring, as Lynn often said, "that I will be an indentured babysitter for as long as I live under that damn roof." Ari mainly referred to them all as "hey you," except for the L.H., who really was in a reprehensible class of his own.

She took a deep breath. She still felt unsettled, but if Lynn wasn't worried, maybe she could relax.

"Seriously?" she said.

"No doubt. He'll drink another bottle of paint thinner and forget about the whole thing."

"Are you going to tell your mom?" Ari asked. Lynn's dad had taken a job out west a few years ago. Well, that was the story put out there, but everyone knew he wasn't ever coming back. Her mother worked crazy hours up at the school and fueled herself with bottomless cups of coffee.

"Probably not. I don't like to worry her any more than I have to. You?"

Ari thought about her newspaper-editor dad and his tendency to mount protests, call meetings and assemble concerned citizen groups. And her local-coffee-shop-owning mother was even more grassroots organizational. It would be like unleashing a tsunami on a bathtub duck.

"Nah. I can just avoid him," she said, with more bravado than she felt.

"I guess," Lynn said. "Besides, he only comes to town once a month or so anyway to stock up on Vaseline and baby wipes."

"Thanks so much for that visual."

"No prob—" Lynn's voice cut off and she stopped walking.

They were passing a telephone pole plastered with flyers. Ari followed her eyes. "Oh, honey," she said.

Tallulah, Lynn's ancient beagle-mixed-with-smelly-doormat, had been missing for three days.

Lynn attempted a nonchalant shrug, but Ari could tell her heart wasn't in it.

"She's old and confused," Lynn said. "She probably got lost. You know she wanders off around the neighborhood. One of the kids left the gate open." Someone had slapped another missing pet flyer on the pole, which partly covered Tallulah's. Lynn pried it loose, muttering threats against people who used industrial staple guns. Tally's morose, black-lined doggy eyes looked back at them from under a banner announcing: "I am friendly, though incontinent, and much-loved!" Underneath and all around were dozens of old, faded flyers with photos of Mister Socks and Snoopy and Tiger and Tofu Wiener Dog. Ari had never noticed how many there were.

"She was wearing her collar, right?"

"Yeah, the butch studded one from the punk store in the mall."

Ari found a smile for her friend. "Bet she comes waddling back as soon as she remembers that she likes your tummy scratches best."

"Sure." They'd reached the corner of Fox and King. Ari's house was two down on the right; Lynn's was three down on the left. If Ari leaned out her window she could just about see if Lynn was upstairs in her room. When they were little they'd tried to communicate using semaphore flags and Navy code but it had been too complicated. Now they just each had a pirate flag that meant "Meet me on the corner now!"

They paused for a moment and then hugged. "Love you," Ari said. "So much."

"Ditto, bitch goddess," murmured Lynn into her shoulder. Ari gave her one more squeeze and let go.

She watched Lynn walk home, looking into each yard as she passed. Lynn complained about having to clean up Tally's messes all the time, but Ari knew her friend was worried about her dog. Her mom had given her the puppy when she was four and still an only child, in case she got lonely. "Lonely" was not part of Lynn's vocabulary anymore, though "beautiful silence" was. Ari wondered what it felt like to live in such a noisy, bustling house.

The lights were off at home—par for the course when you had two workaholic parents. Ari felt nervous and wasn't sure why, only that the curtained windows looked blank, secretive in some way. She switched on both the overhead and table lamps and sank into the couch.

It was the whole Sourmash encounter, she realized. It made everything familiar look unfamiliar. She couldn't get it out of her head. The deer. The smell of fresh blood. That raw anger that had just poured off him like sweat.

She thought about what Lynn had said about the man. Her friend had seemed so sure about his relative harmlessness, but she hadn't seen the rage in his eyes; she hadn't been close enough to feel his spit hit her cheek. Ari didn't think he was so harmless. She thought that, maybe, he was insane.

CHAPTER SIX

Most kids shoot rabbits, songbirds, gophers, water rats, anything that moves. I was not most kids. It wasn't only about blasting something out of existence. It was so much more than that.

Naturally, I was somewhat trigger-happy at the beginning. I loved the hot smell of the gun when it was fired; I loved the way the bullets reshaped themselves like squashed stars after they had traveled through wood, bone or flesh; I loved the kick against my shoulder, the bruise it left, the aftershock of the explosion buzzing in my ear, the smell of kinetic energy.

For the first couple of hours that first blissful day, I fired without thinking, alert to any movement. Leaves falling, butterflies drifting, hyperactive squirrels—I shot them out of the sky. Exciting, but the bullets reduced their bodies to mush and left me nothing to play with.

I learned something about myself. It was this: I wanted to kill something big, something that would fight me hard for its life. And I wanted to feel what it was like when that life was extinguished. Get close, lie down next to it and feel its last breath caress my cheek, the wild thumping of its heart under my palm until finally that too was stilled, the cloud fogging the bright eye. I wanted to climb into its skin to feel the exact moment of death.

I kept my promise to Pa, in a way. I only used one or two shots for each animal, but I didn't kill them outright. I wounded them, usually in the hind leg or the shoulder above the scapula, and then, when they were too helpless to drag themselves any farther and exhausted from thrashing around in the dirt, I brought out my knife. I tried to feel every last, precious moment.

But I couldn't.

This numbness in me remained. The part of my transformation I had not yet mastered; the lesson still unclear; the eternal mystery, so dark and perfect.

For a time I concentrated merely on the execution of my art—the tableaux I created afterward. What would bring about an ideal result? How could I recreate the lovely pictures I saw in my mind? My sketchbook was my haven, but this was even better. With the tableaux I could engage all my senses, sink into them, inhale them into my body.

I would try to prolong the moment of death but the blood always overcame me. The iron scent, the color of it, rich and intoxicating, washing over the dry brown leaves, soaking the ground until it appeared black, and then the skinned flesh, a pale silvery pink like a wild rose. Once skinned, with their heads, tails and feet removed, you couldn't tell what animal it had been to start with. I amused myself by staging small scenes, posing the bodies around tree stumps as if they were enjoying a tea party, hanging the heads from branches like paper lanterns or curling them around one another like sleeping puppies.

The deer were different though. Like all large mammals there was something almost human about their cadavers, the musculature of their haunches, the thick layer of meat over the rib cage. And I always marveled at the size of the heart.

The intestinal tract and stomach I dumped in the woods for the coyotes, but the lungs and liver, brick red, juicy and warm, I ate raw, feeling that potency flood into my veins. Did you know that lungs were called the "lights" in Victorian England? Did you know that in the original tale of Snow White, the evil queen demanded that the hunter bring back the girl's lungs and liver after he had killed her so the queen could devour them and reclaim her youth?

There is power in these organs.

The hearts I preserved in white vinegar—we always had plenty because Ma Cosloy used it in the laundry and to clean and disinfect the floors and countertops. First I hid the jars under my bed. I'd lie there counting them, sprawled on the rough wood-planked floor, dust from the underside of the straw-filled mattress tickling my nose, while Ma Cosloy yelled for me out in the yard. But then there were so many I dug a trench in the woods and covered them with branches and earth. Tiny crow hearts like Valentine cinnamon candies. Bunched-fist deer hearts like presents wrapped in red ribbon. The deep-crimson velvet of a fox heart. Each one gave me something more and for a time I thrived, fed by my secrets, the biting hunger sated, until I realized that dumb animals are no challenge. Truly, I never saw more than abject fear and sweet confusion as they died. It would be different when I killed something that knew it was going to die and begged me with words and tears not to kill it. Something that could tell me the meaning and flavor of pain.

CHAPTER SEVEN

Her body registered the passage of minutes, but barely. It had been dark. And then it was not so dark. She was cold and then not so much, although her feet and hands were freezing.

Thirst was another constant. She'd licked the wall a few more times and crawled around looking for something that would catch the dew. Could she pee into her cupped hands? Possible? She'd found more bones scattered under the leaves, a whole rib cage thick with the stink of rotting flesh. How hungry would she have to get before she considered . . . ? She kicked it away, huddled back into her nest like a hibernating mouse. Tried not to think of ice-cold water, coffee, pancakes, bacon, comforters, hot baths, movie nights with Lynn, doing the Sunday crossword with her dad, frosting fancy cupcakes with her mom.

Her bladder hurt but it was empty, her tongue was swollen. She couldn't seem to rouse herself completely; she felt sluggish, as if her biological processes had slowed down. This was how death came, wasn't it? Slowly. Organs shutting down one by one. Her kidneys would be the first to go. Did it hurt? Or would she just go to sleep?

She had to force her brain to operate in a linear way. She seemed unable to string events together, and jumping from one to the next felt almost physical, like crossing a rushing stream by balancing on slippery rocks. Still, she fought against the cloudiness, though it made her headache resurge with a vengeance.

"Someone will come for me soon," she whispered. The sibilants bounced back to her and crowded her head with the hissing of snakes.

Amidst the confusion, one belief stood strong.

Lynn would realize right away that Ari had vanished and she would find her. A memory teased at the edge of her brain, like a fly caught in a web—what was it? Something important about Lynn's dog . . .

Tallulah.

ɕ

It was an unseasonably humid Tuesday afternoon, four days after the Sourmash incident. And even though it was late September, it seemed as if half the seniors from school were at the swimming hole. Ari had dragged Lynn there as well, to moon over Stroud Bellows and his chest hairs. At a safe distance, naturally.

"This time you'll speak to him, right?" Lynn had asked.

"Of course," Ari had lied.

They were sitting on the hill above the water. Ari tore her gaze away from the frolickers and relinquished the beer bottle to Lynn, who was sitting beside her with her hand out.

"Finally," Lynn said. "I thought you were hypnotized."

"Shut up. You've been staring at Miranda for half an hour."

"Not Miranda, her boobage. And mostly I was just wondering how she gets that teensy bikini top to stay up." She chugged from the beer and offered it back. Ari shook her head. It was lukewarm, it was "lite," and it wasn't giving Ari the buzz she wanted right now. They'd scored the six-pack from some college guys hanging in the liquor store parking lot.

"So do you think there's Velcro or Krazy Glue attached to those oh-so-perky nipples?" Lynn remarked.

"I don't know. I hate her."

Miranda splashed water over Stroud Bellows and darted away laughing. He shook the water from his hair. God, it was like a soda commercial or something. Ari picked angrily at the fraying edge of her jean shorts. She'd been feeling good. Her new haircut had solved the frizz factor, and Philip had added some red highlights, which did something nice to her eyes and made her brows and lashes appear darker. But now she was just annoyed.

"Why don't you show him how to work that rope swing?" Lynn said.

"Miranda already shimmied up it and hung upside down like that pole dancer you like so much—whatshername . . ." The beer might be warm and barely three percent alcohol, but it had reduced her tongue to a less than limber muscle and slowed her brainpower.

"Jenyne Butterfly," Lynn said. "How dare you disparage her excellence!"

"I just meant that Miranda was doing those stripper moves."

"Jenyne is not a stripper. She is an athlete. It's very misogynistic of you to speak of her that way."

"I'm sorry."

"It's okay." Lynn patted her hand. "Someday I'm going to meet her and wonderful things will ensue."

"Absolutely."

Outraged yells floated up from the pond. Jack Rourke had pushed a fully clothed girl—a freshman, Ari thought—into the deep water. She flailed until Miranda extended a helping hand.

"You're positively not going to go down there?" Lynn said with thinly veiled sarcasm.

"In a minute . . . I just . . ."

"We could have gone to Dempsey's Maze, you know." This was Lynn's absolute favorite destination in the Hollow. Eight-foot walls of carefully tended bush—something Lynn loved to announce—occupying more than an acre of land and planted over a hundred years ago by Thomas Lee Dempsey the elder, one of the town's founding fathers.

In the long, hot summers, a riot of peach, pink and deep-glowing-red roses intermingled with the bristly hawthorn and beech hedge. The contrast between the baby cheek–soft petals and the sharp hawthorn spurs was startling, but at this time of year, when the leaves bronzed and fell and the rosehips had been pruned, the hedge was bare, the branches black against the sky. Beautiful but eerie.

"No water," Ari said.

"No assholes either. Here, let me find you some bravery," she said, digging in her bag. "A-ha!" She pulled out a small bottle and unscrewed the top. The smell of something sweet and artificial filled the air. The sun suddenly seemed too bright, and Ari felt the beginnings of a migraine.

"Peach schnapps?"

"You know it. Courtesy of my mom. It was way back in the cabinet. Probably from the nineties," Lynn said. She gulped some down. "Yum, still good," she said, barely concealing her grimace. "Come on."

"Yeah, I don't think so," Ari replied. Lynn had gone from smelling like coconut sunscreen and citronella bug repellent to Sourmash on a really bad day. Sourmash. Ari had managed to push the memory of him out of her mind until now. She gave herself a mental shake.

"Are you having fun?" Lynn asked.

Ari watched Stroud jump into the water with Miranda clutching his biceps and apparently trying to position her body so that he landed on top of her. The freshman girl stood in her dripping clothes, arms wrapped tightly around herself. After a few seconds, she hurried off. Stroud said something to Jack, who just laughed and shrugged his shoulders. Ari had no trouble imagining what filth Jack had spoken to the girl.

"Not really, no."

"Well this makes everything better," Lynn said with a twisted smile. "Trrruuuusssst me."

Ari reluctantly took the bottle. "Don't smell it first," Lynn cautioned. Ari lifted it to her lips and sipped. It was pretty bad. Sugary. Sticky.

"And another," her friend said. This time when Ari drank, Lynn reached over and tipped it up higher. Ari choked and spluttered. And then a warm feeling spread in her belly.

"Attagirl," Lynn said calmly and took the bottle back. "You know, most guys will choose simple and easy every damn time."

"I'm simple."

"No, you're not," Lynn looked at her under heavy-lidded eyes. "You have expectations."

"So what? I believe the best of people."

"That's scary for a boy if he's not willing to man up. Expectations are heavy. It's like sticking a mirror in front of his soul."

"He's perfect. What does he have to worry about?"

"No. He's not."

"What's the deal, Lynn?"

She shrugged. "I'm not you, you know. I don't have to like everyone."

Ari bit her lip.

Lynn relented. "I'm sorry. That was harsh. I just don't want you to build him up into this amazing, flawless guy when he's not." She sighed. "If he's really who you've set your heart on . . ."

"Yes. So what do I do?"

"You're asking me? The lesbian? I don't know. If he doesn't see what I see, then he's stupid."

"But you see the parts boys don't notice right off the bat."

"You mean everything above your neck?"

"Yes," Ari said with a groan.

"Well, fortunately, you can always distract them with your boobs."

Ari snorted out a laugh. "It's nonstop boobs with you."

"Boobs are a universal truth. B, C, double D, porn pontoons, it doesn't matter. Seriously. Western civilization would be nowhere without them." She raised the bottle. "Here's to the ever-loving bosom. Or is it bosoms?"

"What the heck is a pontoon?"

"A boat? A gun? I'm not sure. But 'porn pontoons' just sounds so right."

"You know, being smart doesn't mean you can just throw any word in there."

"You can if no one knows what you're talking about."

Ari leaned back on her elbows. The grouchiness had melted away, taking the headache with it. The late September sun felt so good. She kicked off her sandals and admired the sparkly purple pedicure Lynn had given her.

Lynn waved the bottle in front of her nose again and this time Ari drank deep and then licked sticky goodness off her lips. "This is delicious. Why don't we drink this all the time?"

"Not a good idea. Intermittent schnapps usage is recommended."

"You're crazy," Ari said, ignoring Lynn's attempt to steal the liquor bottle back.

"Did you have breakfast this morning? Lunch, other than that tiny granola bar?"

"No, I didn't want to bloat."

"Why? It's not like you're ever going into that water."

"I might. After a little bit more of this." She tilted the bottle again.

"Hey, Paris Hilton, schnapps is a sipping beverage. Hand it over."

"Too late." Ari downed the rest of the bottle.

She stood up, brushing dirt from her butt. The earth moved underfoot. She adjusted her stance, feeling the sun beating down on her shoulders, watching the light dance through the leaves. She shook her hair back, suffused by a feeling of almost unbearable happiness. "Look at that Miranda. If I had scaly knees like that, I'd keep them covered."

"Turn down the volume, maybe," Lynn suggested. "And sit back down."

Ari snuggled down next to her. "What would I do without you?"

"You'd be lost."

Ari grinned. "You and peach schnapps are my best friends. I might call my first child Peach."

"Good name. Better than Budweiser or Night Train, though Coors has a certain masculine ring to it." Her voice drifted off. "Speaking of stupid names, Stroud is walking this way."

Ari lurched up so suddenly her head spun. She brushed earth and dead leaves off her T-shirt. Why had she been practically lying in the dirt?

"Just take it off," Lynn said, gesturing at the tee. "Mr. Bubble isn't that sexy anyway."

"It's vintage."

"Boys don't care about vintage. They care about breasts. You're wearing a bikini under there, right?"

Stroud had paused to yell something back at the group at the swimming hole. He had his red water polo team jacket slung over one shoulder, his arm muscles flexed in a way that made Ari want to bite them.

"One-piece."

"Not the god-awful Speedo?"

"No. The new one my mom just bought me."

"Good enough."

Ari stripped her shirt off hurriedly and stowed it behind her.

"Does my hair look okay?" she asked, crossing her legs and then uncrossing them again.

"Very naturally tousled and windblown," Lynn said, picking out a stray leaf. "If you lean back on your arms and arch your back a little, your boobs will look bigger."

Ari tried it and lengthened her legs. She was just fake-tanned enough, without venturing into Orange Land; she'd managed to shave around her ankles without nicking herself. The alcohol was a warm buzz and a sweet taste in her mouth rendering everything in sharp relief, as if she were wearing her dad's reading glasses. In contrast, she felt deliciously blurry around the edges.

He was close, near enough to smell the pond water in his hair—and Ari had lost the capability for speech. Maybe she could mention how last week he'd cut his time on the freestyle? By . . . what was it? Two seconds? Three seconds. She didn't want to get it wrong. He was walking past. Going, going, going . . .

"Hey, Bellows," Lynn said. "How'd you do on that killer trig test?"

He paused, looking confused. "I don't take trig."

"My mistake, I mixed you up with that other do . . ." She let her voice trail away and smiled at him widely. Ari could almost see the unsaid "douche" float past in a speech bubble. She shot Lynn a quick frown that was received with a bland expression, and redirected her attention toward Stroud. Golden Stroud. Even on land, he moved like a wild animal.

He cleared his throat and shifted from foot to foot. Ari gazed at his freckled shoulders, followed the length of his arms down to his strong, tanned hands. Whatever Lynn said about knuckle-dragging apes, those long arms were why he was so good at water polo and swimming, and she wouldn't mind being double-wrapped in them like a straitjacket.

She felt a bony elbow in her ribs and blinked.

"Hi, Stroud," she managed. The sun was directly behind him. It haloed his bright hair, outlined him in light. She was staring but she couldn't help it. She knew she should talk, but the words were stuck.

Droplets of water glistened on his broad chest, just a few hairs curling around his nipples. They were like small brown candies. She blushed and dragged her gaze up to his face. He was looking back at her, his deep-blue eyes intent. His soft, pink lips were opening. Every movement he made was in slow motion, and she felt something hitch under her breastbone and pull toward him, as if he had hooked her with a fishing line.

"You look really hot, Sullivan."

What?! Oh my God. Confidence spilled into her like a flood of warm water.

"You too, Stroud." She wanted to say his name at the end of every sentence she spoke. She wanted to hear her own name in his mouth.

He ruffled his hair and frowned adorably. Oh, how she wished she were that hand.

"You should definitely get out of the sun," he said. "You've got a major farmer's burn happening."

The good feelings deflated like a pricked balloon. She watched him walk up the path. Miranda's tinkling laughter floated on the breeze as she trilled, "Wait up, Stroud," and then flew past them, her shiny blond hair and bikini breasts bouncing in just the most perfect way. The two disappeared around the corner, but not before Ari saw Miranda's arm snake around Stroud's waist, his hand slip to her shoulder and then casually down to her breast. The butterflies were replaced by a bitter feeling, and a weird spluttering sound came out of her mouth, part shame, part something else—something volcanic.

"Gonna hurl?" Lynn said, stroking her arm. "I can hold your hair back, if you want."

Ari jumped to her feet, shaking her head. She had to get away, somewhere private.

"Oh, sweetie. He's not the guy you think he is. You can't see past his whole all-American jock thing. He parties a lot, and frankly he's kind of an asshole, like all the rest of them—Rourke and Dinkwad and Whosit."

Ari bit back a half giggle, half sob. Down the hill a short distance in the opposite direction from the water was a stand of trees growing around what had once been a quarry. People dumped all kinds of stuff in there—garbage, broken appliances and furniture, old cars. She headed for it, fighting the sour bile.

"If he goes for the manky chicks like that he's not worth it!" Lynn called after her.

Ari stumbled along the rough path. That's what girlfriends always said, but it didn't help. Another wave of peach-scented bile hit her. She stopped by a tree, leaning against it, and fought to control her churning guts. How had she gone from feeling so good to feeling like this?

Stroud would never notice her in that way. It was a hopeless dream. The dance, an impossible scenario.

She tried to reason with herself. Why did she even like him? Because he was hot? Because he was tall and broad-shouldered? Because she imagined that beneath the muscular exterior he had the soul of a poet? Lynn was right. She'd wait around forever for a guy who was nothing like she imagined. In her mind, she'd built him up into this ideal. But still, his hands. God, how she wanted his hands on her hips, pulling her toward him, and his mouth crushing hers.

"I'm such a loser," she moaned. "So stupid."

A branch cracked above her head. She looked up and got a shower of grit in her face. Someone peered down at her through the sparse leaves. She jumped back, sick feeling forgotten.

"What the hell!" She recognized the face. Jesse Caldwell. One grade below hers, left back because he'd failed a year.

"Lost, little girl?" he said with a smirk.

Hitching his legs over the branch he was perched on, he grabbed another above his head and swung out, hanging for a long moment, his shirt wrinkled up and baring his abdomen, before he dropped to his feet. He took his time pulling his shirt back down, making sure Ari saw his flat stomach. He was that kind of guy, always preening and posing, leaning against his locker in studied nonchalance, going unshaven and letting his hair flop over his face. He slipped a notebook into the messenger bag slung over his shoulder.

She turned her back on him, noting the unimpeded view of the swimming hole from there. The nausea had subsided but now she had a different kind of queasy feeling. Up in the tree the view would be even less obstructed.

"Spying, Jesse?" she said, swiveling around, unable to keep the sneer out of her voice. The schnapps was playing havoc with her balance and she braced herself against the tree.

Under his shaggy black hair, the tips of his ears turned red, and then he straightened his back. "What's it to you?"

"Hoping for some skinny-dipping? Or for Miranda's bikini to fall off?"

His eyes went immediately to Ari's chest, as if his brain were wired for certain words. She wished she'd grabbed her T-shirt.

"No crime in looking," he mumbled, slanting his eyes away when he caught sight of her angry glare. "We don't all live by the rule book."

Jesse Caldwell unsettled her. Frequently mean, often cuttingly sarcastic, he seemed to delight in making other people feel bad as he slouched down the hallway in his black denim and vintage hats. He'd shown up from God knows where halfway through junior year and supposedly lived with an old aunt, or someone, outside of town. A month after he'd arrived he'd cut some girl's ponytail off in Art with a boning knife because she called his artwork pretentious and derivative. Practically scalped the poor girl. Not that they'd ever found the reputed knife on him, and the girl—Kelly something, Ari remembered—had transferred out shortly afterward. Jesse had been suspended for two weeks and his reputation had been sealed. The word *weirdo* was spray-painted on his locker in case anyone forgot, and he'd taken it as a badge of honor.

"Voyeurism is pretty pathetic, even for you." She folded her arms across her chest, feeling more naked than she actually was.

"You think?" There was an odd light in his blue eyes, a challenging twist to his mouth. His eyes raked her body again, lingering. He smiled, though his face was suffused with anger. "Weren't you doing the same thing? Creaming over Stroud Bellows? Giving Miranda the old stink eye?"

"You were spying on us too?" She felt herself blush. Yes, she'd been ogling Stroud, but that was different. "You're such a pervert!"

He took a step toward her. "You're no better than the rest of them, you know?" he said, his lips a thin line. "Everyone is just some *Breakfast Club* stereotype to you. Cheerleader, Jock, Brain, Weirdo. What about the people who don't fit, and those who don't want to fit? Like your friend Lynn? Even you?"

"What about me?" She couldn't help asking.

"You'll never be part of their group. They're a different species."

"You don't know anything about me."

He looked at her briefly. "They think you and Lynn are a couple—a couple of dykes."

Ari gritted her teeth. "And? What's your problem, Jesse?"

But then he'd swung away from her, moving fast, shoulders hunched.

He had a book stuffed in his back pocket. Edgar Allan Poe. Of course he'd be into that morbid shit.

Anger flooded into Ari's veins. "Dyke is an ugly word, you asshole . . . you freak!" she yelled.

He stopped when he was past the tree line and looked back at her.

His voice was pitched low but still she heard him clearly. Each word was bitten off.

"Sticks and stones, Sullivan."

There were no words. Her brain was totally blank.

He turned and walked away, whistling to himself.

Shaking off the creepy-crawly feeling that being in close proximity to him had given her, she was conscious again of the unhappy state of her stomach. Also, she had to pee.

She stumbled forward deeper into the forest where no one would see or hear her. A hundred yards in, it was hotter under the canopy, the air close and still. Her stomach cramped, the nausea surged back. She could smell something sweet and gassy, like rotten potatoes in a plastic bag. Clouds of flies buzzed with an insistent whine. The ground fell away. She was at the edge of the abandoned quarry. She could see a refrigerator, door removed. Black garbage bags, one ripped open, spilling soiled diapers. The sun couldn't quite penetrate the densely growing trees.

Something dangled ahead. Like a large football. And there were other odd shapes, like fists and dripping wet bags tied to a web of thin rope. Her feet moved her inexorably closer, even while her brain tried to decipher what she was seeing. A swathe of black and white nailed to a tree trunk. Then another, all black this time, curly like her mother's bouclé coat, and one larger—tan, black and white in splotches. A collar, decorated with silver studs, swung from a branch. It was familiar. Next to it Ari saw more collars—leopard-spotted, pink velvet, chain. Her eyes went back to the swathe. Not cloth, but fur.

Tallulah.

And then she saw everything. Red, bloated, misshapen, truncated forms hanging from hooks, the leaves below spattered with brown and red stains. Movement came from one, and she struggled to comprehend what she was seeing. It was dead; it had to be. The skinned carcass, she realized, was wriggling with hundreds of yellowy-white maggots.

A fat fly landed on her cheek and she batted at it, hysterical now. The world tilted and rushed away like the sea going out, a swirl of black and green and red. She leaned over and vomited.

"Ari," Lynn called from close by. "Where the hell are you?"

Ari heard rustling in the undergrowth. She turned, shouted,

"No, Lynn, stop! Stay where you are!" But it was too late. Lynn pushed through some bushes, her face red with exertion. "Are you okay, sweetie? I just saw that creep, Jesse, and I was worried—" Her voice cut off as she looked past Ari. "Holy shit. What the hell is that?"

CHAPTER EIGHT

I'm thinking back to the piglets. The lessons I learned then, at nine and a half years old.

Those piglets are my most personal attempt. And yet I make mistakes, mistakes that still sting my soul even now.

Three months after the chicken debacle, I slaughter all three remaining piglets—Ferdinand's brothers and sister—in a sort of frenzy, not pausing to savor the deaths, wanting so badly to recapture the excitement I felt when I killed Ferdinand. My knife-work is clumsy and rough. I hack at them to get the guts and organs out. I neglect to catch the blood in buckets. Not that we have enough buckets for such a massive quantity. I get a ringing backhand across the head for this, which rocks me back on my heels. Pa loves his fried black sausage with a couple of runny eggs and cornmeal mush in the morning.

He stares at the row of dead piglets hanging by the hind legs in a gently swaying curtain of flesh, the heaps of viscera, the thick pools on the dusty floor below their throats, my arms and torso spattered red. I scratch at some dried blood. It itches like crazy.

"How'd you get them all up there together?" he asks, his voice quieter now. I shoot him a quick look, tensed for another blow. Sometimes Pa shouts when he's about to lash out, and sometimes his voice drops to a

murmur just before the blow falls. It keeps me unbalanced. And always aware of where he is in relation to my body.

There will be a reckoning as always, but for now he is curious.

I show him the knots I tied, the pulleys hanging from the eaves: a complex web of support. My shoulders ache and my arm muscles throb with deep pain. Each piglet was hoisted into the air separately, but once they witnessed what happened to the first of them, they knew what was coming and they fought me. Later, I discover my shins are covered in bruises shaped like small cloven footprints. They remind me of purple cabbages.

"I took each one out of the pen separate," I tell Pa, with my eyes fixed on the ground. "Hung it up. Slipknot around the hind leg." I make a slashing gesture with the edge of my hand. "Knife."

"Your ma won't be pleased." He eyes the carcasses. "Not to say you weren't neat about it. Apart from wasting all that blood."

"We can salt them."

"It's more meat than we need right now." He points to the biggest of the piglets, Glinda (after the good witch). "Had plans for that one around Thanksgiving. Already spoke to Hank and James about helping out with raising the new barn, and hosting a pig roast in return." He gestures at the next biggest, Wilbur, who swings slowly in a big circle, gore still dripping from the scarlet slash in his throat. "Promised 'em a couple of hams too, off of that one."

Skilled hired hands were hard to come by, and often, for a big job, the local farmers got together and traded and bartered for help. Meat was as good as or better than money around here.

He sighs.

"Got nothing for them now. You'll have to help with the barn. Salted meat ain't nothing like good, fresh pork."

I straighten my back and try not to wince as sore muscles protest.

"I can do it." I thrust out my scrawny chest and lift my chin.

"You're gonna have to. Can't see any other way."

He reaches out and places his hand on the nearest piglet. Its eyes are closed tight, fringed in white lashes. It looks touched by frost.

"Need to scald them still."

Scalding takes the tough bristles off the pig skin. "I started the big pot boiling."

"Those ropes you got hung, they gonna help you swing them all the way over there?"

I nod, showing him the special knots I'd come up with. They hold but they are also pretty easy to release and re-tie in a different way. As long as I have some leverage, like a strong support beam, I can manage the weight of each pig by myself.

Pa contemplates the ropes and then spits tobacco juice on the floor. "You're not stupid," he says finally. Though the expression on his face looks nothing like pride or approval.

I shift from foot to foot, and then freeze as he looks at me.

"Got to take care of this first."

He unbuckles his belt and slowly pulls it from the loops. It's good, thick leather with a big brass buckle in the shape of a horseshoe. He weighs it in his hand. I keep my spine straight as I can, though it threatens to bow under the pressure of dread. I know that buckle intimately, the snap and the whistle as it cuts through the air and then the sound of impact, a few seconds before the pain bites bone-deep. He'll use the buckle first, chewing up the muscle beneath the skin, often leaving no visible marks, and then the strap against my buttocks, and for the next couple of weeks at school I'll sit on the edge of my chair, and I'll raise my hand for every question whether I know the answer or not. Just to get the chance to stand up off the hard wooden seat and go to the blackboard.

CHAPTER NINE

Down in the well, Ari saw impossible things coming out of the deep pockets of shadow. Tallulah, skinned and glistening; a cat dragging its entrails behind it. Closing her eyes made no difference; begging her mind to stop replaying the horror changed nothing. She was right back there in the grove.

Lynn hadn't vomited, but she'd gone as white as a sheet and she'd tilted so far over that Ari had thought she was going to swoon. When Ari thrust out a supportive arm, Lynn's entire weight sagged against it. Together they'd staggered a few yards away from the animals and called the police on Ari's phone.

The immediate area was taped off now, shrouded by dense plastic sheeting, but the rest of the space was filled with people: two or three cops, but mostly the kids from the swimming hole, and various townspeople who had shown up by osmosis. She recognized employees from the convenience store, waitstaff from the restaurants, and a handful of others from her daily life. Even her creepy biology teacher was there. Jesse Caldwell paced the shadows along the perimeter, observing everyone with an intense expression, as if he wanted to join the group but knew he wouldn't be welcome.

Ari and Lynn sat on a fallen log, staring determinedly at the distant road, a winding gray ribbon.

"The smell," Lynn said.

Ari nodded. It had been familiar to her too. "Try not to think about it," she said, attempting to block it from her own mind as well.

"Just like the cats in biology class."

They'd started on cat dissection three weeks ago. Lynn had mounted an impassioned campaign extolling the virtues of computer models rather than dissection. But it had been ignored, and so she had dropped the class a few days in, adding AP Trig to her course load. Sadly, Ari needed the science credit, and Biology had rapidly become her most dreaded class. Each time Ari opened her plastic garbage bag, she steeled herself, but unfailingly the odor and the sight of that stiff, unnatural-looking body inside made her stomach twist. Their teacher, Dr. McNamara, didn't help. She favored gross-out humor mixed with science, as if she could desensitize the class by saying "gunk" and "ooze" and "kitty."

"Who would do such a thing?" Lynn said.

"Oh, honey. I don't know."

"My poor Tallulah, my sweet girl."

Lynn was quiet for a few minutes, knotting her fingers together. Ari took her hand. It was icy.

"Are you sure you want to talk to the cops?" Ari said. "You could do it later at home."

"It'll be worse then," Lynn said.

Behind them, they could hear the sounds of plastic sheeting being unrolled, the grunts of physical effort. Ari was having a hard time processing the pictures whirling around in her head.

It had been so vivid. Almost painterly, like the abstract art exhibition her mom had taken her to in Bedford a couple of years ago.

Eight animals—dogs and cats, the officer had told her—though at that point they hadn't matched all the skins together with the internal organs yet. "There could well be more," he'd said with a touch of barely contained glee. Criminal violence didn't come to Dempsey Hollow often. This was a big day for the force.

"They're acting like it was a prank," Lynn said bitterly. The background noise had gotten louder.

Ari's eyes went to where Stroud was standing in his swim shorts and bright-red team jacket. The group around him had swelled. There was the sound of high-five slapping and bursts of hesitant laughter intermingled with the babble of conversation. If not for all the cops and the plastic-sheeted lumps on the ground, it could have been a casual party.

Her friend turned toward her and Ari was shocked by her expression.

Lynn's face was splotchy and flushed, her eyes hard as coal, glittering with tears and rage. "My dog was butchered," she said, forcing each word past clenched teeth.

Butchered. That was the word Ari hadn't let herself speak, not even silently in her mind, but that's what the pets had reminded her of—the deer in the back of Sourmash's truck.

Lynn swallowed hard, and then waved her arm, encompassing all the people standing in the grove. "Look at them! It's like they're not even capable of compassion."

"People deal with things in different ways," Ari said lamely. "Some people kid around when they're nervous or scared."

"How the hell did you get to be so naïve, Ari?"

"I'm just trying to help."

"Saying something stupid is not helping."

"That police officer said it was probably a transient," Ari said, not liking the desperate look in Lynn's eyes.

"Because they know no one wants to believe something really bad—that it's closer to home. And it's not just that." Her eyes welled up with angry tears. "Tallulah. Sourmash. All the racist and homophobic jerks at school like Jack Rourke and his posse. If you start scratching the surface it just gets worse."

An image of a rotting log popped into Ari's mind. Under the bark, a writhing mass of pill bugs and centipedes. Her stomach squeezed. If only they could leave. The officer who'd wanted to speak to Lynn was still busy patrolling the periphery.

Ari wished she could whisk Lynn away, seal her up in a protective bubble. "What about two years back, when Jack Rourke Photoshoppped my face onto all those pornographic pictures and glued them on the outside of my locker?" Lynn said, jumping to her feet.

"You're all fucking assholes," she screamed at the group of teenagers. Their laughter cut off suddenly. Some of the adults muttered disapprovingly, as if such language was inappropriate; the piano teacher was open-mouthed and the local library assistant stared at Lynn like she'd never seen her before.

"Crazy dyke," someone said.

Then, quite suddenly, Lynn slumped and curled in on herself, her hands clasped tightly in her lap, as if the weight of their gazes were too much.

"Everything will be okay, I promise," Ari said helplessly, moving to shield her friend with her body. "I don't want to fight with you."

"Some things are worth fighting about. Sometimes you have to take a stand, Ari. Someone killed my dog, skinned and gutted her. Fucking monsters!"

Ari hugged her and couldn't help noticing how stiffly her friend held herself. "Most people are good, Lynn."

Lynn detached herself and stood up. "I really don't think so." She stood with her back to Ari for a moment and then she wheeled around, her face a mask of stone. "You'd better wake the fuck up, Ari."

ൾ

Ari tasted vomit in the back of her throat. Lynn had been right. There were monsters in the world. Oh God, how she wished Lynn was in front of her right now so she could tell her so and beg her forgiveness. The fight would be forgotten like their squabbles always were.

Something had slipped open in her brain, a tiny door unlatched. She felt as if she were choking on memories, each one triggered by the one before. The shadowed figure had spoken to her. She couldn't remember what had been said, but she was sure she had recognized the voice. It was someone she knew.

A trickle of sweat ran down her back, but her feet and hands were still freezing. She crammed her hands into her pockets and danced around, trying to keep warm. She'd stuffed armfuls of leaves in between her T-shirt and hoodie in an attempt to insulate herself against the creeping dampness, but it didn't seem to be working. She could see better now. The moon must have risen. A few hours ago she had screamed pathetically against the black, but now that she could see her surroundings a little better, she almost wished for blindness again. The cistern was at least twenty feet deep, made of mortared bricks painted white. There was nothing at the bottom of it besides the dead leaves, the remains of a deer—she'd found the skull now and it was unmistakable—and the barely alive Ari. It felt like a tomb.

The reality that she might die down here, with or without Sourmash's help, was very real. And there was absolutely nothing she could do about it; she was just counting the seconds.

How many hours had she been trapped? How many more until she was so weak she wouldn't be able to move and she gave up like that drowning rat? With an effort that felt physical, she forced the hysteria back down. At the bottom of her pocket, her fingers touched a piece of paper. She drew it out, unfolded it.

Four words in her own handwriting: *Dahmer, Gacy, Bundy, Gein.*

Ari made lists. Usually it was to-dos or items her mother wanted her to pick up at the store on her way home from school, but she also jotted down anything that interested her so that she could look it up later, either online or at the library. The library was just somewhere she naturally went. She liked doing her homework and research surrounded by other people. The low buzz of conversation, the rustle of pages, even the tapping of keypads helped her to concentrate, and the Internet connection was faster and less glitchy than at home.

The words blurred and then sharpened before her eyes. These were the names of infamous serial murderers—monsters of men. She thought back to the dead animals at the grove, the ritualistic way they had been arranged, and recollected that many killers start off by torturing pets. The whole picture was still incomplete, but she was gradually filling it in, frame by frame.

As far as she could piece it all together, the Sourmash incident had happened on Friday, the discovery of the killing grove on Tuesday, and then—she remembered!—that following Friday she'd gone to the town library to find out everything she could about serial killers. She couldn't recall if it was a hunch or if something else had set her on this path, but whatever she'd discovered then must have precipitated the events that put her at the bottom of this hole.

Sliding down onto the ground with her back against the bricks, she let muscle memory take her back to the library: its warm honeyed lighting, long tables and round-backed chairs. Cloaking everything was the musty, woodsy smell of books. God, how she loved that smell! It was even better than the pool chlorine.

On that particular day, however, it offered no comfort.

"The late charge on *Anna Karenina* comes to $1.80," Miss Byroade, the librarian's assistant, said in her soft voice, "so your change back is twenty cents." She pushed the money across the counter. "Did you enjoy it?"

"I got about halfway before I gave up," Ari said. "All those Russian names confused me."

"It was a serial, you know," Miss Byroade said, adjusting her glasses and blinking rapidly. "Not meant to be read in one big gulp." Ari half-admired the way today's outfit combined paisley with plaid. Miss Byroade always looked like she got dressed in the dark, and some of her color combinations were a little startling, but Ari dug it in a thrift-store-chic kind of way. Ari felt sorry for the woman without quite knowing why. Maybe it was because she was one of those young people who seemed to have been born old. Ari and Lynn had tried to guess her age once. Lynn had thought she was in her mid-twenties; Ari, closer to thirty.

"Chocolate?" Miss Byroade said, pushing an open box toward Ari. "Handmade truffles."

Ari took one. It was so good she licked her fingers afterward. Miss Byroade smiled at her.

"Tolstoy was like Dickens," the assistant librarian continued. "That's why it's quite wordy. Because they were getting paid to drag it out for as long as possible. But if you just submerge yourself in the story, it will transport you. Do you still have the Bacigalupi?"

"Am I late on that one too?"

Miss Byroade nodded. "The price we pay for our addiction. No school today?"

"No, it's a professional development day for the teachers."

"A holiday for you then," Miss Byroade said, with another smile. "And yet here you are among the books."

Ari glanced over her shoulder and surveyed the room. The library was almost empty. Most people were enjoying the gorgeous weather outside. At least those people not mourning their pets. Lynn was still inconsolable. She was positive she was to blame for Tallulah's death, and was completely wrapped up in the guilt. Not only that but she was still mad at Ari, even though she said she wasn't. "I just feel exhausted," she had said on the phone, in a small wooden voice that freaked Ari out. It was as if she'd reached her tipping point. They still walked to school together, but Lynn wasn't talking much. Ari wondered if a gallon of her favorite chocolate-chunk hazelnut ice cream would help matters.

Then suddenly she noticed Jesse Caldwell hunched over a book in the corner, one leg under the table bouncing while he read. As if he sensed her presence, he raised his head and stared at her. She gazed back at him with a heat that made him scoot his chair backward a few inches before he collected himself and arranged his features into that blank, frozen look she found so unsettling. She wondered if he really hated the world as much as he appeared to.

For a second she looked at his hands. They were broad and long-fingered. Strong. He was too far away to determine whether they were covered in scratches or bite marks.

He'd been so close to the . . . what should she call it? *The killing zone*. It seemed unlikely that the foul odor hadn't alerted him, and who knew what kind of a view he'd had from the top of the tree.

Recently, he seemed to pop up all over the place. No, not all over the place—just where she was, both at school and outside it: the coffee shop yesterday when she was helping her mother, the bookstore the day before, and now the library. He was staring at her again, blue eyes glittering like chips of ice.

With an effort, she flicked her eyes away. *What the hell is wrong with him?* Miss Byroade had followed her gaze.

"Not a nice boy," she said, a touch of steel in her voice.

"No." *Possibly someone who kills helpless dogs and cats and gets a kick out of it*. She suppressed a shudder.

"Was there something specific you were looking for?" Miss Byroade said, looking at her expectantly. "Something I can help you with?"

Ari tried to collect herself. She could hunt for the books herself, but the archaic card catalog and the computers were right next to Jesse and there was no way she was going over there.

She pushed the scrap of paper she'd jotted a few names on across the counter and lowered her voice. "I'm just doing a little independent research. For a short story I'm writing," she improvised. Another reason she liked coming to the library rather than just looking things up on her computer was that Miss Byroade was a surprising source of obscure information. She seemed to know a little bit about everything, and she had every book in the place mapped in her head.

The woman glanced at the paper. Her eyebrows rose and her soft brown eyes widened. "Dahmer. Jeffrey Dahmer, the mass murderer?"

Ari looked around. Her voice seemed ridiculously loud. Jesse's head bobbed up. A group of kids doing paper crafts in the corner snickered.

"Um, yeah. Just for some research."

"Why would you want to find out anything about him? He was a demon." Her fingers tapped the paper. "And these others as well. Sick, sick men."

"I know." She pitched her voice low, hoping the assistant librarian would mimic her tone. The woman had turned to her monitor and now typed in a few key words. Her mouth was twisted in distaste, and she pushed the paper back toward Ari with one finger, as if it were a dead bug. "Criminology. The three-sixties. Behind historical nonfiction."

Ari nodded. She'd done a paper on Leonardo da Vinci last year and spent a ton of time sitting on the floor by those shelves. Luckily, that section was located on the other side of the library from Jesse Caldwell.

Once she'd crossed the floor, she skimmed the shelves. There were at least twenty books on the big killers, most with eye-catching titles like *The Devil in Me, Deviant, An American Nightmare* and *The Stranger Beside Me.* She collected an armful and scooted down with her back against the wall. *Why were the killers almost revered and the people they killed just numbers? What does that say about the rest of us?* Ari wondered. *And how are we any better than these terrible people? The murderers became celebrities, the subjects of best-selling books, but no one even recalled the victims' names.*

She picked up a book about John Wayne Gacy and flipped through it, stopping at various passages that leapt out at her. He'd been an alcoholic and possibly suffered from mental illness. The memory of Sourmash's rage-suffused face popped into her head. Just like that, her mind's eye painted him roaring insults and grabbing for her with those gigantic hands, veins bulging, saliva spraying from his lips.

It was only too easy to imagine him inflicting pain.

She perused another book. Ed Gein nursed his sick mother, but at the same time he was collecting bone and skin trophies from his victims. What made him caring on the one hand and completely inhuman on the other? *How can you tell?* she wondered. *Are there signs to watch for? What turns a normal person into a beast? Is it something that happened to them in childhood? But then every abused kid would grow into an abuser, and that isn't the case.*

The thing about Ted Bundy was that college girls basically threw themselves at him, seduced by his good looks and all-American boyishness. All he had to do was get them into his car, where he raped and beat them to death. He had a successful modus operandi and he stuck to it. It was almost like his signature.

She shivered. With these men, psychosis wasn't right there on the surface. Their eyes didn't tell you what was going on in their heads. If she hadn't been able to evade Sourmash, would things have played out differently? What if she'd run into him in a dark alley? If he'd had the opportunity with no one to bear witness? Right time, right place? Maybe that was all it took.

She shifted her weight on the hard floor in an attempt to take pressure off her tailbone and dumped *The Stranger Beside Me* back onto the pile. Stifling the urge to run into the bathroom and wash her hands, she picked up the Dahmer book and started jotting down information, as if she truly were writing a story.

Serial killers were almost always men. There were scientists who now believed that psychopathic killers had endured some kind of injury to the cortex of the brain early in development, like shaken baby syndrome. Others speculated that a killer gene was sex-linked to the X chromosome and came from the mother. She re-read her notes: MAOA, the killer gene. Weirdly, they thought it came from too much serotonin during pregnancy. The fetuses didn't reap the benefits of all those happy hormones. It was as if the pleasure centers in their developing brains were blown out. So, not only did they not feel joy or love, but they also didn't understand pain, and had no difficulty causing it.

Ari thought it must be like living as a zombie.

And here was another interesting fact. Killing animals was where these killers perfected their brand. It was part of what researchers called a "Triad of Warning Signs in Childhood." Besides animal torture, the list included fire-starting and bed-wetting.

She shuddered and thought of the grove. There'd been something so deliberate about the way the pets were displayed. They hadn't been hacked apart but sectioned neatly and hung like meat in a butcher shop. As if the killer were making an announcement: *Here I am. Take notice of me. Watch what I can do.* The deer in the back of Sourmash's truck had been skinned and gutted with precision too. It had been the work of a professional.

What had her dad said over breakfast? "It wasn't a local." As if it was a fact. It sounded more like a platitude—something to ease the tension.

It occurred to Ari that whenever someone was caught doing something really awful, the neighbors always remarked on what a nice, quiet man he was. "He was so kind to the elderly and the neighborhood children. On Halloween he gave out more candy than anyone!" And in the meantime, his wife was boiling away merrily in three separate pots on the stove and her head was in the refrigerator. Her dad hadn't seen the way Tallulah and the others had been skinned, their fur and heads carefully removed, the corpses arranged in the trees like some kind of horrific Christmas window display. He hadn't heard the resolve in Sourmash's voice as he threatened her.

Was Sourmash an actual textbook psychopath? Wouldn't a true predator avoid being a poster child for antisocial behavior and violence? These other men, they'd hidden their true natures with church socials, neighborhood groups and volunteer work. Sourmash was just so fucking obvious. And yet she couldn't shake this rootless, vague sensation of unease, even if at moments it felt totally absurd. So much so that she hadn't even confessed it to Lynn.

It seemed cold in the library all of a sudden.

"Put those poor animals out of your mind," her mother had said. "It's over."

Ari had tried, but the feeling kept gnawing at her: maybe this wasn't an ending but a beginning.

CHAPTER TEN

"Give me a child until he is seven, and I will show you the man," said some priest or another. I have been wondering about this. In my mind I was a formless thing, dull and uninspired until I took hold of my destiny. Did the Cosloys mold me with their punishments and strictures, or did they just uncover what was already there? Was it a gift from my mother?

There are certainly many pivotal moments in my life—Ferdinand, the piglets and hens, the first time I fired a gun and killed something, later on, the boy in the woods—but there are bitter experiences as well. And those wormed their way into my body and nested, and grew fat until my skin could no longer contain them.

Here, I am eleven.

It is the worst day. When I get home from school, Ma Cosloy is in the hen yard. Smoke billows from the mountain of scrap lumber, branches and trash Pa and I accumulate while we ready the farm for the winter months. I can feel the heat of it crisping my eyelashes. The chickens are huddled in a scared mass by the barn.

"Empty the wheelbarrow onto the bonfire," she tells me, pointing to where it waits, piled with more refuse wood, some odds and ends of rubber tubing, and the mildewed tarpaulin that used to cover the rabbit

hutch—until all the rabbits disappeared. Fox, Pa said, daring me to contradict him with any sign, any flicker of emotion. I kept my face perfectly still. That week I got to shoot as many foxes as I wanted. Their tails hung like pennants from the barn eaves. Their ruby hearts pickled in my treasury of mason jars buried deep in the woods.

I put down my school bag and roll my sleeves up as I prepare to push the wheelbarrow closer to the flames. The heap on the barrow is precariously high, and I steady it with one hand. Once I am near enough, I start tossing things onto the fire. It's been burning for a while. The embers glow deep red. Ma is still watching. I dump the load mechanically, but my mind wanders into the flames. I'm thinking of a story I just read. A tale about a massive golden bear cloaked in leaves that comes out of the fire and assigns an impossible task. Deep within the layers of timber and trash, I glimpse two books, their pages just beginning to catch. The covers are singed but not so much that I can't read the titles. My Tales of King Arthur *and my* Fairytales and Legends from Around the World. *The only two books I own, earned at school for perfect attendance, and hidden safe under the loose floorboard beneath my narrow bed. Read over and over again until the spines snapped and the pages flapped loose, held together by strips of masking tape. How had she found them? And then I see my sketchbook.*

A sound like a wounded animal's cry escapes from my throat. I lunge toward the fire, my hand outstretched. If I can just get close enough I can pluck it from the flames or knock it free.

The teepee of wood collapses in on itself. Ash and burning paper rise on the updraft, dancing like bats. The books are almost buried. I reach again. Flames lick my shoes, my fingers. I feel nothing at first, and then the excruciating agony as my skin begins to burn, but still I try to scoop it out. I reach for a stick, prod a hunk of burning rubber out of the way. Acrid black smoke billows out, choking me. There is a push of hot air against my chest like the invisible hand of God, and everything implodes as the flames soar toward the sky.

Another cry rips itself from my throat.

"Child," Ma says. "Come here." I cannot challenge her. Her voice holds quiet warning. I wrap myself in the throbbing pain of my scorched fingers as if I am wrapping myself in armor and I feel myself disappear into my place of nothing. Later I will suck on them until the blisters pop, and the pain will be as pure as a knife.

With one backward look at the pyre, I go to her.

"I have something for you." She shows me a thick plain-bound book. I don't understand. She burned my books, now she gives me another?

"This is the only book you need. I wrote your name on the flyleaf. You may thank me now."

It is the Bible. I know it well.

"Thank you," I tell her as I take the book, and I wish with all my heart I could bludgeon her with it.

CHAPTER ELEVEN

Ari didn't know she'd fallen asleep until she bashed her nose on the wall with enough force to knock her onto her ass. She'd been sleepwalking. She tasted metal at the back of her throat, and when she put her hand to her face it came back wet. Her nose felt mushy and pulsed with pain. She didn't think it was broken, but at this point she honestly didn't care. Injury, discomfort were small things in comparison to what was ahead of her. Dying by inches.

She'd been dreaming about the maze, running, hiding from Lynn, and then she'd heard the sirens.

She stood up, gripping the wall to steady her footing. Sirens. Police. Coming to rescue her? What else could it be? Hope momentarily robbed the breath from her lungs. She inhaled too sharply and her muscles cramped.

"I'm down here. Here!" she screamed. "It's me, Ari Sullivan. Ari Sullivan!"

She imagined her parents appearing at the well opening, throwing aside the cover, flashlights illuminating their tear-stained faces, a rope ladder lowered, some big cop who could carry her up, warm blankets and hot coffee, her dad's arms crushing her to his chest. Safe again. Saved.

All of this in the past.

She waited, face turned up toward the well cover, that almost perfect circle with the tantalizing crescent of sky beyond it. The sound still pulsed in her ears, but gradually the notes separated and rearranged themselves, becoming purer, wilder. Her breath caught in her throat. Not sirens. Coyotes. Out in the hills, calling to each other, their yips like ice breaking on a pond. Hunting her, probably. East Coast coyotes had bred with wolves and were almost as big. She could smell the sour stink of sweat that permeated her clothing, the fresh blood that had dripped onto her chest; to them it must be a dinner bell.

Her legs went out from under her and she fell heavily. A moment later she was laughing, a thin weak sound that caught behind a rib and ended abruptly.

The only good thing was that coyotes couldn't climb down. Thank goodness all the panthers had been wiped out. She huddled in her pile of leaves, gripping the long leg bone, giving herself up to an awful emptiness that encompassed everything, bringing the walls in closer.

It was paralyzing fear. Until now, she'd never really understood what that felt like. When Sourmash had threatened them, she'd felt panic, but she'd been able to run, to dodge. When she'd first attempted the high-diving platforms at the pool, she'd been able to stop halfway up the ladder and climb back down. Now it was as if she'd been robbed of her free will. She could run, but only in circles. She could plot and plan, but until Sourmash showed himself and she mounted an attack, all she could do was wait and hope that something happened before her body gave up.

The thought of a weakness that was inevitable and that she could do nothing to prevent was terrifying. She would dehydrate; she would starve to death; her body would cave in on itself. She would never get the chance to fight for her life. How fucking sad was that? She could lie under her blanket of leaves and cry until she fell asleep again, but that felt too much like dying.

She thought about the first time she'd ever tried to swim by herself. She was eight.

She remembered thrashing around, the water going up her nose, down her throat, the chlorine burning. From somewhere far away, all echoey and distorted, she could hear her father's voice saying, "Blow bubbles, Ari. Move your arms." But the words made no sense.

And then suddenly she realized that her head was above water, that she was somehow afloat and moving forward as if her body just naturally knew what to do.

She stowed the bone and stood, bracing herself until her knees stopped shaking. Her nose was crusty but it was no longer bleeding. She knotted her sweatshirt around her waist, wanting to feel coolness against the bare skin of her arms. If she closed her eyes she could pretend water was all around her, buoying her body and lifting her. "Push, pull, recover," she chanted as she had so many times before. She swept her arms through the air until she found her rhythm, and although her muscles protested, she felt as if she were flying in her element.

A muffled boom sounded in the distance, echoing around the well shaft and shocking Ari out of her rhythm. Thunder? She waited breathlessly but it didn't reoccur. A gunshot? The hairs rose on the back of her neck and adrenaline spurted, waking up her tired muscles. *Sourmash.* He was on his way back, armed and intent on finishing the job.

Get out! screamed her brain. *Get out now!* She paced back and forth, staring up at the well cover.

She tried not to think of how much she had weakened. That her cramping stomach meant that her pee spot was about to become a latrine. She leaned against the wall, felt the damp groove under her cheek where the water dripped, picked at the crumbling mortar and peeling paint.

"Keep moving," she told herself, unkinking the knots in her shoulders. Her fingers went to the tiger's-eye bracelet. She stroked it; thought of Lynn. Movement meant she was still alive, capable of fighting. Could she climb up? She brushed wet grit from her hand. Was there even the slightest chance? How far to the top? Twenty feet. Maybe twenty-five.

She fell to her knees and scrabbled around, found that one bone again and ran her fingers along the back edge where the mass flattened and curved slightly, forming a rough cup. Probably part of the shoulder blade. The other end was far narrower.

She felt the heft of it, ignoring the sweet stink that clung to her fingers, thinking hard. It could be a digging tool—and a weapon.

She reached high, as far as she could stretch, and began to chisel out a handhold in between the bricks. The crack was only an inch deep but she could cram her fingers in there, she could.

"Fuck yeah," she yelled as desperation turned to possibility. She felt a dizzying lightness in her body, a rush of endorphins.

She dropped down and removed her shoes, retying them around her neck. She'd use her toes too. Just like the climbing wall in gym. *You fell three times*, her enemy brain reminded her, but she ignored it. She had to.

CHAPTER TWELVE

Do you recall what it feels like to be a child? To have no voice, no say, no strength? To be powerless against all those who have authority over you?

I'd never have believed I could change anything. But slowly I have.

No one knows it yet. They can't see past my restless gaze, my quiet demeanor. They don't know the thoughts that seethe beneath this mask I've created. They believe me ordinary. But they're the ones who are ordinary. I am becoming something other.

Proving it to the world would be difficult. I had to choose carefully, lay my plans, wait like a spider at the trap door until I found him. The very first who would truly test my skill.

Here I am, thirteen.

I know him from church. He is a reader, a dreamer. I like that. Maybe nine years old, blue-eyed and blond, with chubby cheeks and skin like milk. His head seems too big for his body, and he has the habit of sucking on his lower lip as he turns the pages. There is a small blister there, like a drop of water on a rose petal. A nervous child and full of fidgets. Still, he comes willingly once I tell him how magical the woods are at dusk. Strangers are big men in big cars, not someone you see every day, someone who smiles and says "hi" and ruffles your hair and is polite to your mother. I know I can handle him. He looks up to me as young children do to those a little older. I speak to him of monsters and fearsome beasts until his downy cheeks flush and his eyes are full of stars. I want to pluck them out and carry them in my pocket like a pair of marbles; I want to peel him like a green stick.

He follows me into the forest. There is a clearing, soft with pine needles, dotted with mushrooms growing in a circle. I tell him it is a fairy ring and that if we wait until twilight, the fairies will come and dance, and the elves will slip their twig-like fingers into our pockets and leave presents of bird eggs and walnuts.

"I don't like eggs. I'm hungry," he whines. "You said there'd be candy. And a gingerbread house."

I show him the gleaming skull of a raccoon I killed, drawing his chubby fingers across the sharp teeth. "It rips fish apart with these," I tell him. "It's a predator." I look into his eyes for understanding but there is none. He wants cookies. He doesn't recognize the wolf even when it sits beside him. In my pocket I find a hard crust of bread I'd been meaning to give the hens. He gnaws on it, still whining.

The sun has reached the top of the canopy and is now on its downward plummet. The air grows cold and still. He is fractious, fussing in the way that only kids can do.

I rest against a tree thinking of how best to kill him, blocking out the small sounds he is making, as if he were one of the barn kittens mewling for its mother. My body is buzzing with anticipation. In my pack with the books I have a length of good rope, my knife wrapped in a pair of socks. All night I had plotted about method, sleeping not at all, staring at the ceiling beams, drawing my knife over the oiled stone until both edges were razor-sharp. Stringing him up on a tree branch will be difficult because he will certainly struggle. I can do it—my muscles are as hard as unripe apples from working on the farm—but he might yell and I might silence him too quickly, as I did with the piglets. I am older but he is a solid, healthy child. If I hit him on the head it will ruin the picture I want to make, the scene I am trying to set. I'm striving for peace, innocence, death like sleep, sleep like death. Sooner or later the world will break him anyway. I will be much kinder.

I will freeze him in this moment so he will always be young and beautiful and naïve.

Despite my careful plans, I have forgotten important items: duct tape, food and water. I force down the anger I feel at myself. It is my first time. I will learn from it, and the next time will be better.

But I so want it to be perfect.

I watch him so he does not know I am watching him. His mouth is downturned, a furled pink blossom. I should have brought a cloth to clean him with afterward. The blood has to be contained; it cannot spill except where I want it to. I envision a single perfect drop balanced at the corner of his full bottom lip, or a trickle from one ear looping around his ivory throat like a thread of red silk. If I can fix it in my mind, I'll be able to reproduce the scene later in the new sketchbook I stole from the general store, and I will have him for always.

He falls asleep next to me, like a puppy, his head heavy against my knee, cheeks flushed and mouth open. He would have looked immaculate except for the slime of mucus around his nostrils, the silvery snail trails of his tears.

I feel the rage rise. He is ruining it all.

What if I suffocated him first? A hand over his mouth and nose, my knees pressed against his chest, holding him down. Two minutes, three perhaps. I recently read a book that detailed the physical changes before death. I had to stop reading frequently to consult a dictionary, but it was enthralling to find out what distress was caused by drowning, hanging by the neck, poison, decapitation, choking. A body that had bled out was almost colorless, just tinged with cyanotic blue around the extremities. How beautiful that sounds: cyanosis! Suffocation or carbon monoxide poisoning were the gentlest. The corpse they left looked as if it were merely resting, cheeks in bloom.

I touch his face. He doesn't stir. He sleeps heavily as children do, taken by it in an instant, sweat-dampened hair curling on his forehead. I find my scissors and snip a lock from behind his ear, where it is thick and unruly, and slide it into my pocket. I hover my hand over his mouth, feeling the shushing of his breath. Just a little closer, press down, and I could stop it forever.

Maybe. It is not quite what I envisioned but it might serve. In my fantasy he would come willingly to the knife, tilt his head backward so that I had easy access to the column of his throat, lean into it as if the blade were extending a kiss.

But I know from the piglets that once the jugular is slit, struggle is inevitable and it is impossible to control the blood flow.

I get to my feet, careful not to wake him, and move back, looking at him from a distance. Does the scene work? How will it look in a couple of hours? The big tree with its branches outspread above him. His face, bone-white, awash in the moonlight, the shadows wrapped around him like a cluster of crows, his small limbs thrown out in supple unconsciousness. The blood, thick, black and almost invisible until the morning sun catches it on fire and turns the drops to rubies. I can't wait to draw it. I think of something and hurry forward. The autumn leaves, red, flame-orange, citrine, are a perfect counterpoint, a foreshadowing. I arrange them around his legs and torso like a patchwork quilt.

I decide to suffocate him. I can use my socks.

But then we are found. Pa Cosloy, his mother—her name is Marjorie, I remember. She is concerned, but laughter drowns out the doubt.

"Look how they built a nest," Marjorie says. "What darlings! What a lovely game!"

Connor is tucked against her shoulder, his chubby legs wrapped around her waist. He hides his face from me. My hand itches for my blade.

Pa gazes at me intently but says nothing, though his fingers are tight around my forearm and afterward there is a band of bruising.

CHAPTER THIRTEEN

Ari hung twelve feet from the ground. She'd already made the mistake of looking down. Somehow it seemed to increase the gravity pulling at her and dragging against her fingertips. She was barely clinging to the wall. And looking up just reinforced how much farther she still had to go. *Half-way*, she told herself. *Almost there*. She thought about how much Lynn hated that glass-half-full expression. She always said they should be full-bottle girls, and it always made Ari laugh. Ignoring the increasing rawness of her skin, she dug into the spaces between the bricks with the bone and used her fingers to pull the loose plaster free. She shifted slightly to reach up to the next ledge when a sudden pain knotted her calf muscles. A sharp inhalation of breath made her dizzy, and she lost all sense of up and down.

The ground came up to meet her frighteningly fast and the impact knocked the air from her body.

For a few minutes she just lay on her back staring up at the well cover, too shocked and defeated to even cry. The top seemed as far away as the moon. She'd never make it out. She would die here. And maybe no one would ever find her body.

Her parents, Lynn, Coach—they'd never know what had happened to her.

With the first breath that came back into her lungs she sat forward and screamed out her frustration. Fuck! This was as hard as mastering the butterfly stroke. She thought of the days when it had seemed as if her limbs would never obey her brain's instructions. But that was a series of complex motions that had to be fluidly linked—this, this was just climbing.

She struggled onto her knees, patting the ground for her digging tool, and then to her feet, renewed resolve flooding her weary muscles. *Up*, she told herself. *You did it once, now do it again.*

Retracing her steps, she clamped her teeth around the bone, trying not to breathe through her nose or reflect on the bacteria scurrying across her tongue. Stowing it in her back pocket and repeatedly reaching around to remove and replace it increased her chances of falling again. And she needed both hands to climb, hanging from one while she used the other to dig out the next brick.

She was past the place where she had fallen the first time. She blinked sweat out of her eyes, transferred the bone to her right hand and scraped out an indentation. Adjusting the fingers of her left hand, she forced them into the shallow crack. A nail snapped and peeled back. She bit off a sob. The smell of blood and the stinging pain robbed her of focus, but she pressed herself like a moth to the wall until the sensation passed.

Coach would tell her to concentrate on her breathing. *Inhale. One, two, three* . . . eight seconds. *Exhale.*

Her world narrowed to one brick. Each one maybe four inches wide—such a small distance to be measuring out in slow breaths. But if she really pushed it, she could move up a couple of feet every time. "Do this precise thing six more times, Ari," she told herself in a fierce whisper. "Climb, Ari. Brick by brick."

She was close enough to smell a breath of fresh air. It spurred her on, but she forced herself to continue in her methodical way. The thought of falling again was terrifying. She was much higher now, and she risked breaking a leg, or worse. If that happened it was all over. Slowly she inched forward. The well cover with its seductive gap was two feet away . . . a foot. And beyond that she saw a dark expanse like a swathe of velvet spangled with diamonds.

The sky. It had never looked so vast to her, so beautiful.

Summoning up the last of her energy, she made for the narrow opening, forcing her ragged fingers to dig and flex and her toes to grip. Another nail split open; she gasped and the bone slipped from her grip. She barely heard the thump it made over the pounding of her heart as she climbed. It was stupid to drop the only weapon she had, but she'd find another.

With the end in sight, she managed to pull herself up and out, squeezing her body through the narrow space, turning onto her back when she could with her fingers flattened against dew-wet grass. She sobbed with relief into the cold air. Her fingertips were chewed up like raw meat by the rough brick, her muscles quivered with exhaustion, and cramps ran up and down her legs, arching her feet and making her want to vomit with the pain. Still, she was on solid ground. Once the dizzying sensation that she might fall off the world and go spinning out into the universe ceased, she sat up.

A full moon hung like a massive silver ball low along the lightening horizon. *That must be east, where the sun will rise.* She could tell that dawn was still at least an hour or two away. The sky was glittering with a thousand stars, the weight of them an almost unbearable pressure on her shoulders. She glanced down at the white paint caked across her sweat-soaked T-shirt. It would make her visible. Quickly she stripped it off and turned it inside out. She wondered if Sourmash was watching her already.

She was panting like a dog, the push and pull of air ripping across her dry throat. The thirst came raging back. It took effort to control her breathing and slow her heart down before she was finally able to struggle to her feet.

She was in some kind of field surrounded by other fields as far as she could see, spread out like a dark patchwork quilt. Single, silhouetted trees stood in sparse lines like black watchers, and, on a nearby hill, more thickly, a small forest. Crickets thrummed, the only noise other than the heavy silence of the waning night.

No car sounds, she realized. *Definitely outside town limits. Not close to any major roads*. No wonder no one had heard her screams.

Move forward.

The ground was covered in stubbly razor grass and weeds. It sliced the soles of her feet. She stopped to put her shoes on, looking around nervously, cursing at the knot she'd tied that her ripped, strained fingers couldn't unpick. Finally she got it loose and shoved her feet into her shoes, wincing as the canvas rubbed over her sore toes. She untied her sweatshirt from her waist, slipped it on and pulled the hood up. The dull color would help her blend in with the shadows. She forced her way through a small gnarled copse of stunted trees and halted.

Just ahead was a square building. Small, hardly more than a cabin. Murky windows; no smoke coming from the steel stovepipe chimney. But she could smell a trace of wood smoke in the air and it made her freeze. *Someone has been here*. Someone had made a fire, recently enough for her to discern it.

This must be Sourmash's place. His hunting cabin. He might own all the acreage around here. A perfect spot to make whiskey or meth, live off the grid—bring a victim.

Aware of her visibility, she dropped to the dusty dirt, though there was no cover, trembling like a baby animal caught in the open. Crouched with her face scratched by coarse grass stalks, she strained her ears, listening hard. Was he sitting there in the dark, watching from the shadows? His long-range rifle with hunting sight fixed on her prone body, some kind of night-vision goggles masking his face?

No, he could have shot her any time while she was stuck in the cistern. Like a fish in a barrel.

But he hadn't. He wanted to keep her alive for some reason.

Or maybe he'd been interrupted. Or maybe he needed to hear her beg for her life.

She had to run. *Now*.

She bowed her head, half wanting to just stay where she was until day broke, like a kid hiding its face. She thought she would die from the fear, but the idea of him finding her splayed out on the ground after how hard she'd fought to get out of that well forced her to her feet.

Careful, Ari. She'd skirt the building, keeping low. There must be some kind of track, an exit road. Sourmash would hardly hike in; he must have driven. Driven them both. She wished she knew how she had come to be there, but that section of the past was still locked away in her brain. Every sense was hyper alert, her muscle aches and thirst forgotten as she studied the shadows around the dark cabin. Her eyes had adjusted to the dimness. Nothing stirred.

Slowly, she crept closer until she was crouched in the gloom thrown by the pitched roof. Everything in her was screaming, *Run away, run away*, but her legs didn't seem to want to cooperate. She peered through the grimy window. A table, a chair, a doorway beyond leading to another room. It looked empty, but he could return at any moment. Her thick tongue clacked in her parched mouth. Maybe there was a sink, water? Her eyes went back to the chair, a red jacket flung over the back. She recognized the brash black-and-white logo for the water polo team, and although folds of material covered most of the chest badge, she spotted the *C*, and knew what it said.

Captain.

God knows, she'd stared at it often enough—when she wasn't staring at the enticing muscled skin beneath it.

Stroud. Sourmash must have taken him too. Oh God, this nightmare never ended.

She hesitated. She wanted to help, of course she did, but she didn't want to risk recapture. She argued with herself. Stroud was big, fit—maybe they had a better chance together? Running blindly into the woods, which were most likely Sourmash's hunting grounds, was a much stupider idea. But she'd go into the cabin with her eyes open and she'd go armed.

She picked up a stick from the ground and weighed it in her hand. She'd have to get in close to use it, but she thought it would do the trick if she swung it hard enough. She shifted her grip so that she held it in both hands and raised it up, formulating her plan. She'd aim a low blow between his legs and then bash him in the skull.

First though, she made a circuit of the periphery, hugging the walls and listening with all her might. There were only four windows, two in the rear, which looked into rooms too dark to distinguish anything beyond shapeless forms, and two in the front on either side of what appeared to be the only entrance. She paused there to gather her courage.

In and out, as fast as possible. She made the list in her mind: *Find Stroud. Run.* Her blood was buzzing in her ears and she was short of breath, but she forced herself to tiptoe to the door. No lock. She twisted the knob, feeling as if her hand were not attached to the rest of her.

The door creaked alarmingly. It smelled musty inside, but the scent of wood smoke was stronger. She noted the small iron woodstove on the far side of the table, the stack of cut logs, felt the heat that was still coming off it. Dilapidated couch, empty booze bottles, no kitchen area. While she'd been shivering at the bottom of the well, forced to pee in the corner, Sourmash had been up here comfortable and toasty. She looked around the sparse room noting drifts of dead leaves that had blown in, the dust scattered over every surface, splotched with a multitude of fingerprints and smears. The heavy wooden top of the table was scored with deep knife cuts. She imagined him sitting there, butchering someone's pet. Perhaps he had sat there just a few minutes ago, plotting what to do with her body. Maybe he was out right now, picking up supplies: garbage bags to stuff her body into, a chainsaw to hack her limbs off with, kerosene to burn her corpse.

She hurried over to the jacket and shook it out. It was

Stroud's. She felt something hard in the pocket. His cell phone. She turned it on with clumsy fingers. The battery was almost completely dead and there were no bars. She shuffled to the window; still no bars. She clicked it off and then on again. The screen brightened and died almost immediately. *Useless.* Still, she slipped it into her jeans' pocket. His jacket, she stroked and then put down. She needed both her hands free.

She fidgeted on the balls of her feet. There might be a phone, a landline, but where was it?

She spotted a black electrical cord stapled to the wall. It could be a phone line. Quickly she followed its path, trying not to feel as if she were chasing bait.

It took courage she didn't even know she had to creep through the doorway into the dimly lit adjoining room, but she ordered her feet to move as her eyes skittered around, checking out every dark cranny for an attacker. There was little furniture: a steamer trunk, the heavy lid open to reveal a heap of dark clothes—navy-blue sweaters and camouflage pants, all looking as if they belonged in the bins at an army surplus store. A heavy peacoat, furry with mildew, hung on a hook. It wasn't a regular clothing hook; it was curved with a wicked point on the end, like something from a butcher's shop.

A picture of blue-eyed Jesus and his exposed bleeding heart hung on the wall. Beyond, a bed covered with blankets, and a bare-bulb lamp propped on an overturned milk crate. The shadows cast by the light animated the darkest corners and made her heart leap in terror.

Keep moving, stay alert. There, the cord.

She tiptoed across the room. Rough wood planks squeaked underfoot and the sound seemed deafening. The black cord ended in a frayed clump. She stifled a sob. No landline then. And where the hell was Stroud? She pictured him bound and gagged, helpless, in a closet maybe?

She glanced at the bed and froze, sealing her mouth with her hand in an attempt to cut off the rising scream. There was someone there, beneath the piled blankets. A patchwork quilt with a design of red, yellow and orange leaves was tucked in tight, but one socked foot protruded. Sourmash?

The seconds seemed to pass with agonizing slowness as she remained paralyzed in terror, the air molecular in her ears. She slid her foot forward. The figure under the covers didn't move.

She raised the stick in her fist, ready to strike if she had to, and stretched her other hand out, willing herself to touch the edge of the brightly colored quilt and twitch it aside. Six inches, two, her fingers hovered just short. She swallowed hard, her upper body half-turned in the direction of the front room, her weight on her toes, ready to run.

Steeling her nerves, she gripped the edge of the quilt and pulled gently on it. Slowly the material slipped aside. Her breath left her throat in a gasp.

A young face, dimpled. Mouth slackened. Eyes closed. "Stroud," she croaked, dropping the stick from her nerveless hand.

CHAPTER FOURTEEN

I only looked back once when I reached the crest of the hill. The glow on the horizon resembled an early sunset but I knew it was the house fully alight. A few yards farther on, the farm road dropped into the valley and was swallowed by trees. The nearest neighbors were almost five miles away, hidden by another rise. Only a few wisps of smoke scudded across the darkening sky, and carried with them the inconspicuous smell of burning. People burn everything out here; no one would pay it any mind. It's country folks' way of cleaning up after themselves.

I arranged them in their beds up in the attic under the pitched roof and moved my own little bed from the curtained hallway alcove to the far corner of the room. I pushed them all close together, as if we were a happy family. My bed would remain empty, of course, but I laid my pajamas out neatly anyway. I took some time to fold their hands in their laps, place Ma's Bible nearby, even though I knew no one would ever see this tableau. I wanted to add it to my sketchbook later, so the appearance of it before I struck the matches was important.

There was little blood. I was proud of that.

I struck Pa with a blow to the back of the head while he was crouched over mending the chicken wire that went round the henhouse. He squawked once and toppled like a tree. I used the splitting maul. It's a long-handled steel ax with one side of the head resembling a sledgehammer. I left him where he fell.

Ma was in the kitchen doing the breakfast dishes when I crept up behind her. I'd taken some time to consider the knife and how good it would feel to hold it against her throat, but it was too risky, so my foster mother got the hammer too. I put all my weight into it, in the way Pa had shown me when we split firewood. It made a hollow sound when it landed, but my aim was good and it didn't get stuck as it sometimes did when I hit against the grain. She swayed and turned to look at me. Her hands were lathered with dish soap and her mouth made an O. I'd never seen that expression on her face before. It smoothed out all her hard edges.

"Ma'am," I said.

Her eyes opened very wide and time seemed to stand still, and then she just crumpled, dropping the plate she was holding. It was one of her best plates and it shattered on the wood floor. I didn't bother to clean it up.

Dragging them up the stairs was hard even with the ropes I looped around their upper bodies. I made a simple pulley using the doorknob and stair rail as anchors for leverage and I heaved with a steady rhythm, as if I were competing in a tug-of-war, counting the thwacks their heels made against the steps. I knew from the piglets what dead weight was like, but determination gave me strength.

For seven hours I contained the flames to the small area where they lay, dousing the surrounding boards with water so that the fire would not spread. I filled every container and bucket I could find, hauled them and lined them up in rows. I kept the window closed even though it was always hot under the eaves and the fire made it close to unbearable. I was trying to drive the temperature up as high as possible, turn the room into an oven.

I had to cover my face with a wet towel when their skin began to fry. They made the same popping sounds as green, sap-heavy wood makes.

The smell reminded me of a pig roast. I had wondered if their skulls might explode when their brains sizzled but they did not.

Pa made those beds out of red maple and pine. Ma sewed the dense mattresses out of straw and striped cotton tick. I always hated how lumpy they were, the sharp ends of the straw sticking into my body, as if restful sleep were a sin. They went up like they'd been doused in gasoline. I was half-afraid the roof would catch before I had finished what I needed to do, but Pa had used hard hickory for the beams.

The beds collapsed in a flurry of embers and sparks, and still I waited. It took the full seven hours. I needed this to look like an accident. "A stray spark flew from the fireplace." "The old place went up like a torch." "Timbers half-rotten. They didn't stand a chance." "That poor, poor child." That's what I wanted people to say.

I took the pliers from my pocket. I'd chosen my top back molar. I got a good grip and wrenched and it came free with a ripping sound and a surprising gush of blood. I spat on the floor and tossed the tooth into the flames. I'd never been to the dentist in my life, but a child's tooth was easily identified.

Once the skeletons were exposed and nothing remained but a veneer of greasy blackened flesh, I broke the bones apart with the maul, scattering them around. Bone gets brittle and continues to burn if it's agitated, leaving nothing but shards. This would happen naturally, but I thought it safest to hurry the process along.

After I'd hauled the empty buckets back downstairs and stored them in the shed, I set fire to the woodpile that was braced against the outer wall of the house. I'd stacked it myself and the wood was well seasoned. It caught quickly, the pillar of flame crisping my arms and driving me backward. From there, the fire spread in all directions like some golden tornado, sweeping up everything in its path, leaping onto the old shingled roof. The walls must have been insulated with old newspapers or horsehair. I threw the splitting maul into the inferno so there wouldn't be any sign of wrongdoing. I watched until I was sure there was no stopping it, and then I gathered up my pack, heavy with the jars of pickled hearts I could not abandon, and I walked away.

I'm a couple of weeks shy of my fourteenth birthday and if everything has gone to plan, I have ceased to exist. A few teeth will be found among the bone remnants, but no way to tell if there were three bodies or only two.

I pick a town at random. My eyes closed, finger poised above the map of the northeast.

Albany. It sounds like a place I could lose myself in. For a while.

CHAPTER FIFTEEN

It was as if he were asleep.

"Stroud? Stroud?" Ari murmured. He didn't stir. *Is he breathing?*

She wasn't sure, but for a moment she couldn't bring herself to touch him. For such a long time she had dreamed of it and now. . . . In the dim light, his skin looked so pale, like marble. There wasn't a mark on him. She placed a trembling hand on his cheek. It was cool. She pressed a finger against the vein on his neck, searching for a pulse that she couldn't find.

A tiny moan escaped her lips. Her thoughts tumbled like leaves in a windstorm as fright overwhelmed her, punching the air from her lungs. *Stroud is dead.* The fight-or-flight instinct took over and she ran to the front door.

She wrenched at the handle. She knew it was not locked but still she wrestled with it for precious moments, sobbing, blinded by tears. Outside, it was a little lighter now, and she could see the rough semicircular track gouged and scarred by heavy tires, the ground hard as iron from the dry summer. She followed, praying it led to somewhere safe. Fifty yards farther along, concealed in the shadow of some trees, was Sourmash's camo-painted truck. Ari lurched into a deep tire rut, flung both hands out, failed to catch her balance. She remained on her stomach, staring at the back window of the truck. Empty. Her eyes traveled over to the cluster of trees, the hilly terrain beyond it. He must be out there somewhere. She struggled to think clearly.

The muddy track seemed to widen just ahead. Surely that was more than just a deer path. It must lead to a main road. Where else would it go? She slowly stood up, completely disorientated. Maybe it just led further into the wilderness? Exactly how far out was she? She tried to visualize what the outlying areas around Dempsey Hollow looked like. Farmland, woods, strip malls and box stores on the outreaches. The nearest town, Ross, was about twenty miles away; Wallace, twenty-five in the opposite direction. They were both picturesque, historic, much like Dempsey Hollow. Quiet, sleepy, safe places. At least, they used to be.

The sun would rise at her back, so that was east. She was currently facing west, and that meant that the track, which headed roughly north, could, in fact, join up with the North West Road, which traveled through her hometown, linking all the neighboring towns like beads on a string.

She watched the truck. Nothing stirred. No noise but the wind whuffing over the hills, the strident music of bugs that echoed the tautness of her nerves.

She inched forward, half-crouched, limbs heavy, her heart in her mouth. The bumpers and wheel wells were caked with dried mud. She rose up, feeling her thigh muscles protest. There was no deer in the back this time. Just a bunch of filthy sacking and a ton of empty beer bottles. She circled the truck and peeked in through the partially open passenger window. A smell like firecrackers hung in the air.

It was still dark, the window glass fouled with more mud, but she caught a glimmer of something metallic.

The keys dangled from the ignition. Ari's chest heaved. She could drive out of here. Checking once more over her shoulder, she ran around to the driver's side and carefully opened the door. The overhead light came on.

At first she thought it was just a huge pile of dirty clothes heaped on the seat. But then she saw a hand, fingers curled. She stared at it, the swollen knuckles, the grime jammed beneath each yellow nail, furred wrists poking from his khaki jacket. Her eyes traveled up to the ruin above his neck. And the gun propped up against the steering wheel, pointed at his face. Or where his face had been. Suicide? She remembered the boom she'd heard earlier. It had been a gunshot, not thunder. She could see something obscenely red, like a mound of hamburger meat, and the waxy curve of one ear.

Once she'd noticed these things, her eyes flicked back and forth to each in rapid succession. The blood spattered across the vinyl of the passenger side, the white shards of bone, a mess of glistening pink and gray, which had hit the right side of the windshield and dripped down onto the dashboard. His brains, she thought, but outside his skull. Everything forcefully rearranged and displayed. She bit down on the inside of her cheek, suppressing a hysterical giggle. One eyeball hung loose against his ruddy cheek and she was mesmerized by the sheer wrongness of it. She took a deep breath, gagging on the sour, meaty smell of the air, unable to turn away or shut her eyes and wanting more than anything to do both those things.

The rest of his face was mercifully hidden by his broad-brimmed baseball cap, but it didn't matter. Her imagination did the work for her. Something foul spilled across her tongue and finally she did retreat, swallowing convulsively, her fingers gripping the side mirror as the ground seemed to tilt under her shoes. Somehow she managed not to vomit. She tottered a few steps away and sank to the ground, wrapping her arms around her knees and hugging them close to her chest, feeling cold and hot all at the same time.

She tried to process.

What happened here? Did Sourmash kill Stroud in some drunken spree gone wrong and then blow his own head off? Her stomach churned. She clenched her teeth and fisted her hands, breathing shallowly through her mouth. *Remorse?* It was sickening but it made sense.

The hairs on her body were still standing up. She craned her neck and peered through the open car door.

Sourmash hadn't moved. *He's definitely dead, right?* She shook herself. *Yes, of course.* This wasn't a horror movie, even though it felt like one. No one was coming back from a head wound like that.

Unless they were a zombie. Her laugh, watery and nervous, definitely sounded on the verge of hysteria. If she gave in to it, she'd never stop.

CHAPTER SIXTEEN

Cruelty is everywhere. Endings. Waste. Our bodies are so temporary. Our lives, short threads easily snipped off. Death comes like a thief in the night and steals us away. But not me. I made a pact with Death a long time ago.

One morning in winter, I opened the grain barrel. It was bitter cold and still dark. My boots crunched through hard-frozen mud in the trail I'd made from the house to the barn. Bats swooped in the gray sky searching for furtive insects, their night extended, daylight held prisoner for a couple of extra hours. Ma had sent me for some bran to stir into the oatmeal we ate every morning during the winter months. She never salted it. It lay like soupy plaster in the bowl and set like concrete in my belly but it kept me full.

I pried the lid off and there on the bottom was a huge brown rat, its pink tail coiled behind its fat haunches like a snake, its belly bloated. I recoiled in disgust, and as I did, it came for me, narrow teeth bared. It must have been very desperate to attack a human but attack it did. I ducked as it scrabbled to the top of the barrel, balanced there for a moment and then launched itself at my face. I felt the pinch of its claws against my neck, the warm-blooded weight of it, and then a lucky, wild swipe dislodged it onto the floor. In an instant all the barn cats were upon it—a frenzied swarm of orange, black, brown and white fur, a furious hissing like steam escaping from a kettle. Slowly the hisses subsided to meows and wet, smacking sounds. And afterward nothing remained of the rodent but its wormy tail, which was carried around triumphantly by one of the kittens for the rest of the day.

You might think that I am like one of those cats. You would be right. I am the hunter in the shadows. But I am also the rat—cornered, and forced to play my hand too early.

CHAPTER SEVENTEEN

A surge of determination shocked the hell out of her. She stood up, looked back at the cabin. The dark windows seemed to stare back at her. No need to go back in there, though she felt weird and sad about leaving Stroud alone. *He's dead too. You can't help him*, her brain whispered, and she shook her head violently, trying to clear it. She needed a plan. Her eyes fixed on the keys dangling from the ignition. Could she . . . ? She'd have to move Sourmash. He was a big man: two-fifty, maybe even three hundred pounds. She'd heard of mothers who lifted cars off their trapped children. Somehow they found the strength, and so would she. Should she just haul him out and leave him in the dirt? It didn't feel right. She thought of Stroud tucked up in bed. And the truck was the scene of a crime or something. Desperation made the decision for her. She had to get out of here. The seat was bench-style; she could just move him over to the passenger side.

She could feel the cold of him, even through his heavy hunting coat, though he couldn't have been dead for very long. He was heavy and the angle was awkward. She withdrew her hands, wincing as his limbs fell against the seat with a dull thud, went around to the other side of the truck and opened the door. Pulling on his upper torso was easier than pushing him up and over the gear stick. *Shit*. She registered that it was a standard. She understood the mechanics of how to drive a manual shift but she'd only done it once, at the lake with her cousins in their beat-up Cabriolet. *How hard can it be?* If she had to, she'd just pop it into first and drive. But before that she had to make room. She found an oil-stiff rag on the truck floor and threw it over Sourmash's pulpy head. Then, steeling herself, she grabbed fistfuls of his coat and heaved. Her grasp slipped and she fell backward, landing heavily on the rocky ground. She felt something break in her back pocket and drew out Stroud's cell phone. The glass screen was spiderwebbed. She considered tossing it but decided not to; maybe the battery was not completely dead. She stowed it in her hoodie pouch and grabbed onto Sourmash again, slipping her hands under his arms this time. He seemed to weigh a ton, but slowly he slid forward onto the passenger seat. She closed the door, went back around to the driver's side, and yanked and shoved his legs until she'd managed to push them out of the way. Would rigor mortis stiffen his body in this uncomfortable, graceless pose, his right leg bent at an unnatural angle, his arm contorted behind his back? Even though she knew he was dead—and it was *Sourmash*—it still seemed . . . undignified that she should see him like this. Worse than if he was naked.

Her brain was going all over the place. *His brains went all over the place.* She breathed hard through her nose. *Don't think about it. Focus on getting out of here. Of driving faster than you've ever gone before even if it is only in first and just hope that a cop will pull you over for shitty driving before you get too far.*

She eased her hands out. Sourmash slumped against the window, and what was concealed by the cloth hit the glass with a soft, dull sound like overripe apples falling from a tree. The gun clunked onto the dirty carpet on the passenger's side, and she jumped back about ten feet. *Is it still loaded?* She knew nothing about guns other than that they were lethal. It could have gone off. She left it where it fell, not wanting to rummage around in the papers and garbage on the floor. *Don't think of him as* him. *Think of him as* it, she told herself as she slid into the driver's seat.

Her fingers were fumbling sausages, her shoulders tight and painful. Sweat had dried, leaving her feeling cold and clammy. The ghostly moon was very low now and a wash of pink blushed against the horizon. It felt as if the longest night of her life was finally coming to a close.

She sat on the edge of the seat, set all the way back for Sourmash, who was much taller than her. She didn't want to adjust it. It would feel as if she was crushing his—*its*—body, so instead she scooted forward to the edge. She reached for the pedals with her feet, tapping them to see how they felt. Brake in the middle. Gas on the right, clutch on the left. She thought that was correct. She blew on her fingers to warm them, and then turned the key in the ignition. It clicked over and then caught. She gave it some gas. Too much. The engine roared, the truck jerked forward, and died. She'd forgotten to release the emergency brake. *Put the clutch in and then start it*, she heard her cousin Clare say. She leaned forward, feeling like a little kid going for a joyride—except instead of a partner in crime riding shotgun (ha ha), the lifeless body of a killer was sitting uncomfortably close—and jammed her foot against the pedal.

Right foot poised above the gas, she cranked the key again. The truck came back to life. Ari slowly let up on the clutch and the vehicle shuddered into motion, heading straight for a row of trees and a deep culvert. She braked hard again and the truck died. There wasn't room to turn around.

She could barely see over the dashboard. The part directly in front of her, which was spatter free, was littered with pine-cones, branches of dried leaves, a small animal skull. She hastily brushed it all aside onto the floor, cluttered with empty beer cans, take-out containers and magazines. If she kept her eyes fixed on the small rectangle of glass, she could avoid looking at the mess that had dripped down and pooled like old, gray oatmeal on the far side of the dash. If she breathed through her mouth and leaned into the crisp air hitting her cheek, she could avoid smelling him. *It*.

She focused. The rough track was definitely a road, but first she had to back up. It took forever to figure out reverse. Twice she thought she had it, only to discover after the engine juddered to a tooth-chattering halt that she was in fourth. Finally, with an awful squeal, she found the gear, floored it and shot backward. *Brake! Brake!* She glanced in the mirror. She was lucky she hadn't crashed into the cottage. She jimmied it into first, although from the terrible engine noises, it might have been third, gave it some gas and pointed it straight ahead. She steadfastly avoided looking at the shrouded mound next to her, gluing her eyes to the odometer and the immediate area in front of her tires.

The track forked. She took the left branch, thinking it looked more traveled. She drove until she reached a road—a real road with split lanes and mileage markers—and only then did she allow herself a terrified giggle. The sound of her hysterical laughter reminded her of Lynn, and that un-dammed a flood of tears that threatened to drown her.

CHAPTER EIGHTEEN

This might be surprising but people don't always notice me. It's like not registering the UPS man when he's out of his brown uniform; it doesn't matter how tall he is or how short—all they notice is the outer shell. Sometimes a flicker of familiarity will cross their faces if they see me in the convenience store or around the school, but unless they can put me into context, their eyes just slide right past. I'm not invisible but I am camouflaged. That's ideal. I've spent most of my life trying to find the right uniform. How easy it is to slip it on and off.

The poet T.S. Eliot said: "Let me also wear / Such deliberate disguises / Rat's coat, crowskin . . ."

If I had my way, I would just keep pretending to be exactly who they think I am, continue this feat of acting, dumb myself down, but it has become harder lately. She sees me, even though she's not quite sure what she's looking at. He sees me. Even my hidey hole, this desolate place with its overgrown track road, sheltering woods and nondescript cabin, has become unsafe, though my name is nowhere to be found on the ownership paperwork.

I had my beautiful plan in place and then it all began to go wrong.

Ma always said, "Trouble never comes alone."

First it was the girl, Ari, with her questions and snooping around. It was unfortunate that she stumbled across my killing grove in the woods by the swimming hole. I wasn't ready to let the world see it yet; I had my eye on a bumbling Labrador retriever puppy that always tangled itself in my feet.

Ari is kind and naïve and easily influenced.

Ma Cosloy used to say "needs must" when there was some unpleasant but necessary chore on the agenda, and those were the words I spoke to Ari just before I pushed her into the cistern. It bothered me that her death would not be glorious in the way I would have liked. The timing was all wrong for my tableau; I already had my choice picked out and Ari would decompose too badly to be used for future installations. I felt guilty for being wasteful again, but my intention was that her body never be found and nothing would link her disappearance with the others to come.

Both the blow and the fall should have been fatal but I could hear the small whimpers of pain she made as she lay there, and I knew she was still alive. I'd have to climb down and strangle her and for that I'd need a good strong rope.

I was already back in the cabin, collecting what was necessary, when the other one came sniffing about. I had barely enough time to clean up a few things, strip off my gloves and make it onto the outside porch with the door firmly closed behind me. I cursed myself for not installing locks.

"Wasn't sure anyone was home," he said. "Couldn't see a vehicle." That was because I had parked in an overgrown gully invisible from the track.

I pasted a smile on my face, concealing my impatience. It made little difference, really. Ari would die of exposure or from injuries sustained in the fall. I could tie up the other loose ends, the mess in the cabin, and no one would be the wiser. Obviously I could never come back here again.

"You've got privacy at least. Could get up to all kinds of trouble out here, hey?"

He leered and I kept my expression noncommital, but my senses leapt to high alert.

In the wild, the bear recognizes the wolf and keeps his distance. Each establishes his own wide territory and their paths rarely cross. Bears are stupid and quick to anger. I am the wolf.

"My place is just a few miles down the road thataway," he said, gesturing vaguely. "Good hunting in these woods." He squinted. "You don't seem like the type."

"You know what they say about books and covers," I said.

He showed all his stained teeth when he laughed, and his breath had the odor of a longtime drugger and drinker.

I leaned against the door and watched him as he prowled around the cabin, trying to peek inside through the dingy curtains. I knew he'd see nothing but still I kept one eye on him.

My mind kept wandering to my special project. The girl I have chosen to be my work of art, my princess. I was itching to get back to fine-tuning my plans for her. I could feel my anger rising but he showed no inclination to leave.

"You and I are the same," he proclaimed, scratching the hairy belly spilling over his waistband. "Survivors. We make our own rules, am I right? Help each other out." He stared at me and I stubbornly met his gaze. The implicit threat in his voice was crystal clear.

Sometimes I forget that the rare person notices as much as I do. Drugs had brought me into his sphere. I had crossed the line. And once he'd tracked me here, he left me no choice. I had to dispose of him. He made it so easy. Said he wanted to show me something, led me over to his truck, sat down and pulled out a gun from under the seat. "Look at this gorgeous thing," he said. "Gets me hard just holding her."

I forced a smile, held out my hand. "Let me see it closer," I said.

"Careful. Safety's on but it's a light touch."

I clicked it off and shot him with his own gun, right there in the cab of his truck. The weapon was a beauty, small bore, wood stock, far too good for the likes of him. I hadn't planned on it, but the foul words streaming out of his mouth, the stink of booze seeping from his pores, brought the gray veil down over my vision. In one smooth motion, I leveled the muzzle against his temple and fired.

The report of the gun at such close range made my ears buzz for a day or two. I didn't mind. It was like being trapped in the busy hive of my brain where I savored the shocked look in his eyes, reliving it over and over again.

I just wish he hadn't died so fast.

Next time, I promised myself, I would draw it out longer. Not give in to my anger. I would be calm, every movement controlled, precise. I would paint lovely lines with the tip of my knife, cleave flesh with surgical precision, compose a masterpiece.

CHAPTER NINETEEN

Ari almost drove into the ditch. She'd fallen asleep again without being aware of it. The rattle of loose gravel and earth clods woke her and at the last minute she was able to wrench the steering wheel over enough to avoid taking a nosedive. The engine shuddered and died. She leaned her forehead against the window. All the adrenaline that had been propelling her since she climbed out of the cistern had vanished and she felt weaker than she ever had in her life. There weren't even any words for the exhaustion that had descended on her like a load of bricks. Her legs were trembling and she couldn't hold the pedals down anymore. And she was so thirsty, as if every single cell in her body had shriveled into dust.

Where were the people? Were they all asleep? She thought about her own street. Dog walkers were up early, but no one would walk a dog all the way out here. There was hardly any space along the road, and the ditch on the other side.

No cars. No buildings. Fields, grassy hills, potholes filled with muddy water and the occasional meandering barbed wire fence. The only signs of civilization were the telephone poles and a highway marker—23—a designation that meant nothing to her. The houses must be down rocky tracks, tucked away out of sight. If there were any houses.

How long had she been driving? Long enough for the sun to come up. Half an hour? More?

She glanced over at Sourmash. Her driving maneuver had shifted the body slightly so he now leaned back against the seat as if he were dozing. His arm lay disturbingly close to her leg, and she folded herself up as tight as possible. *It*, she reminded herself. There was a narrow space between its legs and the glove compartment. She wondered if there was anything helpful inside. A walkie-talkie, maybe? She could picture him using one. She slid her hand in, avoiding any accidental contact, and felt around until she found the button. She popped it open and drew out a wad of stuff. Dumping it in her lap, she started going through it. Auto manual, map, mini tool kit, beef jerky, a half-empty plastic bottle with a red screw cap. She held it up. A cloudy yellow liquid sloshed around. *Fuck.* She ran her tongue over cracked lips. Old apple juice? Urine? *God, let it be juice.* She opened the cap and took a cautious sniff. It smelled fruity. *That's good, right?* Before she could second-guess herself she'd lifted it to her mouth and drained it. Her stomach heaved and settled. And now, her thirst temporarily assuaged, she realized something else. She was *starving.* She opened the beef jerky packet with her teeth, tearing into it like an animal, using both hands to shove a piece of jerky into her mouth. She was almost too tired to chew but she choked it down, ate another one, and another, barely pausing in between. Swallowing hurt. She caught a glimpse of her face in the rear-view mirror. It was pale, with planes and shadows and grooves where there had been none before. Hair hung in rats' tails.

Blackening eyes. Blood streaked the side of her head. It had congealed under her reddened nose too, like a macabre mustache. She tilted the mirror away.

"Fuck you fucking fuck, look what you've done to me," she screamed, bits of jerky spraying from her lips. *Did his hand move on the seat?*

The smell of the meat was overpowering all of a sudden. The taste, greasy and rotten on her tongue; and the juice, rank, too sweet. *Was it his urine after all?* She gagged. The cab felt too small. She cranked her window down further and leaned out, gasping for fresh air to clear the stench, but it was too late. The jerky hurt as much coming up as it had going down. She got out of the truck and collapsed against the side, ribs heaving. She tried to spit but she was still too dehydrated.

She shoved her hands in her hoodie pouch and pulled out Stroud's phone. Her grip was slack and she dropped it into a mud puddle near the truck's front wheel.

"Fuck," she screamed as she yanked it out and wiped grungy water onto her sleeve. A few shards of glass fell out onto the road. She powered it up with no real expectation and stared in disbelief. Two bars.

What was the landline number? It took a few seconds for her to remember.

Her hands were shaking so much that she flubbed it the first time. *Come on, come on,* she told herself furiously, forcing her fingers to cooperate.

Her mom answered on the first ring, "Hello," and Ari heard it all in her voice: fear, grief, desperation, hope.

"Mom," she said. "Mommy."

There was a moment of silence and then her mother's voice rose in register higher than Ari had ever heard it.

"Ari! Where are you? Bill! Bill, it's Ari!" she screamed.

"Highway 23."

"We're coming. Stay right there."

She collapsed onto the tarmac, in the shadow of the truck, making herself as small as she could. She kept the phone tucked in both hands until it died, and then she counted in tens to one hundred over and over again, folding her fingers down like a little kid. The wait seemed interminable.

ɞ

She heard the sirens before she saw the police cars, a whole phalanx of them coming up over the hill and screeching to a halt, and then she saw nothing at all but her parents running toward her.

CHAPTER TWENTY

I was eleven and a half when the grays first started seeping in. My world with the Cosloys had always seemed monochromatic and dull. A washed-out environment that made the occasional flash of color appear exotic. But this was different. It was not the tilled earth and the blank sky and the weather-beaten old boards bleached by wind and rain that faded around me. It was my own eyes that slowly failed.

Not everything vanished all at once. At the beginning it was almost imperceptible. Blue went first. So sad when every sky becomes a cloudy, dismal one.

When the reds finally faded, slipping away completely in my sixteenth year like blood on the water, I mourned them.

Even though I couldn't see the glorious red his blood made against the glass, still I could feel the heat of it. Taste the peppery richness in the air molecules. Smell the copper tang. It shines as bright as a new penny.

The sense of red. And blue. Yellow, and green; the idea of pure pigment is still locked away in my brain's memory. All the gradations—the subtle change in shade from red to orange, the explosive quality of crimson, the inky perfection of indigo—I can close my eyes and still see them.

Cone monochromacy is exceedingly rare.

It can be caused by shaken baby syndrome, yet might not present until later in life. That's what I read.

When I was about ten, Pa and Ma Cosloy sat me down after church and explained a few things to me. They told me about my mother. They told me about the foster home. They told me about the hospital reports.

Ma Cosloy's gray, dry lips were pressed so tight together they disappeared into the weather-beaten skin around her mouth. "Your mother," she said, "was no good. Happens sometimes but it's a waste of time to fuss over it or worry about the past. She got herself in trouble when she was barely fifteen, not more than a child herself."

I felt my ears grow warm with shame.

"In and out of the hospital you were. Month after month, from birth. Lord, they must have thought you were the clumsiest child there ever was. Always rolling off the changing table, falling down the stairs or tripping over your own two feet." She snorted and then was quiet. The bone in my wrist twinged. When I came to them, my left arm was in a plaster cast. The break still bothers me on cold, wet days.

"'Member that hunting dog I had when you were six or seven?" Pa Cosloy said. "The black and brown? Went after the chickens all the time?"

"That dog would eat the laundry off the line if you let him," Ma said with a grim laugh.

I nodded. Captain had the softest fur, with swirls of feathery hairs around his paws and between his toes, and a pink tongue that snaked into my ear if I leaned down close to him.

"You can't really blame the dog. It was his breeding, his nature. Something got twisted up inside him, passed on in the blood, something that couldn't be fixed."

I shifted on the bench so that I could sit on my hands. Under my left palm I felt the head of a nail. I pressed down hard upon it, willing the pain to drown out my anger. Captain used to meet me off the school bus, his tail wagging so hard it shook his whole body from rump to head. He was the only thing I had ever felt affection for.

"It was a kindness to put him down," Pa said.

"He went willingly," Ma said.

I remember the furious struggle, the whining and heartrending yelps as Captain fought to free himself from the rope staked in the ground. The piteous look in his eyes, tail forlornly wagging, and the whiplash crack of the gun. But I said nothing.

"Don't know anything about the boy who dunnit to her," Pa Cosloy said. "He quit town fast enough after she made it known."

Ma stared out at the dusty brown fields, but she seemed to be looking past them. My shirt collar was too tight and itched at my neck but I ignored it. Ma hated when I fidgeted, said it made her feel jumpy.

"You were just a little bit of a thing when we came down to the foster home. Scrawny for your age. Always sitting in a corner away from the rest of the children, clutching at a book though you had no idea how to read."

"Most of the time you were holding it upside down," Pa said. This was the closest he'd ever got to making a humorous remark in my hearing. "You never smiled. Never cried neither."

Ma cleared her throat and Pa went back to worrying his worn wool cap between his fingers.

"Fussing never amounted to anything," she said firmly. "Better to trust in God, put your head down and trudge on."

"Blood will out," Pa muttered.

I dared a question.

"What was her name?"

"Who?"

"My ma."

"She was never your ma," Ma Cosloy said sharply. "I told you that. . . . Never paid you no mind except when she was mad about something and then she paid you plenty."

Pa put his hand up and Ma closed her mouth with a snap.

"Gwendoline Maddox," Pa said, finally. "Big old name for a tiny slip of a girl."

"Gwendoline," I sighed. It sounded like a name from a book.

ɞ

I wished so hard that I could recall her. My body did. The fractures up and down my arms and across my collarbone, they remembered. And the pain I sometimes felt in my feet, where the skin grew hard and tough over old steam-iron burns. Her touch was emblazoned on my flesh but I couldn't picture her face.

She must have seen me as some pathetic thing that took from her. And so she beat me and shook me and eventually she robbed me of my colors.

When I was fifteen—the same age she was when she had me—I tracked her down. It wasn't hard. I used one of the computers at the coffee shop where I was bussing tables and washing dishes and googled her. Her name and the small town where she lived popped up. I'd have had to pay for a background check to get her full street address and I didn't bother. Gwendoline Maddox is not a common name, and most people never stray too far from the area where they were born and raised. I found her no more than fifty miles from the burned husk of the Cosloy farm, in Roseville, a town that was barely bigger than a truck stop. I hitchhiked there; it took all day. Asked around at the gas station and was told that, in fact, Gwen had worked at the truck stop, when she wasn't working at the bar, heh heh. The man who told me this was short and red-faced with a belly that sat on his belt like a sack of flour, and he waggled his eyebrows when he spoke the last part of the sentence but I didn't get his meaning. It was only later that I realized he'd been saying my mother was a whore. Something Ma and Pa Cosloy had told me too, in a different way.

She may have been a slut but she didn't waitress anymore, nor did she spend time at the bar.

It didn't come up when I searched for her on the Internet. If it had, I wouldn't have bothered making the trip, dangerous as it was. I had changed my appearance drastically, growing my hair long and dyeing it brown. I'd shot up a couple of inches and I'd even chosen a new name for myself. I went unnoticed most of the time, but still there was the risk that someone local might recognize me.

Her name wasn't Maddox any longer. Just recently she'd gotten married and changed it to Braverman—Gwendoline Braverman. And that's how the newspaper had listed her. Though the marriage had only lasted a few months, I guess she'd wanted to make a fresh start. That hadn't worked out too well for her.

My mother was dead. Carcinoid tumor, the obituary said. When I found out, I was cognizant of extreme disappointment. Once the hues began to bleed from my world and I knew there was nothing anyone could do about it, I'd dreamed of slicing her up myself and taking her heart as a keepsake.

So perhaps I could blame her for everything that had happened and was going to happen. And maybe I could thank her for it as well.

CHAPTER TWENTY-ONE

Ari felt numb. The drive in the police car had been a blur; then a bustle of activity at the hospital—a nurse poking and prodding, checking every inch of her body, including between her legs, bandaging her head; a lady cop, Officer Tremblay, taking her clothes as part of evidence collection; Dr. Elliott performing a series of tests to determine the severity of her head injury. She'd even asked if there had been any sexual assault. Ari had violently shaken her head, cracking open the pain again. At least she'd been spared that.

"She has a concussion," Dr. Elliott told her parents. "No sign of permanent trauma, though sometimes a head injury can lead to ocular migraines later on. If her headache becomes severe, or she has vomiting or a seizure, bring her back immediately and we'll do a CT scan. She was lucky."

Lucky? Ari had almost dissolved into tears right then.

"She might have some trouble sleeping because of trauma-related shock. Keep an eye on her and try to keep her fed and hydrated and calm. The more normal things are for her, the better. She may have some short-term memory loss," she continued. "If she does experience any pain, double the usual dose of acetaminophen. She's young and healthy; shouldn't be any problems."

"You can darkroom her for a couple of days until she begins to feel more like herself," the nurse said. She had very small hands and feet, like a child's, Ari had thought, though she'd avoided looking at the latex gloves the woman wore. What was it about the rubber covering that made hands look paw-like, inhuman?

"Darkroom?" her mother asked, helping Ari slip on the change of clothing she'd brought with her.

"Yes. If you can, block the windows in her bedroom with blackout blinds."

Ari imagined the darkness of the well, the feeling that the walls were closing in on her. She swore she'd sleep with the light on if she managed to sleep at all.

Now she sat in the chilly police station, covered by a thin blanket they gave to unfortunate people like her, bracketed by her parents. The blanket smelled strongly of detergent but there were underlying odors of tomato soup and hair and it made her feel a little nauseated. Her parents had argued against her being brought in for questioning immediately, but after Dr. Elliott okayed it, they'd conceded.

"Ari," her mother said gently. "Can you answer the question?"

With effort, Ari focused her attention.

"So you moved the body?" Captain Rourke asked. "Sorkin Sigurson's body." Ari had to think for a moment. Oh yeah, that was Sourmash's real name.

Ari looked at her mother and father and then at her hands; she'd washed them repeatedly but the tattered nails were still filthy, gummed with gore and flecks of white paint. She'd picked at her cuts until they oozed but she couldn't seem to stop herself from doing it. In the station bathroom, her wounded eyes had stared back from the mirror and found her unrecognizable, this creature with tear-grimed cheeks and horror trapped in her gaze.

"Ari," her mother said again. Raising her head, she became aware that they were all looking expectantly at her.

"You moved him?" Captain Rourke asked again, his tone sharp. Ari flinched. Although she had done nothing wrong, he made her feel guilty.

"Yeah. So I could drive the truck." Even to her own ears, her voice sounded mechanical and guarded. The last time she'd seen the police chief he'd been with his son, Jack, on the sidelines of the school spirit rally. Jack had been yelling obscenities at the players on the other school's team, including some attacks on their masculinity. She remembered his dad thumping him on the shoulder in a manner that seem more amused than anything else. Jack had never been seriously punished for the pornographic photos he'd tacked all over Lynn's locker, although he'd boasted about it plenty. Just a week's suspension and some community service. Of course, this had happened before Lynn's mother became the school principal.

"Can you give us any idea where the cabin is located? Any landmarks?"

"Umm . . . I didn't notice . . . fields . . . it was dark. I just drove."

Captain Rourke tapped his pen on the desk. He looked annoyed.

"You drove for about twenty or thirty minutes, you think? That's a pretty big area for us to cover. I've got my men out there looking but . . ." He sighed.

Ari didn't know what to say. He seemed to be blaming her.

"And where was the gun?"

"It was propped up on the dashboard. It fell when I—" She flashed on the memory of Sourmash's shattered head. The gore. His eye hanging from a few threads like some kind of gelatinous aquatic creature. Her brain had perfectly preserved the images and seemed intent on showing them to her over and over again in sharp staccato bursts. The fluorescent lights overhead were too bright. A headache pulsed behind her temples and the two painkillers she'd dry-swallowed in the squad car were doing nothing to ease the agony.

She drew a deep breath and tried to compose herself. She pulled the woolen hat her mother had given her further down over her ears and wished she could crawl inside it.

"The gun fell on the floor of the truck," she said.

"Did you touch it?"

She shook her head. "I don't think so. I don't remember. Maybe."

"Why does that matter? He killed himself, didn't he?" her father interjected. "Ari found him like that."

"There were no prints on the gun. None. Not even Sorkin's," the captain said.

"So it wasn't suicide?"

Captain Rourke shook his head. His eyes fastened on Ari's face. Her father followed his gaze.

"You're not suggesting . . ." He was half out of his chair in an instant.

Captain Rourke held up both hands. "She was checked at the hospital. No powder burns on her fingers."

"So what are you saying then?" her father growled.

"She's a witness. The only one, at present," Captain Rourke said. "You need to allow me to do my job."

"Ari had nothing to do with it! She's the victim here."

Ari quivered. Her nerves zinged like strings on a guitar, wound too tight. She couldn't concentrate. Her surroundings kept graying out and their voices coagulated into buzzy background noise.

"That could well be, but I still need to ask these questions," Captain Rourke said. "This is a criminal investigation."

Her father goggled at him, the veins standing out in his neck.

"Ari only needs one parent present during questioning," the police chief said. "I could tell you to wait outside, Bill."

"Bill, for God's sake!" her mother said, pointing to his chair.

Captain Rourke flipped a couple of pages back. "We sent a uniformed police officer round your way to ask a few questions. Your neighbor, Mrs. Fisk, said she saw you at approximately 2:30 p.m. on Friday, alone, walking toward the town center." Mrs. Fisk was a total curtain-twitcher; she knew everyone's comings and goings.

"Do you remember anything about that, honey?" her mom asked.

"I went to the library to look some stuff up." She thought about mentioning the subject of her research, but Sourmash was dead, so what did it matter now?

"And afterward?" Captain Rourke said, making a note of it.

Ari shook her head.

There was nothing to say to this. Whatever else she might have planned on doing that day was forgotten, irrelevant. She'd been taken. Sourmash must have snatched her off the street.

"It's a blank," she said.

"So, just to bookend the times, you were last seen on Friday afternoon at 2:30 p.m. and you called your parents this morning at approximately 8:30 a.m.," Captain Rourke said. "That's eighteen hours to account for." The pen hovered above the page. He seemed to be waiting for her to confirm but her mind was empty.

Once again she just shook her head. "I was in the cistern."

"We should have known something was wrong," her mother said, stroking Ari's hand. "It's our job to look after you."

Her words pierced Ari's heart. No one could possibly know when something bad was going to happen, because if they did, then they would safeguard against it. She'd heard about people being stalked, kidnapped and hurt, and the stories had made her sick, but at the same time, part of her had wondered how someone could end up in that situation. Like, how much was their own fault?

Captain Rourke was talking again. "There were some photos found in Sigurson's truck." He placed his hand on a white-labeled, sealed plastic baggie. "Did you notice them?"

"No. There was a heap of garbage on the floor, magazines and cans and stuff. The gun fell down there." Ari tried to look at them now but the captain covered the bag with his palm.

Her mouth was so dry, her tongue stuck to the roof. "Are they of me?" She couldn't remember anything. She was unsure about everything. And she must have keeled over a little because she felt her mother's hand tighten around her arm.

"For God's sake, Fred!" Ari's dad yelled. "What are you trying to do? She's not a criminal."

"Sit down, Bill," the captain said.

Her father sat on the edge of his chair.

"They're candids"—Captain Rourke stressed the word—"of the same group of kids. Some individual shots of kids at the swimming hole. Girls. Boys."

"Is Ari one of them?" her mother asked.

"Yes."

Ari's dad pushed away from the desk and bolted to his feet, knocking over his chair.

"So he was spying on our daughter and doing God knows what. Why weren't you onto him?"

"He hadn't done anything illegal."

"Abduction, kidnapping. And what about the animal killings? This seems right in line with that."

"That's a separate case, Bill."

Ari's dad made an explosive sound. "Oh for God's sake!"

"I have to follow the facts. And Ari is not exactly a reliable witness. We know that there were kids who got their party favors from Sourmash—alcohol, drugs." He stared at Ari. "Were you one of those kids, Ari?"

"No! I wouldn't. Why would I?" Ari said. Her brain was so sluggish. She felt off balance and uncertain and it came through in her voice. Captain Rourke seemed accusatory. As if he thought she was complicit in some way. There had to be a reason for all of this, but what was it? She kneaded her temples and tried to remember, but it was useless.

"Why are you protecting him?" her father yelled.

"I have to build a case, Bill. I can't question him, can I?" He sighed. "We've searched his trailer. We found a rudimentary darkroom up there. Some pornographic magazines. A still. Drugs."

"He was a criminal. He kidnapped Ari. It's likely he pushed her into that well. So why does she have to suffer through any more of this?" her father said, bunching his fists and pounding the desk. Ari jumped. Usually Dad was controlled, quiet. It was her mother who cussed out telemarketers who called during dinner and halted in the middle of the pedestrian walk to deliver a diatribe against people in cars who didn't stop. Her father was the calming influence in the household.

"Because somebody killed him, Bill. And Ari was there, and from what I can tell, she went voluntarily."

"No!" said Ari. "I would never!" Her mother made comforting sounds.

The phone on the desk buzzed. Captain Rourke picked it up. "Great. You found it. Out there west of Wallace roundabouts. Good. And?" He made a surprised noise. "You don't say. No sign. Okay. Yup. Tape it off. Get the white coats in there." He directed a searching look at Ari.

She felt herself buckling under his gaze.

He put the handset down and almost immediately the phone rang again. His thick eyebrows rose as he listened, and he grunted.

"Yup. Okay. No trouble? Sober 'im up. Process him. Yeah. Good. I'll be down in a couple of minutes," he said and then replaced the receiver.

He leaned back in his chair.

"We've found the cabin. Out near Wallace. Private road.

And we made an arrest. Ronald Balboa. They call him Rocky. Known associate of Sorkin Sigurson. Had multiple priors for a whole bunch of stuff including methamphetamine possession, petty theft, public intoxication and resisting arrest. They picked him up, wandering about a mile from the cabin, under the influence of something. We're holding him pending further investigation." He held up a warning finger. "We haven't charged him with murder yet but I'm expecting we will."

Ari felt the tension drain out of her parents. She remembered zoned-out Rocky in the truck, remembered how he cowered in his seat as Sourmash yelled his name. He seemed so shrunken, so twitchy, so incapable of movement, much less firing a gun. He'd probably been so amped up on drugs that it had lent him a kind of psychotic strength.

"That means he probably killed Stroud too," she said, awash in the horror of it.

Captain Rourke looked down at his hands and grimaced. "The problem is, Ari, things sometimes get jumbled up when you've sustained a head injury. I'm trying to make sense of everything here but it's just not adding up."

Directing a stern look at her, he continued, his tone clipped and officious. "You don't remember how you got out to the cabin. You can't account for your actions on Friday. You never even mentioned Ronald Balboa, yet it seems likely he was there at the same time. There's evidence of illegal drug and alcohol consumption. And now this thing with Stroud Bellows." He shook his head.

"What's going on?" her dad demanded.

"There was no body," Captain Rourke said. "There was no sign of Stroud Bellows in the cabin."

"That doesn't make sense," Ari said. "I touched him."

Captain Rourke just looked at her steadily.

"His water polo team jacket," Ari stammered. "It was hanging on a chair. That's why I went into the cabin. I have his phone." She reached into her pocket and then remembered that they'd taken her clothes. "You took it with my clothes. I used his phone to call my parents."

"It was a pre-paid phone. A burner phone, they call it on the streets."

"Like what drug dealers use?" her father said. He was a big fan of *The Wire*.

"Yes. No way to trace any calls in or out. No way to tell if it belonged to Stroud Bellows."

"It was in his jacket. The jacket with the *C* for 'captain,'" Ari wailed.

"No jacket, no prints other than yours that we've found yet, no evidence of his being anywhere in the vicinity," Captain Rourke said with finality. His voice echoed weirdly in her head, words jumbling together until they made no sense at all.

She heard her father ask, "Will you talk to the boy?" and the heart went out of her. Her father didn't believe her.

"We haven't been able to locate him yet but his grandmother isn't worried," said Captain Rourke. "He's often out and about on the weekends, she said."

"He was there. I saw him," Ari said, waving her mother's arm away and sitting forward. The blanket slipped to the floor. She closed her eyes for a moment, little lights sparking in her periphery like struck matches. "He was in the cabin." She could hear the hysteria in her voice but she couldn't help it. "I saw him!"

"Baby, hush, hush," her mother said.

"Can you let us know if there are any further developments?" her father said, slipping his arm around Ari and enfolding her against his shoulder.

Ari heard some more paper shuffling and then Captain Rourke sighed heavily. "Sure. Why don't you take her home now."

CHAPTER TWENTY-TWO

Here begins my education.

Albany is a cesspool.

I found some things out pretty fast.

There are evil monsters in the world.

Kids are powerless. Nothing but prey. Fodder. I lost everything in the first few days. My meager belongings, my coat, my precious jars and sketchbook, and when those things were gone, the predators went deeper and possessed the parts of my body that were unprotected by armor. I suffered it, went to my quiet place until they were done with me. It didn't take long and sometimes they bought me a bowl of hot soup or a coffee following the act, as if we had actually conducted a social transaction. And once, the man threw a crumpled twenty-dollar bill onto the ground near me before he walked away zipping up his pants. After that I made sure I got paid something for my services.

I sold drugs and I sold other stuff that looked like drugs to stupid college students. I stole what I could and flogged it in the back streets and the alleys behind the restaurants, and I made sure to hide my money in my boots and sleep with one eye open. The shelters were the worst for beatings and muggings and so I avoided them and found places under bridges and in abandoned warehouses.

No one will hire you. But if you volunteer or work for free you can get in the door. No one asks too many questions if you practice invisibility and learn how to forge signatures.

And eventually getting the necessary ID papers is not impossible. If you can pay. People see what you want them to see. I became adept at becoming what was needed or expected, and no one seemed to care overmuch. Such is the nature of this busy, bustling world we live in.

Once I'd scraped up enough money I took a room in an old lady's house, Mrs. Randolph. She had no husband or family but she did have various properties, lung cancer and cats. Nine of them, mostly inbred tabbies with extra toes, so that they walked splayed on fat cushions. They slept on her bed with her and about a hundred throw pillows. She was submerged, as if the bed were swallowing her up, as if all those cats were suffocating her. Who knows what would have happened if I hadn't come along?

It was serendipity. I was walking by; she was out on the porch trying to coax a tiny black-and-white kitten down from the roof. I climbed up on the railing and grabbed it by the scruff of its neck, ignoring the sharp pinch of its claws.

Much later, I trussed it up by the legs like a turkey and left it under my bed for twelve hours. It never scratched me again after that, though it would hiss and spit at me from the safety of the mantel.

Mrs. Randolph was glad for the company, and the little bit of money I was able to pay her augmented her disability checks. No family of her own, or at least no one who gave a crap that she was drinking milk well past the expiry date and eating canned okra every day. The cats ate better than she did: beef chunks with carrots and peas, or chicken in cream sauce.

I told people she was my grandmother, and maybe she even came to believe it herself. She certainly didn't make trouble or try to kick me out.

I picked up her mail, learned to forge her signature and cashed her support checks for her (skimming a little off the top), and ate her groceries. Sometimes we shared a can of cat food, if things were tight that week. I warmed it on the stove and told her it was stew. Her eyes were too bad to read the labels by that point and she trusted me.

I sought out the jobs that no one else wanted, where references were not needed, where I didn't need to prove my age and, most importantly, where I could work alone. Collected bottles and cans for the deposit money; worked for the city park spiking up garbage with a pointy stick; helped out at a soup kitchen feeding the lost souls, where I learned how to become as ignored as they are. Some janitorial work if I could get it. Drug dealing. And, one particularly low summer, handing out flyers and standing around in a giant dog costume shilling for a hot dog chain. That at least allowed me plenty of time to observe people without their knowing. Perfect anonymity. I thought a lot about killing them one by one and the exact way I would let out their blood and I captured those fantasies in my new sketchbook.

I had many jobs, but it wasn't until I started working in a Polish meat shop that I felt any interest in my work.

They were hard, tough men, who'd been working since they themselves were kids, and they saw nothing wrong with employing someone who was just a few months past sixteen as long as my social security number appeared to be in order. I could pass for seventeen in any case: old enough to have dropped out of high school.

Every movement they made conserved energy, and if you didn't know any better you'd think they were graceless. You'd be wrong.

When my boss, Jarek, butchered a cow, it was like watching a dance between two perfectly matched partners.

You think of the word butcher *and you think of someone in a bloodstained white coat with big, brawny arms and a ruddy face. Someone who looks like a marbled side of beef himself, who wields a big knife and hacks away at a carcass. But Jarek was a whip-thin, hairy man about forty years old, and he was a poet with a knife. Butchery requires an economy of motion, grace and strength in perfect balance. The blade becomes an extension of your arm and then of your will. I didn't think I'd ever seen anything so beautiful. All of it. The loops of intestine like shiny rubber tubing, the soapy fat, the great balloon stomachs, the lungs like angel wings.*

And nothing shone brighter than the knives.

The sharpening becomes second nature, with foreknowledge that meat and hard bone have dulled the edge and it needs to be honed again. The knife hisses against the steel and is pulled in the direction of the body, toward your own hand and your own guts, as if the danger of accidental injury is all part of the ritual. The old, silvery scars on my thumb bear witness to its proximity.

The knife is small, maybe six inches, with a fine, thin blade. You only use the tip of the boning knife, and then, later, a larger blade for slicing. There's no hacking, no sawing. Just clean, deliberate sweeps. You know the internal structure of the animal; you know exactly where the different parts are and how they fit together, as if they were your own organs. The point glides along, following the natural contours of the muscle and the ligaments, and then it's just a flick of the wrist to sever the tendons, the meat falling away beautifully. I felt like a conductor. I heard music—heard music too beautiful for most people to decipher.

By the end of a year I could portion out a cow by touch alone, my eyes closed.

But first I swept the floors. Then I cleaned intestines for sausage, sluicing them out with cold water, hanging them from lines to dry like transparent holiday streamers. And lastly, as my final test, I disemboweled one hundred and fifty turkeys, one after the other, in preparation for the Thanksgiving weekend rush.

Jarek called me over in the morning and told me, "You gut these."

I put down my broom and trotted over to the pile. It was barely 6:00 a.m. but I loved my work and I came in early.

"All of them?" I couldn't help it. They were everywhere—great, pale, floppy carcasses with that tart smell that all dead fowl have.

"You want to be a butcher?" This was a rhetorical question. He was a man of few words.

He was grinding raw pork for sausages, adding spices, tasting all the while. They did that, the Polish men, not caring about trichinosis, trusting always in the quality of their meat or the iron of their stomachs.

He showed me how to use my knife—a secondhand boning knife that had still cost me a month's pay and which I kept always in a sheath on my hip—to slit the abdomen. He grabbed my hand in his, easily enveloping it. "You shove your hands in, scoop up along the ribcage to separate the lung tissue from the bones, and then pull," he told me in heavily accented English.

He guided me, clenching my fingers around the slippery innards, and then he drew his arm back and my hand came out too, fisted around a whole mess of guts.

We used our hands so we wouldn't pierce the bowel with anything sharp.

I still remember the smell. Warm, ripe, the slight tang of iron though these birds had been bled dry already, and something else, slick and biologic, slurpy like a thickness in my throat. And I remember thinking: this is not something I should smell. That's the inside of something's smell.

It was more difficult with the mammals. With them I had to carefully cut around the anus before I could remove the lower intestine. One nick of the blade and a spurt of excrement would spoil the meat. But done properly, with care, the entire digestive tract including the stomach, all bloated and glistening, and all those feet of silken gut could be lifted out, cradled in my arms and deposited into a bin, leaving the rib cavity empty and perfectly open before me like the framework of a boat.

It gave me such a feeling of achievement to strip everything unnecessary away and be left with only the bones and meat.

It took me eight hours to gut those birds. They were cold. The room was frigid. By the end of the day my fingers were numb and my hands were chapped and raw. When I flexed my hands I bled from a dozen small wounds like stigmata.

But the next week, as if I had done penance, Jarek let me slice sirloin steaks, cutting in long strokes against the grain of the meat. I could imagine the rich tint, like polished cherrywood gleaming in the sun. There was care and precision and honor in how the meat was handled.

And soon after, he gave me the pigs—the meat, the cuts the butcher shop was famous for. The reason people lined up on Friday morning to get the best we had to offer. And I took infinite care with them, making no unnecessary slices, wasting nothing, remembering the mess I'd made of Ferdinand and the rest of them and feeling ashamed at the fledgling I had been and how little I had known of artistry.

Sometimes I saw Jarek watching me with a slight frown, and in those moments I would press my lips together and hold the intense pleasure inside where he could no longer read it on my face. Sometimes, in my dreams, I killed everything in the world, making beautiful pictures out of the vivid flesh and hides and dead eyes. My sketchbook was full of such drawings.

I brought thick chops home; cooked them rare for my dinner and Mrs. Randolph's, though her appetite was miniscule and she'd lost most of her five senses. Feeding her was a waste of good meat.

She had no more secrets now. Not even her shame was private. I wondered if life was worth living once things got that bad. I wondered if she could even smell her own urine anymore or if it was just something she had learned to abide. In the wild, the young and healthy would have turned on her, old and toothless as she was, and ripped her belly out. It would be a mercy but I would hate the feel of her skin on my hands, so I let her live.

CHAPTER TWENTY-THREE

It was nightmarish. The town, the familiar shops, the quiet street that Ari had grown up on looked completely different. In eighteen hours it had become ominous, even though it was the middle of the day, as if she were seeing it through filmy black gauze. The distance between her house and Lynn's seemed insurmountable; the bushes and thickets of trees, places where evil and evil-doers could hide.

Something was wrong with her eyes. It was as if she were looking down a long dark tunnel, and sometimes there was a disorientating shimmer, like a heat haze. She stroked her bracelet. Maybe she could send a telepathic message. And Lynn would somehow know that Ari needed her.

Lynn, she whispered in her mind, wanting to see her friend so badly but knowing she wouldn't be able to make her legs walk all that way, unsure if she could even find the words to make a phone call because the telling would unbottle the tears inside and she was scared they might split her open. Shock. Traumatic injury. Concussion. Her body was betraying her.

If things weren't so completely fucked up with Tallulah's death and the aftermath, Lynn would have been waiting for her on the front steps, her arms opened wide, ready to give and receive a hug. But she wasn't.

"Ari," her mother said gently. Ari refocused her eyes—she'd been staring at the beige back of the car seat—and realized that her mom was just standing there holding the door open and had maybe been standing there for a long time, saying her name over and over, if her stricken expression was any clue.

On feet that seemed miles from the ground, Ari left the warm safety of the car and went into the house.

She felt frayed, as if the fiber of her being were unweaving itself. Twice on the way home she thought she'd seen Sourmash, his bearlike bulk leaning against a tree and then standing on the corner of an intersection, hot eyes blazing, a rifle in his hand. And a few times she'd caught a glimpse of Stroud's bright-red jacket hurrying down a side street, only to blink and look again and see nothing. Could she trust her eyes?

"I'll just get you a glass of water, honey," her mother said. She caught the murmur of her parents' voices as they walked toward the kitchen.

She heard the words *side effects*, *PTSD*, *darkroom* but the rest all sounded like feedback to her. She curled up on the sitting room couch, piled the pillows around her body like a fort. *Stroud*, she thought. The last time she'd seen him alive had been in the grove. She was positive she had seen him in the cabin, no matter what the police said. Round and round flew her thoughts, making her feel as if she were trapped on a carousel, with the speed and music cranked up to ten. Stay on and ride, or jump off and risk breaking something irreparable? Was her brain completely and truly fucked? What was real and what was not real?

"Mom, Dad," she called.

Her parents appeared in the kitchen doorway. They looked guilty, and she knew they'd been discussing her.

"Can you try to find out about Stroud? See if he's come home? If I just knew—for certain . . ." Her voice cracked.

"Of course. We'll make some calls," her father said.

"You should get cleaned up. Change out of those clothes. You'll feel better," her mother said brightly, handing over a glass of water. "Let me run a soothing bath for you."

"A bath sounds good." Ari took a sip and put the glass down. Her tongue felt like a slab of something dead in her mouth. Just forming words seemed impossible.

She got up, her wobbling legs like jelly. Her stomach was rolling and she was worried she might spew jerky again. Her dad hurried forward to give her his arm. "I'm fine," Ari said.

She dragged herself upstairs, her mother one step behind as if she was afraid that Ari might fall backwards. They parted in the hallway and Ari went to her room and shut the door. Her parents' hovering was totally freaking her out.

She wished she could hear their familiar brusque voices, the fond but abrupt things they shouted over their shoulders as they passed each other in the scant minutes between rushing to their jobs, on quick visits to the refrigerator, the last thing at night; small snatches of conversation, blunt words of love that rang true.

She realized she'd been walking around her bedroom in overlapping circles. Just like back in the well. "Get a grip, Ari," she said with force. She was too anxious to sleep, too wired to read or listen to music. She needed an anchor, something to root her into her life. That was Lynn. Reflexively she reached for her cell phone before letting her hand drop, empty. The cops hadn't found it in the cistern or the surrounding area.

Maybe if she screamed loudly enough, gave voice to the fear festering in her belly, Lynn would hear her and come running. But no, she was sick of screaming. Instead she went to the window, threw open the sash and leaned out, perched on the sill. From here she couldn't tell who was home at Lynn's. The driveway was empty, the yard silent, the windows like empty sockets. The world seemed too big. It scared her. It didn't seem to matter how many times she told herself that it was over. Sourmash was dead. They'd arrested Rocky. But Stroud? Dead? Alive? She remembered the clammy feel of his cool cheek. Could it have been a hallucination? Could hallucinations be sensory or were they always just visual?

Post-traumatic stress disorder. My mind is playing tricks on me and I can't trust it. What I think I know, what I think I see might not even exist outside my mind.

"You hurt your head, honey. It's no wonder you're confused," her mother had said in the car on the way home. "And the horror of driving that truck! It's no wonder you're traumatized. Give it time and let us look after you."

"You're safe now," her dad said firmly, as if by saying so he made it true. "Just take it as easy as you can."

Ari had just stared at her black-stained fingertips. The last thing they'd done at the police station was take her prints. "So we can eliminate you from the investigation," Officer Tremblay had said. *Eliminate me like Sourmash tried to. Make me cease to be.*

There was so much she couldn't remember. She felt like she was standing on an ice floe in the middle of the ocean. How had she gotten from the library to Sourmash's cistern? Why would she go anywhere with him? It didn't make sense. She was missing some fundamental piece of information. Something was deeply wrong. It just was.

She needed Lynn's strength and help. The methodical way she always attacked problems. She would believe Ari, and together they'd figure it out.

"Does Lynn know what happened to me?" she'd asked when they had arrived back at the house.

"I talked to her mother but Lynn was out. I'm sure she knows now," her mother had replied.

"Why isn't she here?"

"We asked people to give you room. A little quiet today. Time to heal."

"Lynn is not people. She's my best friend. I need her." Ari's voice cracked. Her head was spinning.

"She can come tomorrow," her dad had said. "We're sorry, Ari, but the doctor recommended a peaceful environment. We have to keep a close eye on you for the next twenty-four hours."

Her mom knocked on the door and stuck her head in. Ari jumped, hitting her head on the window frame.

"Oh, honey," she said, worry quirking her eyebrows. "I thought you were going to soak in the tub. I ran it for you. Nice and hot. It's full now."

Ari looked down at her hands. They lay limply in her lap like dead fish. *Right.* She'd come upstairs to take a bath. Somewhere along the way she'd spaced out again.

Ari focused on her breathing. She imagined she was on her back in the water looking up at the shimmer of lights high above, everything around her made of cool blue. Quiet.

Her mother's voice brought her into the present. "Honey. Please." Her attempt at a smile was ghastly. It didn't jibe with the deep grooves in her forehead and the purple bruising under her eyes.

"Go soak in the tub. I'm making real macaroni and cheese for dinner. With extra cheese. And we'll eat early."

Ari couldn't bear her mother's stricken expression. She forced a smile. The longer she allowed it to remain in place, the less fragile it seemed. She took a deep breath. "My favorite," she said. Her mom smiled in response as she eased the door shut, and Ari felt as if she'd really accomplished something. Something normal.

She stood up, stripped her clothes off and kicked them into a heap in the corner of the floor. Her worn terry cloth robe was rough under her scraped-up fingertips and heavy on her strained muscles. She felt unclean, like she'd been touched by something perverse, as if everything bad had forced itself under her skin and now rotted there. Who knew what Sourmash had done to her while she was lying at the bottom of the well? He could have climbed down. He hadn't raped her but he had put his hands on her. She remembered them now, reaching for her as she dodged around his truck—broad and hairy, muscular with sinew. And then sheathed in black gloves, pushing her into the well as she plummeted, screaming. The two images shuddered in her brain as if she were seeing with doubled vision. She couldn't just sit in the bath, she needed a shower first, hot enough to scour a few layers of skin off.

The bathroom was steamy. The mirror fogged. She was glad of that. She knew she'd look different, changed at some deeply personal level, and she wanted to fool herself for a little while longer. Keeping her bandaged head clear, she stood under the shower with the dial cranked all the way around until she couldn't stand it any longer. Then she climbed into the bath.

Slowly her taut muscles relaxed. She added more hot water over and over again and stayed in long after the water had cooled down, her toes wrinkled, unidentifiable bits of scummy stuff floating on the surface. It wasn't until she stood up, muscles like strings, that she realized she'd completely forgotten to use any soap. Tomorrow she would clean herself properly. She'd change the gooey bandage on her head. Tomorrow was another day. When she finally got out of the tub, there was a thick ring of gray sludge left on the porcelain. She lacked the energy to do anything about it but she was certain she'd get a pass.

She heard the phone ringing and froze, hoping that it was Lynn and she'd hear her mother calling up to her, but there was nothing.

"Brick by brick, Ari," she told herself.

She slipped on the robe again, tying it tight as if it could keep her from falling to pieces, and went downstairs holding on to the banister like an invalid. She made a detour into the hall and picked up the phone. At first she couldn't remember Lynn's cell phone number. She was so used to just pushing the "1" button. She focused and entered the digits. The call went straight through to voicemail. Either the battery was dead or Lynn had turned off her phone. She did that sometimes—declared she was going to be a Luddite and give up electronics.

Ari couldn't verbalize a message. How could she sum up all that had happened in one snappy voicemail? Instead she just said, "It's me, Ari." She didn't care what the doctor or her parents said; she needed Lynn. Lynn would bring her back to normalcy. Lynn was all the good stuff in her life.

Her parents sat stiffly at the table. She looked at the wall clock. It was barely 4:00 p.m. She wanted to get into her bed but she was scared of night falling, terrified of waking up in the middle of it. The darkness would transport her directly to the well.

"Sorry," she said. "I took too long."

"No worries," her dad said, pulling her chair out for her and awkwardly patting her arm. Her dad wasn't a touchy-feely kind of a guy except for special occasions—birthdays and holidays—but ever since the hospital he'd continually reached out for her, as if he were reassuring himself that she was still there. Ari didn't know if she was there. It felt as though some part of her had been left back in the cistern and the cabin. Her sense of self was shattered, leaving just a shell.

"Perfect timing," her mother said, sounding like she was talking to a guest. Ari wondered how long they'd been sitting at the table waiting for her, heads turned toward the ceiling, listening to the water running.

The big casserole of macaroni and cheese was covered with a glass lid. Condensation had formed on the inside, and when her mother served, she shoveled out congealed wedges of glued-together pasta. Clearly the food had been ready half an hour ago.

"Who was on the phone?" Ari asked. "Was it Captain Rourke? Did they find Stroud?"

Her mother froze in the middle of serving and exchanged a glance with her dad, who carefully unfolded his napkin, clearly stalling for time.

"No, it was Carl from work," her father said.

"The police may not need to talk to you again, Ari," her mother said.

Ari's mouth fell open. "But I might remember something else. And Captain Rourke said he'd let us know when they find Stroud and what's going on with Rocky."

"There's been no time for anything new in the investigation."

"Try not to think about it anymore," her dad said. "Let the police do their job."

She stared at him. How was that even possible? "Not think about it?" She knew she was shouting but she couldn't help herself. "I want to know. I need to know. Everything. So I can understand what happened to me."

She stabbed at her macaroni with her fork.

Her mother's voice gentled. "Some things don't make sense no matter how hard you try. They just don't."

Ari's mouth was dry. She swallowed a gulp of water and spluttered as it went down the wrong way. Her father leaned over and rubbed her shoulders.

"I can't just be a victim. I can't let Sourmash do that to me."

"You're not a victim. You're strong, so strong. You saved yourself, Ari," her dad said, putting his water glass down forcefully.

Ari hung her head. That was the thing. She felt like it was her fault. As if she had asked for it. What was it about her that screamed victim? Was it a weakness that predators could sense?

"Okay, Ari?" her mother said, sliding the salad bowl across to her. Her expression was pleading.

Ari nodded, not wanting to upset her any further.

As her parents tried to change the subject, she listened to the buzz of mundane conversation without really paying attention. This was how normal people dealt with trauma, but Ari was beginning to think she would never be normal again. By moving her food around and forcing down a few more tiny mouthfuls she made enough of a dent in the huge mound to soften her parents' worried faces. When she put her fork down, they both exhaled, although she didn't think they were aware of it. They likely had no idea that their concern felt like even more weight on her; the stress of having to pretend that she was all right or would be all right soon, as if there was an ETA for recovery.

"I'm tired," she said, pushing her chair back and feeling guilty for not being able to absorb her parents' worry.

"You get some sleep," her mother said, getting up to give her a hug and a kiss. Her father embraced her too and dropped a kiss on her forehead, something he hadn't done since she was young. She felt the scratch of his unshaven chin through her hair when he tucked her under his chin. She bore it for as long as she could, but she could barely stand the pressure on her skin. It reminded her of the doctor prodding and poking at her. Mumbling an apology, she fled upstairs.

Ari sat on her bed, clutching her pillow. The sun was going down. The shadows lengthening. The tree outside her window sent long black fingers creeping into her room. She had never felt less tired. She needed to talk to someone about all the crazy feelings she was having because otherwise they would swallow her up. Like the bottom of the well, like her darkening room, turning into a vacuum of nothingness, a vast pit of despair, the world as she had known it disappearing around her.

She snuck downstairs and called Lynn's cell phone but it went to voicemail again. She tried the landline. The recorded message came on, Mrs. Lubnick's brisk inflection and some childish ruckus in the background, but Ari hung up without saying anything. The black hole got bigger. Where the hell was Lynn? Lynn had borne witness to all of Ari's freak-outs over the years, had talked her down from numerous ledges of anxiety and fear of failure. Ever since she could remember, they'd seen each other daily, or spoken at least twice. There was no way Lynn would abandon her now.

Up in her room, she logged onto her computer and started typing.

From: Ari <O2BASparrow@onederkind.com>
Subject:
To: Lynn <sassyfreakingass@hottamale.net>

For a long moment she looked at the blinking cursor, tears blurring her vision.

Please come over right now.
Ari

She went back to her open bedroom window. Lynn's house was dark. Ari reached out and hooked up her pirate flag, closing her window behind her. She tugged the curtains closed and sat at her desk, tapping her fingers nervously on its surface.

The notes she'd taken at the library were piled in a heap. She spotted the name *Dahmer*, with all its evil associations, and pulling open a drawer, she swept the papers into it. God knows what she'd been thinking! Sourmash had been a sick fuck but he hadn't had some grand plan. She pushed the drawer closed and leaned against the desk. After a long moment she began to pace.

CHAPTER TWENTY-FOUR

I don't dream often. Never have. But when I do, it's about my mother, or at least I assume so. She's always in darkness, like a person delineated in charcoal, like someone pieced together out of the deepest shadows. In the dream she locks me in the closet. I can't visualize her face, but I remember the closet with the lock on the outside and the hard linoleum floor, the smell of mouse shit, and those wire hangers above me, clicking against each other, moved by some unseen force. How cold it got in there, with the drafts pressing against the thin plywood back wall of the house and coming in through invisible cracks. Sometimes I pulled down a mildewed wool coat and drew it over my ears, but the clothing in there was old, from previous tenants, and it smelled bad—like sick, elderly people. That's what remains in my memory: the dark, the pungent odor and the scratchy feel of wool against my neck.

I chose this place because it has no closets. Instead, my coats and sweaters are stored inside a large cedar chest with a couple of bolts on the outside. The wood panels are good and solid, an inch thick, reinforced with slats, and the chest is certainly big enough for a girl who barely measures five foot three.

After Mrs. Randolph died—of the cancer, though it's possible her cats suffocated her to death while she slept—I was homeless again.

Fortunately I had a little money saved, thanks to one of Ma Cosloy's many strictures. "Always save for a rainy day," I seemed to hear her say. Mrs. Randolph's house—mortgaged and re-mortgaged to pay her medical bills—went to the bank. The cats, those who survived her, were delivered straight to the pound in a cardboard box.

I admire cats. They pretend affection but really they are devious creatures. Have you ever noticed that a cat will always sit on the lap of the person in the room who hates them the most? It's because they are manipulative and filled with cruel intent. You have to trick a cat to catch it, whereas dogs will just come to anybody. The black-and-white cat? The one that scratched me? I held on to it and practiced my knife-work until it gave up every one of its nine lives.

Then I left town again, hitchhiking, sleeping rough, scrounging together a little money.

I already had Dempsey Hollow in my sights. I'd found mention of the neglected hunting cabin in Mrs. Randolph's papers, but I needed a place to live full-time, something that matched up with the dreams and goals in my head. A small, cozy place on a dead-end road, with a river nearby that would drown out sounds. A sanctuary not too far outside town. And I needed a certain kind of old lady. The type of human who believes in basic goodness without thinking too much on the inverse. Evil. One who accepts people at face value and is glad for a little help.

I found both just outside the Hollow. That was old lady number two, Mrs. Klein. Between her house and Mrs. Randolph's cabin I had all the security and privacy I needed.

CHAPTER TWENTY-FIVE

Sunday morning. Ari had barely slept all night, just experienced that uncomfortable sensation of falling and then jerking awake again, her vision suddenly graying out. Per the doctor's instructions, her parents had come in every few hours to wake her, although in Ari's opinion they could have skipped it. She wasn't going to die, although lying on her bed felt like being in a coffin, and closing her eyes felt like death. Instead of curling up on the mattress, she'd piled her comforter and blankets in the corner of her room and burrowed into them. She'd put her bedside light on the floor, turning the shade so that it threw a warm circle of light. In some visceral, primitive way she felt safe within that circle. From her corner she could keep both the door and the window in her line of sight. She'd thought she wanted her mother's comforting touch, a throwback to her childhood, but that was just a reminder of how things used to be, how foolish and naïve she had been. Lynn was the only person she wanted to talk to. She didn't have to hide her dark thoughts from her friend.

Ari stared at her laptop as if she could will it into activity by the force of her mind. It was open to her email account: no new messages. She clicked over to her Sent folder. There was the email she'd sent to Lynn an eternity ago. No reply.

The last time Ari had seen her, at least as far as she could remember, was after the discovery at the grove, those dismal, silent walks to and from school on the Wednesday and Thursday. Lynn had been so devastated, and then so angry. They'd argued about the town and the people who lived in it. And then Lynn had stormed off.

Had Lynn just checked out? Had she become so disgusted by everyone who lived in Dempsey Hollow that she'd detached? And did that mean from Ari too? Ari should have been there for her.

They'd only ever had two or three bad fights. And those had all occurred when they had been much younger, but Ari remembered that this was what Lynn did. She took some time to cool off. Was that what was going on now?

Less than two days since Ari's world fell apart. How short that seemed. And somehow also interminable.

She'd checked the news online, although she was sure her parents would have shielded her from it if they could. *Dempsey Hollow resident found dead under suspicious circumstances. Evidence of illegal drugs. Suspect in custody. Local teenage girl with head injury discovered near the scene. Identity withheld.*

Identity withheld. She barely knew who she was anymore. Lynn knew her better than anyone; Lynn would be able to remind her who she was. Not this person blindly going through the motions, this girl who couldn't remember how the hell she even ended up out there, at the cabin. She noticed that there was no mention of Stroud.

She looked at the clock: 7:54 a.m. She was startled by a

sudden surge of anger. Mrs. Lubnick had spoken to her mother. The story was on the freaking web! There was no way Lynn didn't know what had happened. What the fuck?! Ari would never treat her this way. She slammed her laptop closed and stood up. She was going over to Lynn's. Once she got things clear in her own head—with Lynn's help—she'd fill her parents in.

Although . . . she paused and replayed the conversation she'd had with her mom last night.

"Your father and I have been talking," her mother had said, sitting down next to her on the bed. "We wondered if perhaps you might want to speak to someone. Someone professional. Captain Rourke strongly recommended it."

"You mean a psychiatrist?" Her lips felt numb. There was a tremor in one of her hands. She tucked it under her leg. Maybe she should see someone. If you were crazy, you probably didn't know you were crazy, right?

"Someone who has experience dealing with PTSD. It's nothing to be ashamed of. It could help with the confusion you're feeling, these memories. Like Stroud." Her mother stroked her hair, and then, lightly, her face. Her fingers were cool on Ari's cheek. Ari could remember her mother caressing her just like this when she'd been four years old and had chicken pox. Then it had been soothing; now it made her skin prickle unpleasantly, as if her nerve endings were too close to the surface. Sensory memories were so much stronger than others. She sat up a little straighter and put a couple of imperceptible inches between herself and her mother. Stroud's face had been cool to the touch. Her fingertips remembered the sensation acutely.

"I had Stroud's phone though. Doesn't that prove he was there?"

Her mother said, "The police didn't think it was his phone, Ari. It was a burner and probably belonged to Sorkin."

"Oh yeah . . . but I took it out of his jacket," Ari couldn't help saying.

Her mother stiffened. "I believe you think that, Ari, but Captain Rourke called. They reached Stroud's grandmother. He's been out at the lake fishing and camping this weekend."

All figments of her imagination? What about the feeling of those hands pushing against her chest, the blow to her head, the muffled voice speaking to her? What about the certainty in the pit of her stomach that something was still seriously wrong?

"Mom? The doctor said I might have some short-term memory loss, right?"

"She said your recollection might be fragmented and the loss might be temporary."

Ari thought about this now as she eased her bedroom door closed and stepped into the hall, carrying her shoes by the laces. Fragmented? That meant patchy, not that her brain would make things up. If she just backtracked she might be able to unearth the rest of the stuff she had forgotten. But she couldn't share this with her parents.

She went downstairs, careful to skip the one step that squeaked. Despite the argument they'd had, she had to talk to Lynn. Lynn had been the one to point out the evil things people did, how the world was not always a safe or particularly nice place, how small towns harbored bad people as much as big cities did. Not that Ari had listened at the time, and she probably owed her a huge apology. Yes, Lynn was a realist, verging on a cynic, but she was always, always in Ari's corner. She could go to Lynn with her half-baked suspicions and her cracked brain and she could say, *Something is wrong. Somewhere, buried deep in my memory, I know something.* Lynn would accept it and together they would figure it out.

Slipping past the kitchen where she could hear her mother clattering pans, she went out the door, grabbing a knit cap to cover her bandaged head.

ɕ

Half a block, three hundred steps, five houses, all with pretty gardens and painted fences. One small dog chained in the shade of a tree. It started barking when it saw her and Ari shushed it before walking up Lynn's front path. She entered and went straight to the sunny sitting room like she always did. Neither she nor Lynn bothered with door knocking or bell ringing. The whole *mi casa es su casa* thing held true for them, and in this bright, familiar room smelling of toast and tomato sauce, the scene of so many cushion fights and marathon movie sessions, she felt the tightness in her throat ease a little.

"Lynn," she yelled. "Lynn!"

Her friend didn't appear but a whole gaggle of grimy kids did. The Shits and the rest of them.

"Hey you, where's Lynn?" she asked the gaggle, not bothering to identify a specific individual.

As a pack they shrugged their shoulders and managed to communicate *wedontknow* without enunciating any one word clearly. She felt a flash of irritation.

"What do you mean you don't know where your sister is?"

"She's gone," said one of the Shits. Nelly.

"When did she leave?" Ari asked, resisting the urge to slap her.

"Days and days ago. She's been gone Finidee time."

Finidee. Infinity. Translated into kid speak that could mean anything from an hour to a week. Where the hell was she?

Ari wanted to scream. There were no straight answers. The kids couldn't seem to care less though; a couple of them peeled off and disappeared deeper into the house.

"Did she take her cell phone?" Ari asked Nelly, who shook her head.

"I dunno. I don't care."

Ari looked around the room. Cushions were thrown about the floor and blankets were draped on the furniture. Chairs were stacked in precarious towers. Forts. Paper plates with half-eaten sandwiches were strewn everywhere and juice boxes leaked onto the carpet. "Who's looking after you Sh—" She broke off before she cussed in front of them.

"Babysitter," said Nelly.

Ari stared at her. This was odd. Lynn always looked after her siblings. It was one of the unfairnesses she ranted about most.

"Well, where is she?"

"I dunno."

Sounds of water running came from the kitchen, the clatter of dishes, tuneless whistling. Ari hurried into the room. A college-aged girl with dark hair looped into knots was standing by the sink.

"Hey, I'm Ari," she said. "I'm looking for Lynn."

"Colette. She's out, I think," the girl said, stripping off a soapy pair of yellow rubber gloves. "I've lost track of the time, to tell you the truth. I stayed over yesterday and I'm here until 7:30, 8:00 tonight." She grinned. "If I make it that long."

"Was Lynn here when you arrived?"

"Nope. Mrs. Lubnick was here for about half a second. She left me written instructions. Three pages' worth. Want to leave a note for Lynn? I'm sure she'll be back soon." She held out a scratch pad. There were markers everywhere. Ari scooped one up and scrawled a quick message. *Where are you? I need to talk. Xx Ari.*

"Can you see that she gets this as soon as she comes in?" she asked Colette.

"Sure. Just leave it on the table."

Ari looked at the papers and craft supplies spread all over the surface. One of the kids had been painting. Portraits of Tallulah mostly. Ari's heart squeezed. She cleared a space and put her note down where it would be visible.

"Thanks," she said.

"Sure, no problem."

"Can you tell Lynn I came by?" Ari asked Mark on her way out. She wanted to double up on the messages just in case her note was lost. He looked like he was old enough to pass it along.

"If you give me a dollar."

"I don't have a dollar on me. I'll owe it to you."

"Well then, give me ten dollars."

"What?! Why?"

"For secret information." He smirked horribly, showing gaps where he'd recently lost a couple of teeth. "About Lynn."

"Tell me."

"What about the money? You gonna pay?"

"Yes. Yes. Just tell me."

"She got a phone call yesterday. She said she was going to go see you."

"From who?"

"Dunno. She didn't say a name. Except yours." He sniggered. "Are you her girlfriend?"

Ari ignored this. "How do you know about the call?"

"I was hiding under her bed. Listening. I do that all the time."

Ari contemplated what he'd said.

"Are you sure she said she was going to meet me?" she snapped, resisting the urge to grab the Shit by his dirty collar.

"She said your name a bunch of times."

Yesterday Ari had been dragging her exhausted body out of the well and then sitting at the hospital and the police station. At that time no one besides Sourmash and maybe Rocky had known where she was. Had either one of them called Lynn? How did they get her number? Or had they used Ari's own phone to make the call? She never bothered with the lock or the password or anything. Lynn's number was right there at the top of a very short list.

Where was she now? Hurt? Ari couldn't bear the thought of it.

"No!" she said out loud, ignoring Mark, who stared at her open-mouthed. There was no way Lynn would take a call from those men and no way she'd agree to meet them.

She felt the beginning of a pounding headache pulse at her temples.

Perhaps Lynn had left something in her room that might tell Ari where she was. She ran down the hallway and threw open the door, ignoring the signs that warned of dire consequences to her siblings. Lynn's room was usually neat to the point of OCD—her books alphabetized and grouped according to genre, her posters of Ada Lovelace and Pythagoras framed and aligned, her bed made and her closet arranged by color—but today her covers were bundled at the end of her bed, her closet was open and her nightshirt and slippers lay where they'd been thrown. Lynn had obviously left in a hurry. She flipped open her laptop: 1 new message from Ari. Unread.

Ari raced back into the kitchen. "Mrs. Lubnick wasn't here last night?" she asked Colette, breathlessly.

"All-day seminar, and a dinner. She wasn't sure how long it was going to run so she had me stay over. I think she got in about eleven."

"Where is she now?" she asked.

The babysitter looked up from the magazine she was reading. "She said she had a bunch of errands. She left early."

Shit. "Can I call her?"

"Sure, her cell number's right here." She moved some papers. "Or it was right here."

Ari stifled her impatience while Colette searched through the mess.

"Here it is." She handed Ari a bundle of papers stapled together. The number was at the top of the first page of instructions.

Ari went to the kitchen phone and dialed the number. Voicemail. Goddamn it, did no one answer their phone anymore?

"Mrs. Lubnick, it's Ari. I think something has happened to Lynn. I'm going to the police."

Ignoring Colette's stunned face, she hung up and ran out of the house.

It was only about ten blocks to the station but before she'd gone two, she had to slow to a crawl. She walked with one hand pressed against the cramp in her side, trying to breathe it out. It was a mild, sunny day and tons of people were out on the streets, shopping, running errands. She was having a hard time keeping a straight trajectory and she kept bumping into people. Finally, keeping an eye out for Lynn's mom, she abandoned the sidewalk and took to the street. She wished she had a pair of sunglasses. The glare off the shop windows was doing a number on her eyes. The anonymity might have been a good thing too. People were staring. She wondered if it was because she was moving like a drunk person. Her vision was blurring and a couple of times she stumbled on the curb. She pulled her hat down further.

She walked past the chain-link fence and the park. A bunch of teens were playing basketball on the court, hooting and yelling insults at one another. She scanned the group for Stroud, just in case, but he wasn't there. She recognized Jack Rourke and a couple of others from school. Miranda was sitting courtside and she turned to look at Ari. Ari raised a hand in greeting but Miranda didn't acknowledge the gesture and turned her shoulder to her. That wasn't unusual. They were mutually contemptuous even though they'd been classmates since kindergarten. She wondered how much the group knew. Everything probably. Jack was a conduit straight from his police chief father. A tall figure peeled off from the group and kept pace with her alongside the fence. Speak of the devil. Jack Rourke. Ari sped up a little. He sped up too. She slowed down, ducked her head. From under her hair she could see him glaring at her. He had slowed his pace to match hers.

"Hey, Sullivan, I want to talk to you!" he yelled. Suddenly he threw himself at the fence like a chimpanzee in a zoo, slamming into it with his chest. She skipped backward. It was foolish, just a prank, but there was such an air of menace in it. She bolted, relieved when a turn in the fence forced him to stop.

Her thoughts were racing. What would she tell the police? How would she convince them to take her seriously? Where was Lynn? Every second felt like an eternity. She was waiting impatiently at a red light when someone gently touched her shoulder.

"Ari," a soft voice said.

It was Miss Byroade, the librarian's assistant. For a moment Ari stared at her, confused to see her outside her domain. She was wearing a purple plaid tweedy skirt, sensibly knee-length, with an emerald-green cardigan and a yellow-flowered shirt. A red tartan cap balanced on her head like a fried egg, and she carried a bag mostly filled with books. She was such a strong *good* reminder of the past, the nice things about Dempsey Hollow.

She flashed a quick smile. "Miss Byroade. Sorry, I was somewhere else."

"Wool-gathering. Such a happy term." Her expression grew concerned. "You are very pale, dear. Are you sure you should be out?"

The librarian blinked at her, her soft gaze drifting over Ari's face and then to the bandage just visible under the knit hat. Miss Byroade's hand went up to the side of her own head as if she had a wound there as well, and she winced.

"I'm fine," Ari said. "Thank you." This must be the longest light in creation. She appreciated the caring note in Miss Byroade's voice but it made her want to cry.

"Ari, I have to tell you. People are saying the most awful things." She drew Ari aside and her voice dropped to a hush. "About the cabin, that terrible man, the things he was up to."

Ari managed a nod. The words made her throat close up.

The librarian leaned in close and looked into her eyes.

"They're saying that you were there. That you're the teenager who was injured." Again her eyes went to the bandage.

"Who's saying? How do they know?" Ari blurted out. Maybe that's why people were staring. It wasn't her imagination. She wished more than ever that she could be invisible.

Miss Byroade sighed. "It's Debbie, who owns the Dollar Store. Her cousin Morrie cleans at the police station. He's a gossip. She's even worse. I heard them talking when I went to pick up my birdseed. It's the downside of living in a small town. Idle talk, rumors, no one can have secrets here."

But that wasn't true. Sourmash had kept his secrets.

The librarian reached out and took Ari's hand, frowning at the roughness and stroking the ruined pads of Ari's fingers. "Poor girl," she said. "You look so ill."

Ari was touched, but she felt odd having her hand caressed. As soon as was polite, she extricated herself.

"Listen, thanks," she said, "but I have to go now." It was blunt but she couldn't afford to waste any more time.

Miss Byroade looked a little hurt. She removed her hand and stood there rubbing her arms as if she was cold.

"I just have to go," Ari said again.

"Of course. But, Ari, just promise me you'll be more careful."

Ari nodded and broke into a shambling run, gritting her teeth against the excruciating soreness in her leg muscles. Two blocks down, one block over. The station was just ahead.

She saw the cop cars parked before the blocky, ivy-covered brick building and crossed the street diagonally, remembering that the last time she'd jaywalked she'd been holding hands with Lynn. And Sourmash had almost run them down. She crashed through the door and headed straight for the first uniform she saw.

"I need to talk to Captain Rourke," she gasped, leaning against the counter and trying to catch her breath. The front desk officer looked up from his computer screen. He was heavyset with black hair buzzed down to his scalp. He took in her disheveled appearance.

"Why don't you tell me what's going on?"

"It's important. Please, can I just talk to him?"

The officer—Rojas, according to his badge—said nothing, just narrowed his eyes. They were very black, the iris indistinguishable from the pupil. She took his silence as a negative.

Ari felt tears of frustration surge. "Captain Rourke knows me. I'm the girl who was in the well."

"That investigation is ongoing." He sounded like a robot.

"I know. God. I'm trying to report another kidnapping. My friend, Lynn Lubnick. Please."

His eyes softened. "Slow down and tell me. How long has she been missing?"

"Since last night, I think. I'm not exactly sure."

He put down his pen and notebook. "Miss, we don't file missing persons reports until they've been gone for more than twenty-four hours. Most of them turn out to be runaways."

"She would never run away," Ari said vehemently. "You don't understand. I was kidnapped and I think the same person took Lynn."

"We have a suspect in custody for the murder of the person who kidnapped you. He's been sitting in a jail cell since yesterday morning."

"I'm not saying it was Rocky or Sourmash, I mean, Sorkin Sigurson, who took Lynn."

"Well, it couldn't be Sigurson because he's dead," the officer said, sighing heavily. "You're saying that there's another kidnapper out there? In Dempsey Hollow?" He muttered something under his breath. She heard "Holy Mother" and "God" and then some Spanish words. "Listen, you understand that you can't mislead a police officer. It's a crime."

"No. Yes. I mean . . ." Her head whirled. "Can I just sit down?" She was sweating but her skin felt clammy. Officer Rojas came out from behind the desk. He took her by the elbow and helped her into a chair.

Ari stared up at him. "I'm not explaining this right. Can I speak to Captain Rourke?" She felt like she was hyperventilating. She closed her eyes, trying to gather her thoughts.

"Captain Rourke isn't here."

"How about Officer Tremblay? Please." Officer Tremblay was the one at the hospital who'd taken her clothes for evidence. She'd seemed more sympathetic.

He crossed his arms over his chest. "I cautioned you, right? Don't go wasting her time."

Ari shook her head. "I swear." He walked back over to the counter and picked up the phone. She couldn't hear the conversation, but after a minute he hung up, turned back to his computer and didn't pay her any more attention.

Ari stared at the FBI wanted posters on the wall across from her. Murderers. Kidnappers. Rapists. Was there an identifying characteristic? Something in their eyes?

"Miss Sullivan?" Officer Tremblay said from close by. Ari hadn't noticed the slight woman approaching. "Shouldn't you still be recuperating?" she asked, looking at her searchingly. "Forgive me for mentioning it but you don't look well."

"I'm fine," said Ari, wishing she didn't have to keep saying it.

"Rojas said you might have some information pertaining to the case?"

"My friend. Her brother said she was coming to see me, which is totally what she would do, but she never showed up."

"Okay," said Tremblay. "Is there more? Can you give me something to go on?"

Ari told her about the phone call Mark had overheard. She explained how close she and Lynn were and how they saw each other every day and how Lynn would never abandon her at a time like this. "She's missing," she said, and she thought of something else. "Have you found Stroud yet?"

"It's a big lake, lots of islands. He's got a canoe and his grandmother wasn't sure where he was camping. We're still looking. It won't be long now."

"Maybe they're both missing," Ari said.

Tremblay was quiet for a long time. Finally she said, "I know that you believe this, Ari, with your whole heart, but—"

"No, no buts. I know it sounds crazy but there's something there. Some real stuff. I just can't see it yet. But if you investigate you'll be able to. And if I'm wrong, then why don't you find Stroud and Lynn and prove me wrong!"

Tremblay was shaking her head. Ari half reached for her,

wanting to grab onto her until she listened. "I'm calling your parents, Ari. This anxiety you're feeling, your anger, your confusion—all are signs of post-concussive syndrome and trauma."

"No! But none of that matters. Lynn is gone."

"Ari!" The shout came from the doorway.

Like a hallucination, Ari saw Mrs. Lubnick storm in, laden with bags, her glasses slipping down her hawk-like nose.

"Ari, I got your message. What the hell's going on? Where's Lynn?" She gave Ari a quick, hard hug with one free arm. "God, you look wrecked."

Hot tears spilled over Ari's eyelids. "She didn't come to see me."

Mrs. Lubnick blinked. "What do you mean?"

The bags went flying, spilling groceries all over the floor, and Mrs. Lubnick sank down on the chair beside Ari.

"What are you saying? She was on her way over to you before dinnertime yesterday. It's two hundred yards." Her ruddy face blanched.

"I've been trying to tell Captain Rourke that she's missing," said Ari, "but he won't talk to me."

Mrs. Lubnick stood up. She skewered Officer Tremblay with her forefinger. "You tell Fred Rourke that my daughter is missing. You tell him right now."

CHAPTER TWENTY-SIX

I watched her all the time. She was perfect. Beautifully rounded arms and legs, glossy hair and eyes, a rosebud of a mouth, the thick vein that pulsed in her neck. I could imagine how vivid she is, though my poor vision rendered everything in gray. I could feel the heat of her, smell her musk. She reminded me of a deer. Bold and shy at the same time, victim of her own insatiable curiosity.

I observed and learned her daily patterns. I noticed the others who noticed her and I hated them for it. I stalked her outside the school, in the park, at the convenience store where she bought red licorice and root beer. Once I was close enough to breathe in the sweet tang of her breath when she spoke to someone. My sense of smell has strengthened with my loss of color. Another time, a curl brushed against my hand as I held it outstretched just so, as if by accident. That soft contact sent chills up and down my spine, shooting electricity into my groin. I can only imagine what it will feel like once I have her under my knife and can bend her to my will. Her skin like velvet, the silk of her blood, the scent of her, a flawless red apple. My tired foggy eyes will see clearly again, I just know it. The color will seep back into my world as it pumps from her heart, leaving her as bleached as silver driftwood on the sand.

Lynn. *Such a mediocre name for such a gorgeous creature, such a spirited, vital thing. I have her safe and I will never let her go.*

CHAPTER TWENTY-SEVEN

A crow squawked and Ari's head jerked. She took in her surroundings. How had she gotten here? She'd left the station with Lynn's mother and walked almost all the way home again before she'd decided that sitting quietly and waiting for news was the last thing she wanted to do.

"Hang tight, Ari," Mrs. Lubnick had said on the corner, giving Ari another one of her bone-cracking hugs. "They'll find her." Ari couldn't help but hear the note of desperation in her voice. Captain Rourke had sent cars out countywide and they were putting up flyers with Lynn's picture. Ari tried not to think about Tallulah's furry face staring back at her from telephone poles, and failed.

She'd stalled until she saw Mrs. Lubnick stride up her garden walkway and throw open the front door, and then she'd spun on her heel and headed back to town. She'd lost another small chunk of time; from early afternoon to late. Her feet hurt as if she'd been walking for miles, and she supposed she had, though mostly in loose circles and figure eights, threading through downtown and out again.

And now she found herself here. Dempsey's Maze looked like a wall of thorns, something out of *Sleeping Beauty* after the world fell asleep and the wilderness crept back in. It was as if she were half-asleep herself, caught in a nightmare, Ari thought, fighting to suppress the panic that deadened her limbs and made her feel she was trudging through waist-high brambles. Her headache was back, the twinkling distracting lights too, as if her brain were misfiring on all cylinders.

She sank down on a bench and watched a curled brown leaf skitter along the path, caught up in an invisible breeze. Pushed and pulled, taunted and teased, helpless before a force greater than itself. Ari felt like that too. *Are we all just victims?*

Something stirred in her brain and Ari grabbed for it. Last night, just before she'd fallen asleep, in that weird halfway-between state, she'd been back at the cistern. The forest quiet and still, not a breath of air, and there had been someone else there too. She strained to remember something, anything—a feature, a voice, a recognizable item of clothing. It had been dark, the bottom of the hole shrouded, and she'd felt a cold updraft. But she had not been afraid then.

She sat up straight, her heart leaping in her throat like a trapped bird. She had *not been scared.* Surely that meant she'd known the person she was with, had trusted whoever it was. You don't go out in the woods with someone you don't know; you don't freely stand at the edge of a pit deep enough to kill you if you fall. There was no way it could have been Sourmash. *A friend? Absolutely not, but perhaps someone who didn't pose an obvious danger.*

Excitement flooded her veins, obliterating the terrible anxious feelings that seemed to encase her, mind and body, in ice.

This memory rang true. It was fact. A memory she could share with her parents. Something she could tell the police that they would have to take seriously.

Or would they? She gnawed on a shred of skin near her thumbnail. Would they question her until she no longer knew what was the truth? *Holy shit, you could argue yourself out of breathing*, Lynn would say. *Make up your mind!*

Her friend's voice was so clear, so loud, so familiarly exasperated that Ari looked around, expecting to see her. This more than anywhere else in town was Lynn's place.

She knew the trick to navigating the winding paths. Ari always got helplessly lost.

It was almost as if Lynn could see the maze from above, track the most direct route to the exit. On the few instances when they separated—not by Ari's choice, but because Lynn sped off without her, casting taunts over her shoulder—Ari usually ended up facing a towering dense wall. One of the many dead ends. Like now.

She wondered what had possessed her, coming in here without her guide. The paths seemed as convoluted and twisted as the pathways of her brain, clogged, a gnarl of questions so tangled she could not straighten them out. She thought of the story her father had often told, of why her parents had named her Ariadne. Her namesake was a clever Greek princess who helped a hero find his way out of a perilous maze by using a ball of thread. "She was a little more proactive than most of them," her mother had said wryly. Maybe if she just found the end of the thread, she could pull on it and everything would unravel and become linear again. Her feet rustled through a carpet of leaves, and the shushing sound seemed as if it were emanating from inside her head. *Whisper, whisper, whisper.* Perhaps, she thought, she'd find Lynn here, walking, thinking, figuring out the next step in her life.

Somewhere out of sight, she could hear the sounds of feet thudding, yelling, a ball game being played out on the adjacent field. She pressed against the thick interwoven branches. They pushed in and then sprang back. There was no way to force her way through. The scent of mold and dry leaves crept into her nostrils and scratched at her eyes. Her brain crackled, the ever-present lights flickering at the edges of her vision. She felt a wave of weakness, remembered she had eaten nothing since she had picked at her mac and cheese. The blood thundered in her ears, like the ocean advancing, retreating. There—she could almost see Lynn, in a bright-red sweatshirt, running ahead, a flash of color at the next bend, her laughter drifting back.

Catch me, catch me if you can.

Or no, it was Stroud.

Ari started to run. She ran until she was out of breath and sobbing. She ran so blinded by tears that she almost missed the gap in the hedge that marked the exit and the boy who stood there, beanie cap pulled down over his hair, craggy shoulders hunched.

"Stroud!" she yelled.

The relief was almost as big as if Lynn had appeared. Stroud would be able to tell her what had happened up at the cabin. Fill in the empty spaces.

"Jesus, Sullivan. Does anyone else even figure in your pathetic world?" Jesse snapped, whipping his hat off and smacking it against his leg as if it were dusty. His hands were encrusted with dirt, and more stiffened the knees of his jeans.

It took a moment for Ari to clue in. How had she mistaken him for Stroud?

"What?" she said, feeling even more disorientated. What the hell was he talking about?

"You walk around oblivious. Like a victim. It's so sad." Why was he taunting her? Did he know that she was the girl in the well? Of course he did; it was exactly the kind of juicy morsel he would uncover and gloat over. What kind of asshole delighted in someone else's misery?

Ari felt rage bubble up. It was a relief. "What the fuck is your problem, Jesse? Do you think I don't know how things really are?"

He blinked at her.

She was just getting started. "It's not all gothic and romantic, you moron. The world is a truly dark place. People are fucked." Her breath caught on a sob. "I don't have time for your small-minded bullshit."

"Fine. Get the hell out of here then."

For a breathless second she stared at him. "Fuck you, Jesse Caldwell!"

CHAPTER TWENTY-EIGHT

I draw her blanketed by the blackness, as if the shadows are slowly feeding on her. Only her perfect face floats there like the moon.

I sketch the beautiful bones under her skin. I surround her with eyes and the drift of her hair and she looks like a constellation mapped out in a dark sky.

CHAPTER TWENTY-NINE

Ari bunched her fists. She felt high on a heady mix of rage and adrenaline and exhaustion. Summoning energy from who knows where, she'd launched herself at Jesse Caldwell's smirking face, using her shoulder as a battering ram, and she'd knocked him flat on his back.

For once he'd had absolutely nothing to say. He'd just stared at her from the ground as she walked away, his eyes darkening from shock to hatred.

She was still trembling with the force of it now, standing at a busy corner. Part of her wished she'd gotten a few kicks in as well.

There were tons of people around, too close, brushing against her shoulders, her back. She could smell fried onions, hot dogs, sweat. Someone laughed, mouth wide, their teeth impossibly large. She stumbled out into the street. A car slammed to a halt, brakes screaming. The sound catapulted her right back to the incident with Sourmash and instantly the buzz of energy left her body, and she sagged.

"Jesus, the light was red," the driver yelled.

Ari followed his gesticulating hand with her eyes. She hadn't noticed a traffic light. All she'd been thinking about was getting away from all these people.

"You got a death wish?" the driver snarled, shooting her a venomous look before peeling away.

She made her shaky way across the street, ignoring the concerned glances and murmurs of "are you all right?" coming from behind her.

No, she was not all right.

Although it hurt her bones, she started running again. Little more than a shambling jog at first, but slowly her muscles loosened and she was able to move faster. It felt good, even though she knew she'd pay later when her body cooled down.

Ari didn't stop until she got back to her house. By that time her feet felt like they were encased in concrete blocks and she couldn't catch her breath.

She bolted through the front door, registering that the car wasn't in the driveway.

"Mom! Dad!" she yelled, ducking into each downstairs room. She paused at the bottom of the stairs and shouted again. Neither was home.

She whirled around in despair. Should she run back to the police station? She didn't want to waste time trying to explain things to Captain Rourke again. She'd tell him she knew the person who had pushed her into the well and he'd just look at her with that skeptical expression and when he asked for a name, she wouldn't be able to give him one. It would be better if she were accompanied by an adult.

She picked up the phone and called Mrs. Lubnick. Colette

answered on the first ring. "Lubnick residence," she said wearily.

Various kids whooped in the background. It sounded like a war zone, battle raging full force.

"It's Ari. Is Mrs. Lubnick there?"

"No. She's getting some people together to put flyers up around town. She has her cell phone with her, and she's been checking in every hour." Colette sounded desperate. "She's got us on lockdown. Can't leave the house. The kids are going a little crazy."

Ari felt some grim satisfaction. At least Lynn's mom was taking things seriously.

"Do you want to leave a message? Your cell number?"

"I don't have a cell. I'll call her back," Ari said, hanging up. A thought had occurred to her. She had lost her cell phone near the well, although it hadn't been recovered by the police. But she could still check her messages remotely. From any phone or computer. Maybe there was something that would jog her memory, a clue to what she had done on Friday.

She punched in the access number and then her password.

Three new messages. One from her coach reminding her to work on her delts, a telemarketer asking if she was happy with her cell service, and then she heard Lynn's husky voice. She almost sobbed with relief. The reception was awful, filled with snaps and crackles and hisses. It took three listens before she could make out what Lynn was saying, and even then it was only snatches of words. . . . *just missed your . . . only . . . one bar . . . could hardly . . . what you said . . . on my way . . . smooches. . . .*

Ari listened one more time and jotted down the audible words and the fuzzy, garbled spaces in between them.

She tried to piece it together systematically, ignoring the thump of her ever-present headache. Lynn had called from someplace where she only had one bar on her phone. But that didn't narrow things too much. Cell reception was notoriously bad in the Hollow, especially since the motion to put up a tower—or eyesore, as some would have it—had been voted down. So she could've been anywhere that was not the downtown core.

Then, filling in the blanks as if she were playing Mad Libs, she jotted: *Just missed your* call. I've *only* got *one bar.* I *could hardly* hear/understand *what you said.* I'm *on my way. Smooches.*

Ari's heart turned over. *Smooches* was so Lynn.

She replayed it, noting the time and date. Lynn had left the message at 5:08 p.m. yesterday. With tremulous fingers, she dialed Lynn's number. It went straight to voicemail.

Ari's breathing quickened. The call must have come from Ari's own cell phone, which was why Lynn hadn't questioned it. She couldn't see Lynn being fooled by a vocal impersonation. Muffled? Text to voice? Perhaps.

She tried to think clearly. What she did know was that there was no possibility it was Sourmash because he'd been dead by then, and there was no way Rocky could have done it either. The police had picked him up while Ari was still at the station. So who then? The shadowy figure who haunted her every thought?

She heard the back door slam.

"Mom, Dad," she yelled. She could hear the buzz of her parents' voices coming from the kitchen. She was just reaching for the doorknob when her mother's voice froze her in place.

"It's a relief he confessed. Now maybe we can put all this behind us."

"It's a dirty business," her father sighed. "Rocky insisted at first that there was someone else there, but after some intense questioning he caved."

"Do they know why he would do such a thing?"

"Drug-related. Fred said they found all kinds of methamphetamine paraphernalia up at Sorkin's place. Balboa had been crashing there too, I guess. They probably had some kind of an argument over money or drugs."

"And he shot him?"

"Looks that way. He'll have to detox in jail. Fred said he's hallucinating. They have him on suicide watch."

"God, Bill. I can hardly stand the thought of it."

Ari burst through the door, brandishing the phone.

Her mother turned, abruptly knocking over one of the bags of groceries on the counter and sending cans crashing onto the floor. "Ari! We thought you were asleep upstairs! What is it?"

"Lynn is missing. The police are looking for her. But she called me late yesterday afternoon. She left a voicemail," Ari said breathlessly. "Someone set a trap for her."

"Ari, tell us calmly," her mother said, shaking her head. "You're talking too fast."

Her father pulled a chair out from the table. "Have a seat. You look like you're going to collapse."

Ari waved him away. She didn't want to sit down. She wanted to keep pacing. "No. Listen to me. She called me."

She dialed up the voicemails again, deleted the first two and pressed the speaker on the handset. Lynn's distorted voice spoke her garbled message.

"And she was returning my call," she told her parents, striving to keep her voice steady. "But it wasn't me. The person who called her must have my phone."

"Oh my God," her mother said. "Karen must be going nuts. I need to get over there."

Ari felt tears of relief come to her eyes. Her parents believed her. Finally. "Lynn's mom's not home. She's got a taskforce putting up missing persons flyers. But we need to tell the police that it's someone with a bigger plan. The same person who pushed me into the well and killed Stroud. It wasn't Sourmash. Or Rocky. Someone else." Her voice was rising with every word. Now they could figure this out together.

Her parents exchanged looks. The worry lines were carved so deep into their faces that they looked like strangers. Old people. Ari felt the excitement rush out of her.

"What? What don't you understand?" It was so clear to her. Lynn would have gotten it immediately.

"Stroud hasn't been reported missing," her dad said. "He's camping."

"Stroud is dead!"

"Oh Ari," her mother said, sitting down heavily.

"It can't just be random. It doesn't make sense," Ari said, stalking back and forth in front of the window. "You're in complete denial. You think the Hollow is some perfect, safe little haven, and it's not. What about the pet killings? What about what happened to me? You need to wake the hell up!" She was barely aware of echoing the words Lynn had spoken to her. Her mother's face had whitened but Ari was in the grip of some kind of fury.

"Just a second, Ari," her dad said warningly. He moved forward and slipped his arm around her mother's shoulders. "We're just trying to help you through this."

"Yes, but don't you see that all this pretending is making it worse for me? It makes me feel like I'm on one side of the wall and everyone else is on the other." She tried to express the feeling of utter loneliness. "The sun is shining where you are and I'm standing in the dark."

"It's the terrible after-effect of what you went through. It will fade away, Ari," her mother pleaded. "Just give it a little time."

Ari set her lips. "You can't just stick a Band-Aid on it."

"Tell us what we can do for you," her mother said.

Ari shook her head, miserable. She just didn't know how to express what she was feeling. "It makes sense to me." She held up the cordless phone that was still in her hand. "Where is she? Why can't anyone find her?"

They had no answer.

"Lynn would never leave me alone to deal with everything that's happened."

"But you're not alone, honey," her mother said.

"I am if you don't believe me."

CHAPTER THIRTY

She is weakening. I have not given her any food for more than twenty-four hours, and she spent a lot of time kicking against the padded lid of the box and screaming curse words before her struggles ceased and her voice wore thin. She begged me at first. I was disappointed. I thought she would be excited about my plans, but instead she railed and moaned and promised me things I care nothing about. I let her tire herself out, strain against the rubber tubes cuffing her wrists, ankles and knees. "You can scream as loud as you want," I told her as I prepared to fit the lid to the box. "You can call me every name in the book." She spat at me and I slapped her across that ripe mouth until she hid her head again.

She has spirit though, and I resist the urge to open the chest and look at her. Her nails gouged grooves into my forearm, and her sharp little teeth tried to bite through my shirt into my shoulder before I was able to knock her on the head just behind her right ear where her thick hair would hide the wound. Funnily enough, it's the same place I hit Ari. The terror in her voice when she regained herself was the purest sound I have ever heard, a single high note played on a violin. It knifed straight into my heart.

Now she is quiet but for some muffled sobbing and snuffling. She reminds me of the piglets. I have given her a bottle of water; until I'm ready for her, she can rest on the old blanket I folded in the bottom. I don't want to risk her bruising her skin or injuring herself; no marks that will ruin the perfection of my tableau. There are new breathing holes drilled in the sides. As long as she calms down and conserves her air, she will be all right. If I press my eye to one of the holes I can see her face, staring up. Her little chin so firm and stubborn, silent tears sliding down her cheeks like raindrops. I can smell her fear. It is intoxicating. The glossy curl I took from her head is tucked away in an envelope in my pocket. I stroked it until static electricity made the dark hairs stick to my skin, and then I moistened my fingers and smoothed it into shape and put it back with the others, subtle gradations of light gray and dark gray. It's the texture that entrances me, various degrees of coarseness and silkiness. I can hear the paper crinkle as I turn my attention to my work.

A few hours later, I set my paintbrush down. Two of the three walls are done. Chaotic violence; a red Milky Way of runnels and burning stars. I can't see the color, of course, but if I place my palm flat against the paint where it has dried to a crust, I can feel the heat of it. Thick gouts, textured like skin, warm as if the flesh and ruin portrayed were living and breathing just a few minutes before. I remember how the slaughtered cows and pigs gave off heat, steaming in the cold of the butcher shop, opened like red velvet–lined purses disgorging their pearly contents. Standing in the middle of the room, I feel as if I am being reborn in blood, like some triumphant warrior. My final transformation.

CHAPTER THIRTY-ONE

Ari leaned out her bedroom window until she could see Lynn's house. It appeared deserted, doors shut tight, but she knew that inside Colette was wrangling little kids for suppertime and Lynn's room was empty. Her mom had had dinner on the table early again and the food—pork chops and mashed potatoes—was sitting heavily in her stomach although she had eaten only enough to appease her parents. She looked up at the sky, the specks of birds wheeling far above. She could pretend they were swimmers and she was at the bottom of the pool. Alone, but safe in her element. It was still light but the sun would set in about half an hour, at 6:30. She breathed deeply for a few seconds, and after she'd filled her lungs with that peace, she pulled the sash down, and then the new heavy blinds her father had installed a couple of hours ago.

She turned around slowly. It was shocking how much they blocked the light. Her room transformed, became oppressive, cramped. It felt like the cistern.

Her breathing quickened as she crossed to the bedside lamp she'd kept on, flicked it off, and made her way blindly to the corner by the door.

She sank down, hugging her knees to her chest. Somehow, choosing the darkness now allowed her brain to roam.

It had all begun in the well. She had become a target for someone and they had put her there. She didn't care what anyone else believed. She knew she was right and she had to confront her fears. The police were doing what they could. Mrs. Lubnick and her parents were taking action, but it wasn't enough. They didn't see the big picture. She couldn't just sit around waiting.

She drummed her fingers against her forehead as if it might loosen the web of her thoughts.

Someone had wanted her dead but she had escaped. Surely they still wanted her dead. Maybe even more now than before. She was a liability. She knew things that were still locked in her brain. That person had Lynn, she was sure of it, tucked away in some hiding place. But perhaps she could draw them out.

Bait. She could be bait.

She inhaled, appalled by what she was thinking but excited too. It was like the moment before she dove into the water, the seconds before the race started. She always knew within a few heartbeats if everything was going to work in perfect rhythm or if it was all going to fall apart.

"Bait and switch" was an expression her mother used laughingly sometimes when describing her cupcake window display. Customers would come in for the sweet treats and leave with a pound of coffee and a decorative mug as well.

Ari could do the same thing, but in reality, she would be the hunter. What did that entail exactly? Making sure she was alone? Walking blindly into dark alleys? She had to do this with her eyes wide open.

She scrubbed at the itchy scab above her ear. The bandage was flapping loose. She peeled it away and prodded the wound. It was healing. It felt crusty but there was no blood. She poked some more and frowned. Had the doctor clipped her hair? No, she'd have remembered that. The sensation of the cold stethoscope traveling over her back was still vivid, the dry, powdery feel of the latex gloves.

She got clumsily to her feet, stumbled over to the bed and switched the light back on, blinking until her eyes adjusted. She had a hand mirror in the drawer, a full-length hanging on her door. She held the hand mirror behind her and aimed it at the side of her head. Carefully she separated a sweaty mat of hair and pushed it aside. Scalp gleamed. She was missing a big chunk.

She recalled her notes on serial killers. How she'd dismissed that research because it was clearly insane and paranoid.

Her thoughts began to hammer her. Trophies. Killers often took trophies from their victims: jewelry, clothing, *locks of hair*. She pulled the sheaf of notes out from her desk, flipping through them until she found what she was looking for. Serial killers often exhibited warning signs before they began to murder people. Pet killings—check. Arson? Had anyone been setting fires in the area? She woke her computer, first checking her email. Just spam. She entered "Dempsey Hollow arson" in the search engine. A page of entries popped up. She clicked on the top news article and read it quickly. Six mysterious fires in the last two years. Two on State Park land, but the rest within town limits, derelict buildings mostly.

This was real information she could share with her parents. They could take it to the police together. She rose, reached for the doorknob and stopped herself. They didn't believe her already. They'd never believe this. Would they force her to see a shrink? Would they put her in a hospital if they thought she was really crazy?

She sat back in her chair and then clicked back over to her email. Lynn. Lynn was out of reach but Ari felt like she had to try. She typed:

You're not dead are you? I can't bear it.

Ari stared at this line for a long moment as her heart heaved. And then she deleted it and wrote:

I'm going to find you.

She hit Send and then stared at the wall, fingers playing with her bracelet. A knock at her door made her jump. She closed her computer.

"Going to get some rest soon, Ari?" her mother asked, peeking in. Her parents had been tiptoeing around ever since her outburst earlier.

"Yes, soon."

Her mother crossed the room and fussed with the blinds. "Your father and I think you should stay home from school tomorrow. Give yourself one more day to rest. I'll be at work in the morning but I can come back for lunch, and your father can stop in in the afternoon." She sat down on Ari's bed, clasping her fingers together. "What do you think?" Scanning Ari's face, she said hurriedly, "Or I can stay home with you if you'd like."

A day, basically on her own, would give her time to figure stuff out. She was pretty sure she wasn't going to get much sleep tonight anyway.

"I think that's a good idea," she said slowly. "I'll be fine on my own though." She summoned up a weak smile. "I know it's super busy at the coffee shop."

"Need anything? Herbal tea? Crackers and cheese?" Ari was relieved her mother hadn't suggested warm milk, as if she were a bed-ridden invalid.

"I'm not hungry," she said.

"Okay," her mother said, somewhat doubtfully. "Try to relax and let your body heal, honey."

Ari nodded as her mother dropped a quick kiss on the top of her head and left the room. Ari listened to the sound of her footsteps descending the stairs. Closing the door, she scooped up her pillow and stuffed it against the bottom to block the light. Her parents checked on her periodically during the night, but usually they just stood in the hallway for a few seconds listening with an intensity that was tangible.

She splayed her notes out in front of her. She scanned down. She'd underlined the following: *Serial killers are 91% male, 54% white, with an average IQ of 113*, which put them way above the norm for intelligence. This was not some alcoholic screw-up or skeletal junkie; this was someone who lived in the shadows by choice, a hunter.

What kind of person was she looking for?

Dahmer. Gacy. Bundy. Gein. All predators who hid in plain sight and were part of society. Sourmash had lived totally off the grid and made no attempt to pretend he was anything other than what he was. Maybe she was looking for someone who was the opposite? Pedophiles sometimes worked in jobs that brought them close to children. It was like the witch in the gingerbread house.

It had to be someone who knew things about her and Lynn, their routines, who had used that information to track Ari and then get to Lynn. It had to be someone who saw them regularly.

Bundy had sweet-talked his victims. Charmed them and played with them. He liked to kill college girls and so he hunted them on campus, blending in with the other yuppie jocks.

She slid her chair out, found a notebook and a pen and scribbled down a name. Circled it.

What were her and Lynn's regular haunts? The bookstore. Ice cream parlor. The park. The school. Who did they see every day? The person she was looking for knew Dempsey Hollow, the grove, the neighborhoods with the most pets, and they were above suspicion. That implied a certain stature in the community. Her pen tapped like a metronome. Or maybe below suspicion. If this was someone who was just starting out on their career path, they could be young. Her own age.

Who did she know who could butcher a family dog? Who seemed capable of acting on morbid thoughts? Had a cruel streak? She wrote down another name and chewed on the end of her hair. She supposed it said something about her that she was writing down the names of possible serial killers living in her town, but she didn't care—her friend's life hung in the balance. *Wake the fuck up*, Lynn seemed to say. *This is a sick business*. She shook off the guilty feelings and returned to her list.

Many people believed that Jack the Ripper had been a doctor. His kills were so precise, so surgical. Ari considered the local family physician, Dr. Prentiss. He was a white-haired, fluffy, doddering man who gave out lollipops to all the kids no matter what their age, and still handwrote his careful instructions though his fingers shook with tremors. He was barely capable of holding a pen, to say nothing of a knife or a gun. Was it an act? She didn't think so. She'd heard her mother and Mrs. Lubnick mention Parkinson's disease and retirement. The pet killings were recent. It made sense to her that the person she was looking for was just starting out and not someone who'd been living here for fifty years. She crossed Dr. Prentiss's name off and threw down her pen. Dammit. Her brain felt encased in sludge. It hurt to think. Power nap, she thought. I'll just rest my eyes for a second. She laid her head down on folded arms. Sleep rose up and submerged her like a wave.

Ari jerked awake. Apart from the bedside lamp and the glow from her computer, the darkness was enveloping, the silence so thick she could hear her blood pumping in her temples. The clock on her computer said 3:47 a.m. Monday morning. She hadn't slept for that many continuous hours since before the cistern. Out of the grogginess a memory sprang to mind, and she fought to capture it before it could disappear back into the murk.

It was three years ago, summertime, and she and Lynn had just finished freshman year. They'd been playing on the street outside Lynn's house. It was some old-fashioned game and Ari didn't fully grasp the rules.

"You touched on Wales," Lynn said.

"Did not," Ari said, pushing her wet hair off her face. It was boiling hot, and the tree they were using had some kind of fungus that had curled and stripped all the leaves off, so it offered no shade. She shrugged her shoulders, trying to unstick the back of her shirt. Her shorts kept riding up in a really annoying way.

"Popsicle run?" she suggested.

"Can't leave," Lynn said with a sour look. "The Shits." Lynn's triplet siblings were seven years old. Thankfully the Littles (Horror, Bother and Monster) were in daycare for the summer.

"Where's your mom?" Ari asked, flopping down on the edge of the sidewalk.

After a moment, Lynn joined her.

"Work, as usual." She sounded bitter. This whole summer her mom had either been taking extension classes in admin stuff or putting in major hours at the school, catching up on curriculum. "She's going for the principal position vacated by our dear, wish-he-was-truly-departed Mr. Oickle."

A car roared by, barely slowing at the stop sign at the intersection before jetting off down the street. Lynn jerked her head up, looking for her brother and sisters, counting them off *one, two, three* under her breath. "Stay out of the road, you dingbats," she called. They had grouped together, shoulder to shoulder, and were staring intently at something just ahead and out of sight. "Get on the sidewalk," Lynn said, in her "I'm deadly serious" voice. It worked maybe half the time, but not now. They weren't shifting. Mark still held a branch in his sticky fist and he was pointing it at whatever it was that had grabbed their attention.

Lynn pulled herself to her feet, muttering. Her capris were stuck to the back of her thighs and she walked a little bow-legged as she tried to free the sweat-dampened material. Ari followed her, flapping her shirt to try to get some cool air circulating. A popsicle would taste so good right now. The smallest girl, Nelly, was crying. At their feet was a small brown-striped tabby cat, not much more than a kitten. It lay on its side, ribs heaving, and then suddenly it lurched to its feet, and then flopped back over again. It couldn't seem to hold its head straight. Lynn cursed and shoved the kids back behind her. She looked up the street where the car had disappeared moments before. "Asshole," she said. Nelly hid her head in Lynn's shirt and wailed, "Kitty!"

Ari was mesmerized by the cat, which was doing a weird, disjointed dance, as if it were being attacked by invisible bees. One of its eyes bulged from the socket but there was no blood or anything.

"What do we do?" Ari said, feeling sick.

"Brain injury," a voice from behind them said. "Car bumper probably clipped it." A woman with curly auburn hair and a voluminous orange sundress had appeared. Ari looked at her and then looked again. She was a new-that-year teacher from school, she thought. Senior biology? That sounded right.

The woman kneeled down, one hand gripping the kitten by the scruff of the neck and holding it still. "I'm Dr. McNamara." Ari stared at the cat. It was trying to bite and scratch but Dr. McNamara didn't even flinch.

"Don't hurt it," Lynn said. She and Ari both had tears in their eyes.

Dr. McNamara looked at her without expression.

"I'm trying to help it. See the distended eye? That means there's pressure building up in the brain."

Ari made a movement toward her. "It's suffering."

"It's dying," the teacher said.

"Christina, take the other kids and go in the yard," Lynn said in a tense voice. For once they listened to her, scurrying across the street and into the yard, where they pressed up against the chain-link fence with transfixed expressions.

Dr. McNamara had shifted her hands; now both were cupped around the kitten's head. Its ears were completely flattened, and its back legs kicked fruitlessly. And then the woman did something, Ari wasn't sure what, a quick twist of her fingers. There was a snap like a twig breaking and when she removed her hands the kitten was still. She laid it down at the edge of the road and stood up, brushing her palms against the material of her dress.

Lynn and Ari exchanged horrified looks. *Oh my God*, Lynn mouthed. Behind the fence, Ari heard Nelly say in a tearful voice, "What happened to the kitty?" and then Lynn had rushed up and hustled them all onto the porch and into the house.

"See you at school," Dr. McNamara said to Ari and walked away.

Ari drew a continuous circle around Dr. McNamara's name now as she thought about the teacher. Yes, most serial killers were men, but there was a coldness about her, a lack of emotion. And she had the knife skills and knowledge of anatomy.

Above suspicion, she thought. Or maybe *protected* from suspicion. She jotted another name down and stared at what she had written so far.

Jesse Caldwell. Completely antisocial. Cold-blooded. Insults, people's negative opinions just seemed to bounce off him. He could be sociopathic. She remembered the rumors about him cutting that girl's ponytail off, and he'd been right there at the killing grove. Admiring his work? She underlined his name.

Jack Rourke. He seemed to be heartless beyond the borders of normal high school asshole-ry, and protected to some extent by his cop father. He liked to antagonize, dominate and intimidate. He had always targeted Lynn with taunts and dirty slurs, usually delivered in a quiet voice. Lynn could look after herself, but still, what kind of guy persecuted the only openly gay girl in school? Someone predatory.

Dr. McNamara. Or Mephistopheles, as Lynn liked to call her. She stifled a nervous giggle and chewed her lip.

Still, she had to admit, the list was ludicrous. Nothing she could actually show to anyone. But if she did nothing, Lynn might die. If she did *something*, perhaps there was a chance. She had to do it.

Three suspects and they could all be found at school on a regular Tuesday.

Next step. What would make the killer reveal him- or herself?

More likely a him, Ari decided. She opened up her computer again and then, gathering her courage, texted to her cell phone. *I'm going to find you and then you're going to pay.* With trembling fingers she pressed Send, jumping away from her computer as if it had suddenly turned into a giant spider.

It was an empty promise, but she was so angry that it fueled her courage and determination. It could be enough to make him let Lynn go and stop what he was doing. Maybe he couldn't operate out of the shadows.

Or maybe it would just shine a big old spotlight on her.

CHAPTER THIRTY-TWO

The Klein house is perfect. I've been here on my own for three months now. Not only is it a legitimate address for any nosy people who come sniffing around but it is also a safe and private place for me. Mrs. Klein agreed to let me live here for free as a property manager after she went into the nursing facility. I still visit her regularly, and all the bills and such are in her name in case I have to disappear again. Always be prepared, Ma Cosloy used to say.

It checks every box on my list. I have all the benefits of a higher elevation, perched as it is at the top of a hill. The windows face the intersecting roads half a mile away, unrolling like long gray carpets; the curtains are thick to help warm the house during the winter months. Most of the time I keep them closed and just peek out if I hear the sound of an engine. If a car does appear, it usually turns around as soon as the driver realizes that the road dead-ends and leads nowhere.

Kitchen, sitting room, two bedrooms upstairs, and a tiny bathroom. And a parlor for visitors.

A short distance from the house is a sparse row of trees, nothing more really than a marker along the field boundaries. A windbreak. Beyond, the land rolls upward at a slight grade toward the horizon. Grassland belonging to some unknown person who doesn't care to farm it. And of course there is the river. Dwindling a little in the hot summer months, but deep and studded with tumbled boulders and wide slabs of slick rock. Close by the house, it twists and turns, boiling over the banks in swift-moving rapids. Roaring. In the spring, I tried to ford it, and found the footing unstable and the currents much stronger than expected. Once there was a drowned deer, one leg pinned under a tree branch, stomach bloated with gases so that it bobbed like a balloon on the water's surface.

I bend my mind to the problem of Ari.

She is a curious girl, and you know what they say about curiosity and the cat. Books and movies are full of characters like her: those people who can't stop themselves from opening the forbidden door, or entering the dark woods, or asking too many questions of dangerous strangers. She is so intent on her own thoughts she doesn't notice that I am observing her. At first to discover how much she recalled of that day, and then, once I realized she remembered nothing of me, to keep an eye on her comings and goings. I've heard that amnesiacs may suddenly regain their memories after the brain settles again. And that conversation we had, just before I knocked her out and threw her into the cistern, was sufficiently traumatic that she could still remember it if her mind allows her to travel back into her fears.

Such an unpredictable thing, the brain. Breathing, walking, swallowing, a hundred functions controlled by a lump of gelatinous goop pulsing with electrical charges.

I'm enthralled by how parts of the brain shut themselves off, like rooms in a house, the way Ari's mind has blocked the truth from her, as if by not knowing it she can be saved.

I have to say it was a shock to find the cistern empty when I went back to dispose of her properly. I'd hit her very hard and the fall was a high one. If I hadn't been distracted by Sourmash, I'd have made sure.

And after I killed him I admit that I lost my head momentarily and left the cabin without covering my tracks. The plan was to come back, kill Ari if she was still alive, and tie up all the loose ends. I managed to get rid of any incriminating evidence, but it was risky, foolish behavior and I was lucky the police were so slow to mobilize.

I'd underestimated her. Her fierce inquisitiveness, her thirst for answers. She found the animals in the grove before I'd finished my tableau. She was an impediment, a direct threat to me, and I had to get rid of her.

Fortunately, her strength of character worked to my advantage and she was easy to lead. I waited until she started heading home from the library that day and then I pulled my car over beside her and rolled down the window.

"Ari, I just saw that guy, Sourmash, with a pet carrier! He threw it into the back of his truck. I could hear squealing and whining. It was terrible," I told her.

She filled in the rest. I didn't even have to hint at anything. "He's a monster," she said, trembling with rage. "I knew it!"

"We can catch him," I said, throwing open the passenger-side door. "Together we can stop him."

She climbed in without hesitation, although she looked surprised when she saw who was sprawled in the backseat.

"Passed out drunk," I said with a small smile. "Safer with us." I pressed down on the accelerator and we sped out of town.

I steered the conversation back to Sourmash. "Men like that never stop unless someone makes them," I said.

She leaned forward. "I don't see him. Is he so far ahead? How will we know where he's headed?"

"Up there, just past the motor home. I caught a glimpse of his bumper."

She sank back against her seat, worrying at her fingernails. "God, I'm freaking out," she said.

"It'll be fine, Ari." I pointed out the bottle of brandy. "Help yourself. It'll calm you."

She took the bottle automatically and swallowed a small mouthful.

"I heard he's got a hunting cabin outside town," I said, drawing her back to me. "He's probably been killing animals up there for years." She was so horrified she didn't ask questions, just accepted what I told her. I kept talking about it, distracting her from thinking about which way we were heading and how far we were going.

"Maybe he kills them up here and then moves them to the grove so people can see what he's done," I said. "What kind of a monster would do that?"

She was so pleased that I cared. She took another sip of brandy.

People are stupid, lazy and gullible. Most of them believe without question. I can put on and pull off masks, appearing one way to one person and completely different to another. On that day I was being empathetic. It's easy if you remember that humans are easily manipulated.

I took the turn off to the cabin and parked the car in a dark hollow shaded by close-growing trees. I grabbed a tire iron from the trunk. "He could be dangerous."

She turned worried eyes toward me and then toward the car. "Shouldn't we . . . ?" She was swaying a little from the alcohol. I liked the fact that she obviously didn't drink often.

"I'll protect you," I said, playing the knight in shining armor.

"I don't see the truck."

"He's probably pulled in alongside the cabin," I said.

Then, pretending that I'd heard something, I started running into the woods. "Hurry," I said, over my shoulder, "I think that was an animal screaming."

Adrenaline was firing in her so strongly that she was caught up in the story I was spinning. "This way," I said, dodging around trees, jumping over small bushes. She was completely preoccupied with keeping up and wasn't paying attention to anything more than preventing the low-hanging branches from whipping her in the face. I purposely chose the overgrown track, trying to wear her out and confuse her sense of direction.

She was out of breath, bewildered and disorientated by the time we reached the edge of the cistern. I threw my arm up, as if to stop her teetering over the side. "Where is he?" she asked, clutching her ribs.

I matched my tone to hers. "I think he ran over there."

"Where's the animal? What did he do with it?"

"I don't know." I let fear creep into my voice, but inside I was giggling with glee. "Did he throw it into the well?"

Immediately she moved forward, perching on the lip, craning her head into the void. Her neck was so smooth and so white. I wanted to bite it. I slipped my gloves on, holding the tire iron in my arms like a baby.

"Ari."

"What? What?" Her voice throbbed with emotion. She was still trying to see.

I let the mask fall.

"I killed Tallulah, Ari."

"What?" She seemed incapable of saying anything else. She cast quick glances over her shoulder, as if she'd find the answer to her question hiding in the trees.

"And all the others. Two kittens the other day, just to see which died more easily—the one in the barrel of water or the one in the freezer. I liked doing it. I want to do it again." It felt so good to admit this to her.

"Why are you telling me this?" she asked, her mouth twisting painfully.

Her eyes, impossibly wide, were fixed on my gloved hands, as if she could suddenly see blood on them. I could hear her breathing—quick pants, like a winded animal.

"Do you think that's funny? Is this some kind of a sick joke?" she said, making a weird sort of sound in her throat.

"Such an old doggie. But still she tried to bite me with her toothless gums."

Her mouth opened and closed. I watched her struggle to understand. The truth was just dawning on her when I struck. I aimed for the base of her head but she turned unexpectedly and the blow glanced off the side near her temple.

I cradled her against my shoulder, saw her eyes flood with inkiness as her pupils dilated in pain. It was like watching the seas rise. Supporting her slackening body with one hand, I quickly took my souvenir, pocketing it with my knife.

"Needs must, Ari," I said as I pushed her hard in the middle of her chest.

In a way, I found her even more satisfying afterward. Her limp body curled like a shrimp at the bottom of the well, broken, utterly helpless. I wish she were there still waiting for me, completely compliant, like Lynn is now.

And inspiration leaps at me. Perhaps there was a reason that Ari survived the well.

There are always two of them. In all the great stories. I don't know why I didn't remember until now. Hansel and Gretel. Kai and Gerda. Rose Red and Snow White. Ari and Lynn are the best of friends. Closer than siblings. Inseparable. The exact opposite of the other and the perfect complement. One a tall, fair, freckled gazelle of a girl. Quiet and thoughtful. I used to think her boring but not anymore; she has teeth and claws. And the other, lush and vivid. Ripe, bursting with life. Together they will be breathtaking. They will make the perfect picture.

Their ivory corpses and, all around them, like an implosion of energy and vitality, my beautiful bloody walls.

And the anguish their deaths will cause this town, their families. An emotional wound that will never heal.

All I have to do is bring them together. And serendipitously, at the moment I think this, Ari's phone vibrates in my pocket. So lucky for me that it fell from her pocket as she ran through the woods.

She's sent me a text. I keep her in suspense for a good long while because it pleases me and then send her one back. "87 School Lane. Tuesday morning. Wait for me, Ari."

And then I write, "Breathe a word and I will kill her." And a quote from Poe. I think she will appreciate it and understand what's in store for her. "We loved with a love that was more than love."

CHAPTER THIRTY-THREE

Tuesday morning. 6:00 a.m. The sun would be rising soon but the blackout curtains gave her no sense of time. She'd spent almost the whole day Monday obsessively checking her computer for a reply to her text, pacing her room and peeking out the window until her parents came home. Dinner was mostly silent, which Ari was thankful for, and she kept her head lowered so that she missed nearly all of the glances her parents exchanged. As soon as she could, she escaped back to her bedroom to circle endlessly. When she did sleep, curled up in her nest of blankets on the floor, it was so heavily and fitfully it made her feel sick— as if she were exhaling and re-inhaling all the toxic fears that had leaked into the air. She woke up desperately every half hour, clawing her way to consciousness and feeling as if she was struggling for breath, reaching for her computer before she was fully aware. No answer. No answer. The seconds moved like snails. His response had finally come in at 12:34 a.m. And after that, she had not slept, just watched the numbers magically roll forward: *1 2 3 4. Is it all part of some sick game?* Even though she knew it by heart she'd read the message again and again.

She squeezed her eyes shut, opened them; the words were still seared onto her retinas. Under the blanket, fully clothed, including running shoes, her fists clenched and unclenched. The darkness gathered around her. She couldn't hear street sounds or birds. It was as if the world outside had ceased to exist. She wished she could stay exactly where she was, cocooned, but she couldn't. She got up, flipped the light on and started to pace.

Bastard. 87 School Lane was the address of her school. That instruction was clear. But it was the other part of the message that slayed her.

Breathe a word and I will kill her. And what was with that intimate postscript? It made her feel like puking but it was strangely familiar too.

She thought about her routine, the small world within Dempsey Hollow that she and Lynn inhabited. A roughly polygonal wedge bordered by school, their homes, the park and downtown. She bet she could make the trips between them blindfolded, it was all so fucking familiar.

Pre-set. Expected. Scheduled. Eight a.m., a straight trajectory down Fox to Laurel, across Main, and right on School Lane. Four p.m., the same route but reversed. A kiss and hug on the corner, home by 4:45 on Tuesdays and Thursdays, by 6:00 on Mondays and Wednesdays when Ari had more swim time and Lynn had Mathletes. Fridays they went to the ice cream parlor, the vintage clothing shop and the bookstore. Lynn hated being predictable in any way, but "What the fuck else is there to do in this town?" she'd gripe. Ari loved knowing how her week was going to play out. If they'd deviated from it at all, maybe they would have escaped notice. But no, you could set your clock by them, and someone *had* noticed. Someone had been watching and now he had acted. She thought about how often they ran into Jesse Caldwell and Jack Rourke when they were out and about and she clenched her jaw so hard it popped.

She thought about how relieved her parents were that she was going to school. They'd stayed close when the police had come to speak with her again, just before dinner. It was Officer Tremblay, and the questions had been about Lynn's regular routine, her interests and activities. Talking about Lynn had kicked her adrenaline into high gear.

"Oh, Ari. It will be good for you to be with your classmates again. To get back to your regular day," they'd said. And Ari had just nodded because at least she was doing something. Now though, she thought she might faint. He would be there too. She felt her chest constrict and her pulse quicken. She collapsed onto the carpet, coiled tight. All of a sudden she couldn't breathe. The air seemed thick and the walls closed in around her. She put her hands down flat on the floor and lowered her head between her knees, forcing herself to take shallow inhalations. She muscled her brain into cooperating. See the blue there before you, Ari. Gentle ripples on the surface. How good it will feel against your skin when you dive, cutting through the water like a knife. Your body almost weightless, your breath coming slow and easy. She heard her coach's voice: *No one can catch you when you're in the water and you're not second-guessing yourself. You're a shark, not a tadpole.*

After ten minutes she was able to uncurl herself; after fifteen she was able to get to her feet and go to her desk. She googled the love quote he'd sent. Edgar Allen Poe. Her fingers tightened on the edge of the workstation. Poe's poems and short stories were studied by all junior and senior English students at her school but she remembered the book sticking out of his pocket as he walked away from her in the grove. Jesse Caldwell. She was hot with anger.

"Everything okay, honey?" her mother asked, tapping on the bedroom door as Ari quickly closed the lid on her computer and swept the serial killer notes into a drawer.

Her mother came in with a folded pile of clean laundry, which she put on top of the stripped bed. "How are you feeling?" Her eyes searched Ari's face. Ari shrugged and turned toward the heap of blankets on the floor, not wanting her mother to touch her. She felt as if the slightest caress would make her implode.

"You look a little flushed."

Ari forced herself to answer, hoping her voice wouldn't betray her racing thoughts.

"I'm still tired but I'm all right."

"No headache?"

"No." Although there was the threat of one. She wondered how her eyes would handle sunlight, and the flurorescents at school. Not to mention the attention she knew she would draw from every kid there. Could she just wear sunglasses? *Diva*, she heard Lynn mutter.

"Karen Lubnick said they've asked the county police for extra feet on the ground. They'll find her, Ari." Her mother said. She was wringing her hands together but her voice was adamant, as if she were willing Ari to believe it too.

Ari wished with all her heart that she could. That someone else could do it for her. Her blood boiled; her stomach had turned to stone. Until she found Lynn, she knew she'd feel as if her insides were slowly fossilizing. The hope was so slim, a thread, but she grabbed onto it as if it were a rope. A rope she envisioned tying around the killer's neck until he begged for his life.

"Your father and I are meeting the rest of the volunteers at the café. Captain Rourke has officers at the school for the students' safety."

Ari's belly spasmed. She had her sheets knotted in her hands. As soon as she noticed, she let them fall.

"Everyone is on high alert. School is the safest place for you right now."

I will kill her. Ari was pretty sure he was going to kill her as well but she had to try. She turned her face away, confident that her mother would be able to see the terror visible in every line.

"The community is really pulling together. We're doing door-to-door today."

Ari forced something approximating a smile. There were posters of Lynn everywhere. The photo they'd used was from her last birthday. Ari had been right beside her but they'd cut her out of the picture. She flashed on a nature program she'd watched. The wolf separating the prey from the herd. She closed her fingers around her bracelet. Was Lynn still wearing hers? Did it give her any kind of comfort or had she given up?

"Are you ready to go?" her mother asked.

No! "I guess," Ari said, zipping up her sweatshirt.

Her mother followed her downstairs, picking up her backpack for her and holding it out. Ari slipped it over her shoulders. It felt like years since she'd attended class. Why had it ever been important to her? There was no future. Everything came down to right now and how she chose to act.

Her father was waiting in the hallway by the front door. Ari evaded his hug by fumbling with her sweatshirt hood, which had caught under the backpack strap.

"Ari," he said. His tone alerted her and she turned to look at him. He searched out her eyes, glancing quickly at her mother. Then he dropped his hand onto Ari's shoulder. It felt like a warm brick but she let it lie there, rooting her to the ground. "I just heard. They've put out an alert for Stroud Bellows," he said.

"They didn't find him at the lake?" her mother asked, sagging against the banister.

"No. No sign of him. Not even his car."

They both turned to look at her and spoke at the same time. "Ari, we're so sorry."

She brushed aside their apology. "Do they think it's the same person who has Lynn?" A wave of coldness fell over her. A thought began to gnaw at her. Where was Stroud? Was she the last person who had seen him? His cheek had been cool but not cold. She hadn't felt a breath when she leaned over him, but she'd been so hyped up fighting the flee instinct with everything she had. Was he alive? Why hadn't he come home?

"They think a predator is operating in the county."

Predator. Yes, that was the word for the killer. Someone wily, patient, a hunter who stalked his victims, unseen until the kill. If not for her father's supporting hand, Ari thought she might crumple and fall. What if Stroud was the predator, not the prey? Now that he was missing too, there was clear evidence of wrongdoing, and the police might actually listen to her, but—*breathe a word and I will kill her.* She felt hysteria start to build and forced her attention outwards.

Dad was mouthing words at her. With an effort she focused on what he was saying.

"You take my car," he said. "Just drop us off at the coffee shop."

It was unspoken that they knew she'd feel safer driving than walking. It was unspoken that they thought of her as some damaged, fragile thing. She hoped they were wrong.

CHAPTER THIRTY-FOUR

It pains me to leave Lynn. She's urinated in the box and I am annoyed. But then I realize she is scared and can't help herself. It doesn't matter how often I try to calm her, how much I tell her I love her. As soon as she hears my voice now, she starts to scream.

Ma Cosloy beat me for soiling my sheets. When I was old enough I had to launder them each morning before the school bus came. I remember the weight of the wet cloth, the struggle to pin it to the line and the bite of the vinegar on my chapped hands.

I will wash her body in the cold water of the stream and all the impurities will be swept away.

I wonder, though. It shows a weakness that I didn't think she possessed. What if her heart gives out before I am ready for her? I can't afford to take that chance.

If she dies too soon, it will ruin everything.

I pull out my sketchbook, look at my recent drawings. The background is rendered in simple lines, the details yet to be added. The girls will be the centerpiece. They will tell the story. I portray them curled up together as if in sleep, hands clasped, hair mingled, dead roses strewn around them, and their hearts, like beautiful offerings.

I remember the first time I saw a diorama. I was living on the streets in Albany. I'd just made twenty dollars from one of my regulars. A man who liked me to kneel in front of him and when he was close to finishing, he'd push my head down into the dirt and put his foot on the back of my neck. He was quick at least and in a hurry to get back to his wife.

It was damp and bitterly cold and my bones hurt.

I'd passed the art gallery often but I'd never gone in, figuring that I'd stick out around all those adults, in my scruffy clothes with my wild hair. But I was huddled across the street in a doorway that smelled of spilled booze and urine, and the window was brightly lit, the artwork displayed. I'd never seen anything like it. It drew me like a moth. I hurried across the street, dodging traffic, and pressed my face against the glass.

The canvases were huge, at least ten feet tall and thickly painted. I couldn't distinguish any color—the reds had abandoned me by then—but the way the paint was applied gave me hints. One canvas was a maelstrom of swoops and swirls, an immeasurable force building under the surface, like a wave on a stormy ocean. One was shiny, slick as patent leather, a mirrored surface that distorted my face. A third reminded me of a thick slab of bloody meat. My fingers itched to touch them.

It was a girl at the counter. The gallery apparently empty except for her. She was young, close to my age, and as I hovered by the window, she looked up and frowned and then gave me a tentative smile. I took it as an invitation.

Her smile slipped a little when I came in. I guess she could smell me. It was almost impossible to stay clean on the street, but I could tell that she was too embarrassed to throw me out.

I found the scent of the gallery to be almost as intoxicating as the butcher shop. Paint, wood and mineral spirits, some kind of lemon cleaner.

More of the large canvases hung on the walls but now my attention was taken by something else. It was a tableau. Life-sized. Partially walled, like an open box. A family sitting at a table, plates and glasses in front of them. Mother, father, two children. A festive celebration, but rather than a turkey, the middle of the table was occupied by a tiny, curled-up infant. All the figures were fashioned out of plaster of Paris. Stark white. Like the negative of a photograph. It felt chalky when I touched it, ignoring a warning gasp from the girl at the desk. The realism was startling. It was almost as if there were bodies of people under the plaster, bones and flesh giving their shapes structure. As if they had been entombed. Diorama *said the card on the wall. Die-orama, I repeated in my head.*

Great art doesn't last; I know this. Nothing beautiful does. But in a way it is the impermanence of it that makes it special.

I am ready. It's time to collect Ari.

CHAPTER THIRTY-FIVE

The student lot was almost empty when Ari arrived shortly after 8:00 a.m., and still she parked at the far end away from the few cars that were already there, just in case someone was hiding, waiting to leap out at her. She knew about girls being abducted as they unlocked their doors, stuffed into trunks and driven away to be tortured, raped and killed. Bundy had faked injury in order to get the co-eds into his vehicle. She'd always wondered how they could be so unaware. So dumb. But she'd been safe in her ignorance too. Now she locked the car with shaking hands, and made sure to check out her surroundings.

The sky felt very big over her head as she hurried toward the school. A few hundred steps later she was stationed on the corner across the street, watching the kids start to arrive, fruitlessly praying for a glimpse of Lynn, and feeling completely cut off from everyone, as if the road were some impenetrable barrier. It was hard not to feel as if she was completely isolated, but harder still to sit down or hang out on the steps near so many people. Plus she spotted two cops standing guard. She couldn't risk being seen by the killer near them. *Breathe a word and I'll kill her.*

Her money was on Jesse Caldwell but she had to be smart and consider all possibilities. She tried to imagine each of her suspects speaking those words. Jesse, Jack, McNamara, Stroud, their faces blurring into the shadow figure she remembered, hands swathed in black. It was like dress-up dolls. She could make each of them fit.

There was a side entrance to the school as well, though most kids found the main entrance more social, gathering there in groups before and after school. Jesse was one of those who preferred the other way in, but from where she stood, she could still see that door. His shit-brown piece-of-shit car wasn't in the lot either. Where was he?

She watched the underclassmen arrive first, most of them dropped off by their anxious parents. They were so small, burdened by their huge backpacks and in danger of toppling over. A squad of football players showed up, traveling in a huddle, and then a mass of students who must have synchronized their schedules and possibly their outfits. Her heart sped up as she picked out a few red water polo jackets. She scanned the cluster for Stroud's profile, his chlorine-bleached head. Her gaze caught Miranda Taylor's. She stood in the middle of the throng, presumably doing the same thing Ari was, looking for Stroud among the various groups of people assembling and intermingling on the front steps. Even at this distance, Ari could see her frown. Turning, the girl searched the parking lot, no doubt looking for Stroud's blue Audi. Ari had already checked; it wasn't there.

The first bell clanged, the noise making Ari's pulse pound. She'd seen none of her four suspects. She paced, stalling for as long as she could, although she could see that the cops were looking her way.

The trickles of students flowed into a few main tributaries heading to the main entrance, and gradually the area in front of the school emptied out. Second bell rang and some late-comers arrived, clutching gaping messenger bags and unfastened backpacks, or strolling nonchalantly because they were upholding a reputation. She heard mutterings as they passed her, caught a few sidelong looks and some pointing fingers. It was obvious that everyone knew she was Lynn's friend. Slowly, those kids disappeared inside as well. *Fuck*. She was vibrating with adrenaline. Unable to stop walking back and forth. One of the cops glanced at her curiously again and said something to his partner. And then, finally, Jesse Caldwell appeared, sneaking around to the side door. She started toward him but he was too far away. He ducked into the crowd and was gone.

She shifted from foot to foot, unsure of whether to chase after him. It felt a little too much like sticking her head into the wolf's mouth. And he'd said "wait for me" in the text. Where should she wait?

"Ari Sullivan, come on, we're both late," a sharp voice said behind her. "And for my class, I believe." She turned to see Dr. McNamara and took a cautious step backward. Suspect #3. Jesse was definitely the front-runner, but it would be stupid to let her guard down now. And Stroud? Jack Rourke? She mustn't discount them either.

"Lots of work to do today," the teacher said tensely.

Oh God, she'd forgotten about the cats.

"Are you back to full strength?" Dr. McNamara asked. "Your parents called the office and let them know that you've had a hard time. Seems a little foolhardy to be out and about."

"I'm fine," Ari said, her voice catching in her throat. Were these thinly veiled warnings? All part of the mind game? She felt very much like a mouse and struggled to find her courage.

"You don't seem fine. You don't seem fine at all."

She searched the teacher's face. Had she always looked so harsh? Ari couldn't tell. She clasped her backpack in front of her chest as if it could protect her.

"We'll go in together," the teacher said, giving her a little shove on the shoulder. "And that way you can avoid getting in trouble."

Ari shot a glance at the cops, and then back at the teacher. She kept some distance between them but she followed her toward the main entrance. Dr. McNamara was humming tunelessly under her breath.

She swallowed, her mouth desperately dry. Sweat trickled down her back. Her fingers fumbled at her bracelet.

Ari thought about dodging into the nearby bathroom to splash cold water on her face and get her breathing under control, but she was half-scared the teacher would follow her in.

On the way down the hall, she darted her head around, so focused on locating Jesse that she almost fell over a library cart pushed against the wall. Special book orders brought over from the central branch.

"Easy there, watch your step," Dr. McNamara said, steadying Ari with a hand to her elbow. Her fingers were cold and Ari jerked loose, muttering some response as she continued to search the crowd.

Safety in numbers, she reminded herself. Miranda Taylor was sticking a folded note through the slats into Stroud's locker. She saw various kids from her classes. More pointing in her direction, more whispering. She hung her head. And then she spotted Jesse Caldwell brooding by the water fountain. He caught her gaze and straightened up. *Was it him?* She hurried toward him, aware of his eyes on her every step of the way. His lips curled into a smirk. "Sullivan."

"I'm ready. I'm here." Her voice throbbed with emotion.

"Frankly, I'm surprised that you came." His expression was so smug. She bunched her fists.

She welcomed the anger, felt it flare in her belly. She got right up in his face. If he had hurt Lynn, she'd kill him with her bare hands.

"What do you want from me?" she said. "Let's get this over with." Her saliva hit his cheek; he wiped it away.

He gave her an odd look and then spun on his heel and strode away.

"Come back," she yelled.

"Come back," Jack Rourke echoed in a high-pitched voice. Ari jumped in surprise. She'd been so focused on Jesse that she hadn't heard Jack approach. He slid his gaze up and down her body and sniggered.

"Where's Bellows?" someone asked him. Ari's ears pricked up.

"Dunno. Hungover," Jack said. "Late, as usual."

Neither he nor his friends seemed concerned. The news must not have gotten around yet. Ari moaned and leaned against a locker. Her stomach was killing her. A tentacle of pain wrapped around her skull.

Jack tossed a paper airplane across the hallway to one of his buddies, making every passerby duck. He threw low and it clocked Ari on the head. She winced even though it was soft and light and no worse than being pegged by an eraser. Still, he'd had this gloating expression on his face and she knew it was no accident. Making eye contact with her, he threw another one, aiming straight for her face. She bent down to pick it up and unfolded it. Lynn's happy face smiled up at her. It was one of the missing persons flyers. A couple of girls nearby breathed in sharply and directed shocked glances at Jack. The whispering got louder, buzzing in Ari's skull. She stared into her friend's eyes.

Dr. McNamara reached over and snatched the flyer from her hand. "Practice some restraint, Mr. Rourke," she said, crumpling it up. She opened the door. "Now, hurry up, Bio 403. Mr. Rourke and entourage, you too. The rest of you," she yelled, "get to your respective classes now." The hallway emptied out.

Ari followed Dr. McNamara in and took her seat. Her heart was hammering and the white explosions had started up in her periphery again, like miniature cannons firing. She felt as if she might jump out of her skin.

On his way to his desk, Jack slowed down. "Girlfriend missing, Sullivan?" he said. "Party too hard? Did you leave her passed out up at the cabin?" He spoke so softly that Ari wasn't sure exactly what he'd said.

"What?" she stammered. "What did you say?"

Dr. McNamara clapped her hands together and Ari started. "Settle down, students. Take your places immediately."

Smirking, Jack loafed over to the back row nearest the bank of windows. He spread his legs wide and swiveled in his chair so that he was facing the door. It also put Ari directly in his line of vision. She lowered her head, covering her face with her hair.

"I have an announcement to make," Dr. McNamara said. "All students must remain on campus for the full day. If you have a spare, go to the library." She then chose two students to start wheeling the garbage cans out of the storage cupboard, and soon the familiar smell of formaldehyde and decay filled the room. It crawled into Ari's nostrils, took her straight back to the grove. She focused on her hands splayed out on top of her desk and commanded her brain to think logically.

Dr. McNamara? The teacher had her back to the class and was covering the board in a series of numbered queries. "Ask yourselves, what is the purpose of this particular organ? What am I looking at?" she said over her shoulder. "And how does it all fit together?" Ari pondered, feeling her brain wake up a little. Facts are incontrovertible, Lynn would say. The teacher was trapped at school. She couldn't just leave. And she'd have had to fill out tons of paperwork and go through criminal checks to even get her job in the first place. She eliminated her from the list.

So what about . . . ? She pushed her hair back and stared over her shoulder at Jack, who just so happened to be looking in her direction. She felt rage start to simmer. Two could play at this game. When you confronted a strange dog, you did not break eye contact first. That was giving over your power. Even though she could feel Jack's animosity, thick as a flannel shirt, she kept her gaze on him until he looked away. *Down boy*, she thought triumphantly.

Next up: Jesse. He'd been following her—no, *stalking her* ever since she'd discovered the pet killings. At the maze his hands had been dirty, as if he'd been burying something out there. She tapped her lip. Stroud was an enigma. Everything was pointing to his being alive. But surely he couldn't just show up here? Not with most of the force out looking for him?

The cops were watching the exits and entrances, though. They weren't patrolling the halls.

She thought of the long corridors between classes, the storage closets, and the often-empty labs. He, whichever "he" it was, had plenty of opportunity. She'd scream, she decided. Even if she couldn't fight him off, she'd scream until there was no more breath left in her body. She felt a scream building now. She couldn't face the cats. Not now, not ever.

Without knowing how, she was on her feet, swaying a little in place. Dr. McNamara stared at her.

"Ari, what's going on?"

"The nurse," Ari mumbled, slipping her bag over her shoulder.

The teacher nodded impatiently and pointed toward the door. "Come back quickly," she said. "We've got a lot to cover."

She felt Jack's eyes on her every step of the way.

At least she knew where he was for the next while. She checked the windows into the other classrooms until she found Jesse. He was tapping his fingers on the desk and staring out the window. Biding his time?

She forced herself to concentrate harder. The killer was toying with her, but he wanted to communicate. He liked issuing the instructions and she was positive he knew where she was right now, so how would he get in touch if he needed to? Another text? She could access a computer.

The computer lab was directly across the hall. It was unoccupied. She went in and powered up the closest monitor, leaving the ceiling lights off so that she wouldn't be immediately noticeable to a casual passerby. Twisting her fingers nervously, she waited for it to come online, and then keyed in her information. She clicked over to her email account and scrolled down the new messages. She let her breath out with a sigh. *Fuck!* Nothing but spam and some social media alerts. It was the waiting that was killing her. She logged out, staring at the blinking dot in the lower corner. It pulsed in time with the headache clamped at the back of her skull.

She went to the nurse's office. At least she could get some meds and an excuse note.

"I have a really bad headache," she told Mrs. Amherst.

The nurse nodded. "Your parents sent in a copy of the doctor's report. Any other complaints? Dizziness, confusion?"

"No, just the headache." It wasn't untrue at this point.

"Do you want to lie down?" the nurse asked, taking a closer look at her.

"Something for the pain, maybe? And a hall pass."

"All right, but let me know if it gets worse," she said, handing over a packet of painkillers and a slip of paper.

Leaving the nurse's office felt like walking with a giant bull's-eye on her back. She wouldn't go back to class but she had to get out of the hallway. She pushed the bathroom door open. Thankfully it was empty.

I look like a crazy person, she thought as she gazed at her reflection. Her eyes sunken into her skull, shadowed and weary, her hair lank, her hands trembling. A tiny muscle twitched in the corner of her eye. She swallowed the pills and leaned her forehead against the cool of the mirror.

Her plan, her detective work, seemed ridiculous now. If Jesse was the killer, or Jack, would they be at school like normal teenagers? Would they be taunting her, playing games, acting like typical assholes? Yes, if either of them were a psychopath.

Gacy held a job, had a family, she recalled. Ted Bundy haunted college campuses. Predators go where the prey goes. She was the hunted, she thought as she stared at her reflection, and foolishly she had thought she had some measure of control. Maybe this was all one giant nothing, engineered to drive her nuts, and in the meantime Lynn was scared, maybe hurt? She kicked the trash bin, mashing her toes but not caring.

The smell of dead cats seemed to cling to her. She splashed her face with cold water and felt a little more alert.

What to do? In about fifteen minutes the bell would ring for next class. His message had said to meet him in the morning. *Make a decision, Ari. Go to your locker and wait,* she thought. *Wait and watch for Jack, for Jesse, for Stroud. Wait for whoever it is to come out of the shadows and play.*

Turns out the sitting duck thing was near impossible to pull off. Ari's muscles were spasming, wanting to move, to fight, to flee. She leaned against her locker and picked at the skin around her nails, counting seconds under her breath, watching the minute hand on her watch crawl around. Very faintly, from the next-door cubicle—Lynn's locker—she could smell the lemony conditioner her friend used. It tugged at her heart.

When the bell rang she tensed, arms wrapped tight around her torso. Students crowded into the hallway, pressing against her, a bustling hive of activity. The fluorescent lights seemed blindingly bright, and the scents of sweaty armpits, new sneakers, hairspray, cologne and cleaning bleach were overwhelming. Impossibly, she tried to avoid contact with the bodies milling around her.

She wanted to scream, *There's a fucking serial killer on the loose and you're all in danger*, but she clamped her lips over her teeth.

The warning bell rang. Jack moved down the hall. She shadowed him to Government class and waited until he took his seat. Unless he left early with some excuse, she was assured of his location for the next forty minutes. Since she was in the general area, she checked out Jesse's locker. The paint spelling out *weirdo* was chipped and fading, but someone had carved the letters into the metal with something sharp. She wondered if Jesse had done it himself. It seemed likely.

She hovered, feeling very conspicuous. He didn't show. Two freshman girls, looking impossibly young, stared at her and whispered behind their hands as they packed up their books. She stared back at them, trying to remember when she had been that clueless and realizing with some sadness that it hadn't been very long ago. Suddenly, she wanted more than anything to protect them. "Be careful out there," she said as they strolled past her. They exchanged incredulous glances, and Ari wanted to sink into the wall.

She darted back into the computer lab and checked her account. No new messages. She scrolled up and down, as if maybe a clue was hiding somewhere on the screen, her fingers fumbling on the keys. Her heart zipped along like she'd OD'd on espresso.

"Hey, you're on my computer," a freckly girl said.

"Sorry," she muttered, and went back out into the corridor.

She checked her watch again. She was going to be late for English, which was on the next floor in the east block. She decided to take a shortcut, going up the back stairs and through the old gymnasium. A new state-of-the-art gym had been built on the other side of the school, but time had run out over the summer to finish the reconstruction on this one. Her shoes echoed on the rungs as she climbed the three short flights and entered the gym through a side door. A window high above was shattered. She could hear pigeons warbling in the rafters, and there were feathers and spatters of pigeon shit on the basketball court.

This had been a huge mistake, she thought to herself. Coming to school, going to class, waiting on tenterhooks for something to happen. Maybe this hadn't been a trap at all, but just a way to fuck with her head and throw her off balance. It was working.

She was so wrapped up in her thoughts that at first she wasn't aware of the footsteps behind her. She slowed, unsure. Was it just an echo? She stopped completely and heard the squeak of a shoe sole on polished wood as someone else stopped too. She froze on the center-court line, waiting to see who appeared. The seconds ticked by, dread building. And now all pretense was abandoned. She ran as fast as she could and the footsteps pounded after her. Across the court to the double doors at the other side. She reached them, out of breath, and pushed on the bar. The doors moved slightly but did not open. She heaved and shoved again, putting all her weight behind her efforts. There was some kind of latch at the bottom, grooved into the floor. She could see the end of the metal bolt, but her fingers were wooden and she clawed at it fruitlessly, unable to dislodge it.

The footsteps halted. She felt the hairs rise on the back of her neck.

She whirled around, throwing her hands in front of her defensively.

It was Miranda Taylor, and she looked angry.

Ari lowered her arms, looking past the other girl. "Miranda! God, I was sure it was him." The adrenaline left her in a rush and she slumped against the door.

"What the hell's going on, Ari?"

"Someone chasing me. Jesse Caldwell, I think," Ari panted. "Did you see him?"

Miranda shook her head impatiently. "I came to find you."

"Why?"

Miranda moved closer. "Do you know where Stroud is?"

"No," Ari said slowly. "Do you?"

"He wouldn't tell me anything."

"And? It's not like he'd check in with me."

"I know you were with him on Friday, partying or whatever."

Ari's mouth felt as if it were stuffed with cotton. "You're saying I was with Stroud on Friday?" Her thoughts were racing. He *had* been at the cabin. That memory was a true one, but why had they been there together, and how had they gotten there? The holes that remained in her recollection of events were maddening.

Miranda made a noise like a small explosion. "Jesus, Ari, he texted me and said you were. He didn't want me to join him. Wouldn't even tell me where you guys were hanging out." She screwed her lips up. "And now he's missing. You're probably the last person who saw him."

"What about Jack? Did you ask him?"

Miranda waved her hands impatiently. "Jack is a liar. He can't be trusted. He actually used that 'bros before hoes' line on me." Her face crumpled. "You must know something."

Ari swallowed hard. "I'm worried. I think something bad has happened to him. The cops have put out an alert." Had it been Stroud who had led her to the cistern? She thought back to the dumbass she had been. She would have followed him anywhere; she would have jumped at the chance. Her hand went up to the wound above her ear. It was throbbing, shooting out spikes of pain.

"Why were you even together?" Miranda demanded. She sounded to Ari as if she were speaking from the other side of a sheet of glass. Ari wondered if she was about to gray out.

Distantly she heard the bell ring.

Miranda gave her one more outraged look and stalked away, her back stiff.

Ari drew a deep breath and steadied herself against the railing. She walked back down the stairs in a daze, assaulted by her thoughts. It was hard not to feel as if they were all walking around in a fog. Only one person knew what was going on, and she had to find him.

She decided to get rid of her backpack. She stopped at her locker and opened it. It was chaotic as always, a jumble of sports bags and books and paper at the bottom. It smelled of chlorine and moldy towels. She was always forgetting to take them home for laundering. The inside of the door was covered in photos of her and Lynn. Every single moment of Ari's life that had in any way been special included Lynn. This was her existence, her trajectory so far, mapped out in snapshots. She stroked a finger over Lynn's face, freckled from the sun, the summer before this one. The lens had caught her in the middle of talking and laughing, a state that was common for her, but even so, Ari could remember what they'd been talking about. Child stars and the fucked up messes they made of their lives.

She dropped the bag and had begun to swing her locker shut when she spotted the slip of paper on the floor. It must have been wedged in the door and fallen out. She picked it up and unfolded it. A handwritten note, with a heart scrawled on one side. She turned it over. *Rural Route 4, exit 20, Tanner's Way at Kissing Bridge. The yellow house. Come alone, Ari.*

She crushed it in her hand, slammed the locker shut with such force that it rebounded. She shoved it closed again and struck it with the flat of her hand, leaning her forehead against it.

What the fuck?! Hours wasted. She hated this feeling of being a pawn, a puppet dancing on strings. *I don't want to go.* "You have to go, Ari." She straightened up.

Tanner's Way. She had some idea where exit 20 was but she was drawing a blank on the rest of the address. She could google it.

She ran down the hall to the computer lab. It was packed with students tapping away at their keyboards, a teacher pacing between the desks. She wanted to scream. Her nerves were worn to shreds and her determination was in tatters. She took a couple of deep breaths, kept walking, looking into classrooms as she passed. Dr. McNamara was in the middle of another lesson, writing something on the board below a detailed drawing of a dissected frog. She kept an eye open for Jack and Jesse but didn't see either one.

Fuck it. Enough of this cat-and-mouse shit, she thought, stopping just inside the entrance to the main floor. She needed to get home to her computer right now. She could look for some kind of weapon as well, even if it was just a hammer.

She remembered the cops standing guard on the steps. How could she slip away? She needed a diversion. Without pausing to reconsider, she pulled the fire alarm.

CHAPTER THIRTY-SIX

I am pondering my recent errors in judgment. Strength has nothing to do with the physical. The body might be strong, as his was, but if the spirit is weak then nothing can keep you alive. He died before I could even get to work on him. I wanted to practice my knife skills on a living subject. Play around with various methods of display. He was drunk and high from the drugs I'd given him, but still conscious. When I sat down beside him, he laughed nervously and tried to move away, but the couch was snug and his legs were weak.

"Man, I've never been so fucked up," he said. The sedatives blurred his eyes and thickened his tongue. "I don't remember how I got here. Ha ha."

He didn't even notice when I took the knife out. It wasn't until I held it before his eyes, letting the lamplight glint on the wicked edge I'd made, that he'd focused. And then that was all he saw. I watched his pupils swell like ink spots, and I told him exactly what I was going to do to him. The honor of it. To be the first under the knife; to become a beautiful picture. He looked at me with confusion, the words taking forever to seep into his brain. And when they did, he was too scared to scream and he was too drugged to run.

But then I heard a noise outside, a vehicle, engine cutting out, slamming door, footsteps. I panicked. I'd already botched killing Ari and now I was in danger of being discovered before I had accomplished everything I needed to. I slipped the knife back into the sheath; it was for fine work that would take many hours. This was just manual labor. My hands were around his neck before he could make another sound. I squeezed with all my strength, thumbs against his windpipe and my face close to his, pressing against his chest with the whole weight of my body. Still, it took longer than I expected. At least three minutes before he made a curious noise, like a hiccup, and his head fell forward.

My hope is that Lynn and Ari will fight much harder.

The weather has changed abruptly. There is a sharp bite in the air. When I went out early this morning to look at the creek, the wind whistled across the fields and numbed my fingers. Even now I can feel them tingle at the tips, and holding the paintbrush is difficult. The creek is swollen. Hidden rain-filled mountain springs have fed it and caused it to burst from its banks. Dead leaves, blackened and slimy, slide underfoot, and the soil smells musty like old coffee. I spend a long time looking at the water, the froth and swirl, the dark depths, the early-morning ice riming the rocks. A tree has fallen, loosened from the earth's grip by the currents. Roots snarled and tangled like a witch's hair.

I think of the deer's submerged carcass, the way the hide loosened and sloughed away, the rolled eye like a slice of hardboiled egg, held captive there in the bright, pure water. I wonder if ice will creep across its surface like a window cracking. Like a silver spider's web.

I imagine my girls trapped under the ice, gray lips, eyes transformed into clouded jewels, skin frosted and pale as marble, and their hair, spread out like seaweed, limned in light.

Back at home, still winded by my escape from the school, I lie down on the floor and press my face to the side of the chest. I can hear her quick breathing. For a moment I match my breathing to hers and see her eyes widen as she hears it. "Ari is coming," I tell her. I admit that Ari surprised me with her fire alarm trick. It showed initiative. Although there is barely any room in the box, Lynn turns away and hides her face. Sobs rack her body. It is all coming together.

The third wall confounded me, but eventually I painted it white with blue shadows like a snowdrift. I couldn't see the color of the paint but I had the man at the hardware store write the shades on the lids. He assured me it was subdued. "November Sky it's called," he said. I will display the dead girls against it, half reclining, backs bolstered by the wall, heads together, fingers clasped. I've decided to suffocate them long enough for a temporary loss of consciousness followed by drowning in the glacial stream, and then I will bleed them out and remove their fierce hearts. Their blanched faces will blend into the whiteness, exquisite china dolls, their eyes replaced by chips of ice like in the Snow Queen story. If I kiss them, will my lips stick to theirs? Will I leave a layer of skin behind, taste salty blood?

I check on Lynn again. She is unmoving, but slowly she exhales. Her hair is lank and there is a sour smell coming from the wooden chest. She has peed on herself again.

"Lynn," I breathe. "You beautiful creature." She begins to cry—jagged, heaving sobs.

"I'm going to eat you up."

And then she begins to scream.

CHAPTER THIRTY-SEVEN

Ari consulted the map she'd printed out from her computer and took exit 20 onto Tanner's Way. It was roughly twenty-five miles from her doorstep to this bumpy one-lane country road. She met no vehicles coming the other direction. Up ahead a few hundred yards she could see the intersection that must be Kissing Bridge. No bridge in sight, nor could she imagine anyone kissing in a place like this. Although there were fields on either side, they were brown and dead-looking and it seemed too quiet. Hardly the spot for romance. Just past the crossroads, a gravel road, little more than a driveway, wound up the long slope, and perched at the very top she saw a two-story house. She rolled down the window. Unseen in the cloud cover, a single bird sang. The air carried an eerie stillness. She thought of the photos she'd seen of John Wayne Gacy's home. They'd torn it down after Gacy was caught, but it had been a little bungalow built out of different-colored bricks with big picture windows and cheery shrubbery. It looked like a house a typical family would live in, but they'd found twenty-eight bodies buried in the backyard.

Was that where she was heading? A house of death?

Lynn was somewhere inside. Ari watched the sun hover at the edge of the tree line and turned her collar up against the sudden chill. It might be safer to hold off until dark, but she couldn't bring herself to wait any longer. He was dictating everything; she'd make what decisions she could. She closed the window, tucked the keys into her hip pocket and picked up the large screwdriver from the passenger seat. It wasn't much of a weapon but it was something. For a second she found herself in agreement with the National Rifle Association—every citizen should be able to carry a gun.

"Just stab him with the sharp end, Ari," she muttered, feeling an insane urge to giggle. What was up with her lately? She remembered Lynn telling her about gallows humor. The oh-so-funny side of murder and death. At any second she could collapse into tears or laughter.

She'd left a note for her parents, telling them exactly where she was going, what time she left, and everything she suspected: there was a psychopath living in Dempsey Hollow; he or she had slaughtered those animals and tried to kill her; and now they had Lynn. Carefully she wrote four names on the piece of paper: Jesse Caldwell, Stroud Bellows, Jack Rourke and, after a moment's consideration, Dr. McNamara. She was doubtful about the teacher, but at this point everyone looked like a psycho.

Halfway up the driveway she paused and scrutinized her shaking hands. Her heart was leaping in her chest and she felt unnaturally cold. This was fear. This was basic primeval instinct. She'd gone over everything that had happened in the last couple of days, everything that her brain let her remember, hoping for some clue to this killer's identity, but there was nothing, just a black silhouette and the gloves, and a voice that sounded like death calling for her. If she knew who it was then she could—what? Figure out her assault plan? She had no plan. It didn't matter if it was Jesse or Jack or Stroud or McNamara; they were all bigger and stronger than her, and all she had was a screwdriver and some serious rage. It would have to be enough. She tightened her fist around the handle and forced her feet to continue up the road, hoping the cavalry would arrive at the last second.

The curtains were drawn, the windows looking out at her like furtive eyes. The yellow hue was off, the sickly shade of a rubber chicken. She stood on the path for a couple of minutes, steeling herself. Taking a deep breath, she walked up to the front door and paused with her hand inches from the wood. Knocking just seemed wrong. *Hello, I've come to be killed. How are you?* She twisted the knob. Locked, solid. *Fuck!* She looked through the glass. A hallway with a couple of doors leading off it, a staircase. *Please God, let there not be a basement!*

No curtain fluttered. She didn't have the sense of eyes on her. She'd ramped herself up on adrenaline and now—nothing. Too quiet. If she hadn't received that message, she'd have thought the house was a summer place, or on the market to be sold. Uninhabited. But someone had raked the leaves from the browning grass and mowed in the recent past. It was well-tended. She walked around the back, ears pricked, nerves hopping. Curtains shielded the back windows of the house too. There was a garage with small grimy windows. Someone had nailed a dead crow to the wall. It was an old farmer's trick she knew. A way of warning away other crows. She tried to peer through the dust-covered windows. She moistened a finger and cleared a patch. A car was parked inside. A blue Audi. All of a sudden her heart was pounding like a jackhammer. It was Stroud's car.

She ran up the steps leading to a screened back door and grasped the knob. It was bolted as well but the glass was up a few inches and nothing but a rectangle of screen barred her way. She stabbed at it with the screwdriver, ripping it loose with her fingers, and reached in to unlock the latch. The wooden door behind it was not bolted from the inside and yielded easily to her hand. The click seemed unnaturally loud but no one came at her, no one shouted. The house appeared to be empty. Should she creep in like a mouse or storm in like the army? She settled for something in between—balanced on the balls of her feet, screwdriver at the ready, prepared to ward off any surprise attack. Her mouth was dry, and she could feel the sweat soaking her T-shirt, though her skin still felt clammy.

The house was cold. Refrigerator cold. She was surprised not to be able to see her breath as she exhaled. From somewhere she heard pipes clanking. An uneven rhythm that seemed to keep time with the uneasy lurch of her heart. Kitchen, cupboards, a small table and chair. The décor, if you could call it that, was minimal, like something out of a *LIFE* magazine from back in the seventies. An electric clock that hummed rather than ticked; a black telephone mounted on the wall. She picked it up and got a dial tone. Working phone. She filed the information away, continued down the narrow hallway.

Floral wallpaper and a diseased shade of yellow paint, the same as that on the outside, covered the walls. Some sections were sun-faded and some were water-stained, but it hardly looked like the scene of a murder. There were no photos though. She did a slow sweep. No personal touches. Nothing that indicated who lived there.

She paused by the refrigerator. Should she open it? She remembered Dahmer and his cannibalism and pulled the door open. Slowly she looked through her eyelashes. A box of baking soda, a small Tupperware container too compact to contain a head. She felt her pulse calm a little. She opened the container anyway. A couple of shriveled potato wedges; no severed fingers. She let her breath out and hunched her shoulders a couple of times to loosen them up.

Slow and easy, Ari.

Now she was by the front door. Stairs to the upper floor to her right. She switched the bolt to open just in case she had to run out this way and glanced quickly outside. She could hear an airplane buzz far overhead, but inside it was deathly still except for the pounding of her blood in her ears.

No creaks of the floor to indicate that someone lurked upstairs. Dust hung in the air and there was a tangy smell that tickled her nostrils. Fresh paint. She turned toward an open doorway, holding up the screwdriver, and stumbled backward in shock.

Red exploded from the walls, paint in thick strands and globs that looked like it had been applied with a trowel. Ari entered the room feeling as if she were going into a cave. A cave made of skin and meat. At first it all looked so random, but as she turned around, she started noticing details. Some areas were painted more densely, like bloody strips of hide, cross-hatched with a sharp implement; others were barely skimmed with color, and it wasn't just deep crimson but other shades closer to brown, orange and purple, which gave it depth and an almost three-dimensional quality. It was vivid, frenetic with energy and a roiling movement like a stormy sea, but the colors were all wrong. It made her heart leap crazily in her chest. It made nausea rise as if she'd stumbled upon the scene of a terrible accident. She suddenly thought of liver. Something her mother brought home about once a year when she started worrying about iron deficiency in teen girls. The last time, Ari had flatly refused to eat it. There was a slimy, shiny aspect to this paint, and a thick, warm smell that reminded her of raw chicken. Organic.

In contrast, one of the three walls was painted cool white and blue, and washed in gray like moonlight on a frozen lake. Cut into it were spiraling lines that reminded her of a maze. She put her hand out and touched her fingertips to the wall. It was still wet. She reached out to the nearest red wall. Dry. And now she saw the faces, tumbled amongst the swathes of color—screaming, distorted faces, like some depiction of hell. She backed up and stumbled against a large cedar chest. The lid was open, a mildewed blanket crumpled in the bottom, an empty bottle of water. And she smelled the sharpness of urine, an odor that catapulted her instantly back to the bottom of the well. A plastic crate sat upended next to the chest, holding a row of books. They were leather-bound, old and worn, their titles stamped in gold. *Grimm's Fairy Tales*; *The Crimson Fairy Book*; *Myths and Legends of Old Britain*. Next to them was a bulky journal. She picked it up, leafed it open. The sketches leapt at her, finely drawn, meticulously detailed, scenes of torture and death. They were exquisite and horrifying. Compelling enough to keep her looking. A dozen pages were all of Lynn—in profile, captured in a hundred life moments, almost jumping off the paper, then body broken, chest cavity split, and pieced together like a ruined porcelain doll. *Her heart, her heart is missing,* Ari's thoughts screamed. The last two pages were sketches of herself, curiously specific, even down to the mole by her right ear, a thin, frayed ribbon tied around her throat. She looked closer—not a ribbon but a knife slash from ear to ear—and let the book fall.

"Lynn," she yelled, no longer caring about furtiveness. She whirled from the room and ran up the stairs, a bedroom empty but for dust bunnies wafting in the corners, a tiny bathroom with a stained sink and dingy toilet. Another bedroom. She stopped so quickly that her feet skidded against the worn floorboards and she had to grab the doorframe to steady herself.

This one was not empty. Her blood thundered in her ears. She smelled something sweet and rank like spoiled milk. A threadbare armchair faced the window. Beyond the high back she could see brown stubbly fields stretching to the horizon. They reminded her of the field she had walked across from the well. She remembered the razor grasses slicing the bottoms of her feet. There was a large hook mounted on the sill, a length of rope coiled beside it. She could clearly see a shirt-sleeved arm and the hump of a shoulder covered in a blanket. Slowly, balanced on the balls of her toes, she made a wide circle around the chair, barely breathing as more and more of the occupant came into view. *Please let it not be Lynn,* she prayed.

The cloying smell grew stronger.

She saw the hummock of a body, patchwork blanket pulled up high, covering everything but a hand, limp as a fish, and the curve of a pale cheekbone, like a sliver of the moon. It felt like déjà-vu.

Stroud.

She backed away, tripping as her foot snarled in the blanket. The cover slipped and she saw the red marks around his neck, the vivid bruising in the shape of fingers. She recalled how carefully he'd been tucked in at the cabin. As if he were a small, loved child. He was dead and had been for some time. There was no mistaking it. His lips were tinged blue and his eyes were open and staring at nothing, the skin around them starting to slough away.

A whimper escaped from her lips. She wondered at the strength it had taken to overpower him, kill him, to get him up to this room. Her eyes went again to the window and the rope.

She pounded down the stairs and out the front door into the yard, where she stood panting and looking in every direction. "Lynn!"

The road, her dad's red car, and then nothing but golden pastureland, wind-burned, rolling into dips and hollows, slashed with shadows that crept and crawled.

She looked toward a line of crooked trees, bent with age and pitched forward, their branches scraping against the ground. Parked underneath, partially concealed, was a grimy brown car. She'd seen it before, leapt out of its path as Jesse Caldwell drove it too fast, horn blaring, into the school parking lot.

She set her teeth in a snarl and re-tightened her grip on the screwdriver.

Jesse Caldwell. She would kill him.

Heart beating wildly, Ari caught the gleam of something among the dry stalks of grass and bent to pick it up. Lynn's tiger's-eye bracelet. Moaning, she slipped it onto her wrist next to the one she wore. Perhaps Lynn had dropped the bracelet on purpose as a clue, believing Ari would search for her.

"I am coming, Lynn. I'm here," Ari said, staring in every direction. But which way?

The scrubland dipped just ahead and she could hear the splash of rushing water. She headed toward the sound. A hundred yards on, the muddy ground fell away along a deep-carved river. More gnarled trees bent to the water's surface, trailing their knotted limbs and obstructing her view.

She stopped and listened hard. Water foamed and roared. The mat of leaves was thick, it was impossible to walk without making crunching noises, but she tried her best to be silent. Birds twittered and rustled in the undergrowth and pecked along the ground. She saw a shallow trench running through it, like a track made by someone who was not picking up their feet. It led toward a thicker growth of trees overhanging the stream. She could imagine Lynn stumbling along it, weak and dizzy. Or being dragged, perhaps. Where was Jesse? Was he watching? Waiting for his chance?

She crept closer, caught a flash of something white on the shore. A bird? A tangle of bedsheets? A person? Lynn? She ran toward the bank.

And then the breath rushed out of her as she was tackled from behind. The screwdriver went flying. She fought back furiously, throwing wild, awkward punches. Hot breath against her neck, her face shoved into the mush of leaves, something bony against her spine, a hand smashing against her lips. She managed to twist her body around so she was on her back; she brought her legs up to her chest and shoved away with all her strength. Jesse's face, red and sweaty, contorted, loomed above her. He opened his mouth and she launched a flurry of sharp-nailed blows at his eyes. He pulled back a little and the weight across her chest lessened, but he still held her trapped beneath him.

"Ari!" he yelled, but she was screaming curses back at him, her blood thundering in her ears as she twisted and fought, using her muscles, her rigid fingers to tear at him. To destroy him.

Jesse settled his weight more heavily, evading the punches she threw at his face. He gripped one hand by the wrist, and she arched her back and bit him in his fleshy palm. He cursed, letting go, and the small victory reinvigorated her. She struggled more wildly. His eyes alight with murderous rage, he tried to pin her arms again with his knees but she kept moving, snaking her torso and lashing out at him.

They were both breathing hard. Her lungs were burning fire.

"Stop fighting me, Ari," he gasped out. A trickle of blood ran from his lip. She felt a huge surge of satisfaction—at least one of her blows had landed.

She didn't waste breath answering him; instead, she struck out with her hands, elbows and feet and felt the reassuring thud of connecting with his flesh. He was tiring. She just had to keep moving.

He backed off. She leapt to her feet, staggering as a wave of dizziness overwhelmed her, and kicked him right in the balls. He fell to his knees and then his side, clutching himself. His eyes squirted tears.

"For fuck's sake, Ari," he screamed. "It's not me. It's her. Her!"

And now Ari saw her, rising out from the concealing shelter of the trees. Her—but not Dr. McNamara.

Miss Byroade. Ari scuttled backward, past Jesse who still lay moaning on the ground. Miss Byroade moved so fast that Ari didn't have time to shout a warning.

There was a length of pipe gripped in her black-gloved hand. It swung back in a wide arc, and then connected with Jesse's skull. He let out a high-pitched yelp and went still. Blood oozed down his forehead like a black slug. Miss Byroade stepped over his prone body, her eyes intent on Ari, the weapon held high.

Ari felt the echo of excruciating pain on the side of her own head.

"I knew you'd come, Ari," she said with pleasure.

And with a sharp inhalation that tore at her throat, Ari suddenly remembered everything. Those terrifying eyes, black pupils engorged so there was no iris visible, like a beast. She had seen that look before.

She retreated, desperately searching the ground for her screwdriver or something she could use. There was nothing but twigs. She pulled her keys from her pocket and held them between her knuckles, the pointy ends spiking out. And then the librarian was on her, as wiry and sinewed as some feral animal, far stronger than Ari was, though her body was slight.

She bore Ari over backward and they both fell to the ground with an impact that knocked the breath from Ari's lungs. The pipe crunched against her wrist and she dropped the keys.

Ari flailed desperately, her arms feeling heavy, her hands

open not fisted, digging into the leaves and soil and hurling them at the snarling face above her. Bucking wildly, she lashed out. Miss Byroade grunted, and the pressure against Ari's body lessened for a moment. Summoning a last vestige of energy, she threw herself aside and staggered to her feet. She backed away, searching for her keys. Too late she saw them in the grass behind the librarian.

"I'll be kind, Ari," Miss Byroade said, with a ghastly grin, raising the pipe in her black-gloved hands.

Ari was mesmerized by the gloves. She forced her gaze up to Miss Byroade's face. Her cheeks were red with exertion, her teeth slick with blood from the gash on her mouth. It looked like she was wearing a kabuki mask.

"Where's Lynn?" she screamed. "What have you done to her?"

"I'm going to take you to her," Miss Byroade said, moving forward.

Ari shook her head, feeling the terror rise and a scream lodge in her throat. Branches scratched the backs of her legs. The river was right there.

There was nowhere for her to go.

Miss Byroade lunged. The impact flung Ari into the air. She hit the ground and instantly the woman was on her again, slick hands tightening around her neck. She jerked her head back and forth, trying to break free. The white bundle was only a few feet away. She glimpsed black hair, a blue T-shirt, an arm. It was Lynn! Knocked out? Dead?

She redoubled her efforts, bucking and thrashing as the librarian's fingers constricted and she felt her awareness begin to slip away.

The ground tilted suddenly and they crashed into the stream, frigid waters closing over her head as the breath was snatched from Ari's lungs and blackness filled her eyes.

She spun and writhed. Utterly helpless.

The librarian pulled her to the surface and pressed her thumbs against Ari's windpipe. Her head felt as if it were going to explode. She struggled to get her feet under her, slipped, gasped and swallowed water. Her hands gripped Miss Byroade's wrists, easing the pressure against her throat. She kicked out and landed a solid blow, and finally she tore free.

Her clothing was soaked, heavy. She tumbled head over heels, unable to fight the inexorable power of the river. Her elbow hit a protruding rock with a crack she felt in her teeth; pain flared along the length of her arm, and then it went numb, hanging useless. Something ripped at her, clung. Miss Byroade had a hold of her again. Ari thrashed and her head smashed into something solid. Suddenly her wrist was free, but she was disoriented, weak. She swirled within the current, unable to fight against it. It would be so easy to give up.

All around was blackness. She was at the bottom of the well again. The surface miles above her head. She stared blindly at nothing. A stream of bubbles poured from her nose and she watched them dance, and then float upward. Her eyes followed the flight of a bubble. She remembered being told in lifeguard camp that that was how you orientated yourself underwater. That way was up.

She kicked her legs, feeling a desperate surge of energy propel her forward, fighting to reach the surface before the air gave out, battling against the current, hardly feeling the impact as her body repeatedly slammed against the rocks.

Her eyes filmed over. Her lungs were empty. And now her leg was caught. She reached for the wavering light above her. How far? Her hands opened and clutched at nothing. And then finally her head broke the surface, and cold air streamed across her face, and someone had her by the leg and was pulling her from the water.

She choked, gasping, and threw up, and then finally she could take a breath. Deep and pure, it hurt her lungs like a shard of glass and still she gasped until she had filled them again.

She collapsed on the muddy bank, chest heaving, water pouring from her nostrils. She had nothing left with which to fight and she lay there waiting for death to arrive. She could hear someone else breathing loudly. After many moments, she raised her head and looked beside her.

Jesse, with a purpling bruise on his temple, lay on his back. His fingers were still clasped around her calf, and near him, Lynn, so pale and sick-looking, curled on her side. Their hands were linked together, making a human chain, and she felt something almost like warmth travel from their bodies into hers, as if their veins were connected.

There was no sign of the librarian.

CHAPTER THIRTY-EIGHT

"Hi. Ari?" said a voice from behind her. It was so whispery soft that it took a moment for it to permeate.

Ari turned around. Miranda Taylor was standing with one hand on the back of the park bench. She looked like she needed the support to stay upright. Ari recognized the expression in her eyes immediately. That stricken, empty, hopeless expression. Oh yeah, she knew what that looked like.

"Can I?" Miranda said, pointing to the bench.

"Sure." Ari moved over a little bit to make room. She had come here almost every day for the past three weeks. It was around the corner from Dr. Barker's office, and she liked the view. It overlooked a long swoop of grass that disappeared at the horizon line. The kind of soft, gentle hill she and Lynn would have rolled down as kids or sat in the middle of making dandelion crowns. There were no trees, no bushes, no buildings anywhere on it. Nowhere for anyone to hide. It made her feel calmer.

The police and ambulance had shown up within twenty minutes of Ari calling them from the phone in the kitchen. It had taken her longer than that to stagger from the house back to the creek. The leaden weight of her body, the weakness of her limbs had surprised the hell out of her and she'd had to take frequent pauses to catch her breath. Neither Lynn nor Jesse could stand up without reeling. Her parents had cried, even her father. Uncontrollable sobs and since then, many hugs, apologies, check-ins and assurances that felt comforting but at the same time oppressive, like a really heavy blanket.

Just breathing the air, listening to birdsong, from a vantage point where she could see three hundred and sixty degrees, helped temporarily lift the claustrophobic feeling that regularly debilitated her.

Miranda didn't say anything for a few minutes but it didn't feel uncomfortable. Ari was just thankful that her mind was quiet for once, and that the sun was warm on the back of her neck.

She scratched at the crook of her elbow where the cast stopped and the itching drove her crazy.

"How are you?" Miranda finally said, her eyes going to the cast. And surprisingly, it sounded like she gave a damn. "We miss you at school."

Ari was doing her classes online on a trial basis.

"A month, two, three, whatever you think works," her dad had said. Ari thought that there might come a day, sooner rather than later, that routine—that everyday sameness—might be better than this limbo. Besides, she had started pining after the smell of the pool and even the chatter of the cafeteria.

"Everything is different now."

Ari shot her a quick look, noticed the swelling under her eyes, the papery look of her skin, the way her hands jittered—too many tears, too little sleep, too much coffee. She'd been picking at her cuticles too. She followed Ari's gaze and shoved her hands into the pockets of her baggy jeans.

"I want to know. How you are."

"I feel like shit," Ari said, tired of pretending otherwise. "My body hurts. I can't sleep. I cry all the time." Admitting it actually made her feel like she could make it through five minutes without crying. Or perhaps she'd used up her quota already in Dr. Barker's office.

Miranda took a deep breath and then sighed so loudly Ari figured she was completely unaware of doing it. "I'm sorry," she said. "I said some stupid things to you. I thought worse stuff about you."

Ari felt uncomfortable. She'd been equally superficial. "That's all right. I mean, bigger picture and all . . ."

Miranda gave a hollow laugh that turned into a sob somewhere along the way.

"Are you scared?" she asked. "Even now?"

"All the fucking time," Ari said.

Miranda shifted uneasily.

"You're not pretending," she said, "that everything is okay."

"I don't think I could pull it off."

"My parents say I need to move on from Stroud's death. The funeral was last week and there was that assembly and the bouquets and candles in front of the school . . . but no one is talking about him. It makes him seem even more dead. It makes it feel as if he was never alive."

She turned a tear-stained face toward Ari. "If we do that, then it's like she won. She erased him."

Ari took Miranda's hands in her own.

"Not as long as you remember," she said. "As long as *we* remember."

6

Ari walked into the café and scanned the room. It was the awkward time between breakfast and the lunch crowd and most of the chairs were empty. There were reporters crawling all over the town, but so far Captain Rourke had been able to keep her identity secret—she, Lynn and Jesse were listed in the news articles only as "three teenage victims." She knew it was just a matter of time though. They—the *survivors*, not *victims*, her brain reminded her—were visibly injured and suffering from shock. People were talking. Jack Rourke had already given a bunch of interviews as the grieving best friend.

Ari grabbed a cup of coffee with her uninjured hand and slipped creamer and a cinnamon bun into her pocket, nodding to Frances behind the counter. The woman's face was full of concern. Ari had avoided her bathroom mirror that morning like every other morning, but she knew she still looked bad. She forced a smile. A purple sunrise, Lynn called it.

"Mom told me to come down for some coffee therapy," she said.

"Okay, love. She's baking in the back. Lynn's been here for a bit, nursing a cappuccino," Frances said and blew her a kiss.

Lynn was tucked in a corner bench by the window. Her head was down and Ari took the opportunity to really look at her, noting her pallor, curved posture and trembling fingers. Lynn had never looked petite to her before.

It's weird, Ari thought, moving slowly across the floor, *how much physical abuse we can take.* Her whole body was bruised and battered, her left arm broken in four places, strips and chunks of skin missing from her knees and elbows. But none of that hurt as much as the knowledge, felt bone-deep, that Miss Byroade's actions had killed the childlike, innocent parts of them.

She cleared her throat, not wanting to startle her friend, put her mug down carefully on the table, and once she saw recognition in Lynn's eyes, she slid in next to her and slipped her arm gently around her thin shoulders.

"Hey, sweetness," she said, hugging Lynn quickly and then moving away a little.

"Too much and I feel like I'm going to shatter in a million pieces," Lynn had told her. "Just knowing you are nearby is enough. Just knowing you came for me."

Lynn straightened her posture and took a deep breath.

"So how was your session with old Barker?"

"He's good at getting me to tell him how I feel. He talks around things. It makes it easier."

"He's got me meditating. He's gonna Zen all the punk rock right out of me."

They both laughed and Ari felt the tightness in her chest loosen a little.

"Sleeping better?"

"Sure," Lynn said. "You?"

They both knew that Lynn slept with the light on and all her windows open. Ari had told her dad to leave the blackout shutters up, and she often woke to find herself curled up on the floor.

"Yup."

They smiled at each other, recognizing the lie.

Fake it till you make it.

Dr. Barker had mentioned sleep aids, but Ari didn't ever want to sleep that deeply again. She wanted to be aware. At all times.

Lynn slid her hand into Ari's and they laced fingers.

Life was full of gaps, Ari realized, like a worn carpet. And somehow they'd have to fill the holes themselves, and rebuild something solid enough to hold them both. She looked at their linked hands. This was a good true thing. A strong thing. In this moment she felt like nothing could ever break their friendship apart. They were bonded.

"Jesse," Lynn said, nodding toward the door.

He spotted them, grinned and limped over.

They'd become a trio without even discussing it. Since everything had happened there hadn't been a day that they hadn't spent together. Not doing anything in particular, just hanging out, not even talking that much.

"I just ran into Miranda," Ari said, grabbing an extra cushion from a neighboring chair. She'd bruised her tailbone while she was in the water. Then, considering, she amended it to, "I mean, I think she was waiting for me. It wasn't random or anything. She thought I could help or something. I feel so sorry for her."

"Stroud was still an asshole," Jesse said, taking the chair across from their bench. "Now it's like he's a saint or something. Even the kids he treated like shit are going around all teary-eyed."

"Better that than that he be forgotten," Ari said slowly. "And all anyone remembers is that he was some kid who was murdered. Most of them don't even know his name." She blinked hard until the tears receded.

"Jack Rourke is totally pissed he had no idea what was going on. It's knocked him off his block," Jesse said with a satisfied grin. "Don't ever tell him he made the suspect list for a hot minute."

Ari shook her head. "I should have known he didn't have the smarts," she said. "But I wasn't exactly thinking clearly."

"How are you?" Lynn asked Jesse, touching the back of his hand briefly.

He smirked and gave their stock answer. It almost felt like the password for a secret club. "We survived. That's always a good day."

"So," he continued. "Did the doc ask you about your chronic bed-wetting?"

"Shut up, you idiot," Ari said with a wan smile. It was just a joke, but she couldn't help but think of the trifecta of warning signs for serial murderers. Bed-wetting, fire-starting, pet killing—just some of the knowledge she had acquired in the last month.

"What? Mine asked me. I never did wet my bed, but he seemed so disappointed I told him I did."

Lynn flicked some coffee foam at his face. He raised his hands in mock surrender.

"Anything come back to either of you?" she asked. Part of Lynn's self-prescribed therapy was piecing together all the different parts of the puzzle that was Miss Byroade. Time was divided into Before Miss Byroade and After Miss Byroade.

"I remembered how I got to the cabin," Ari said. Dr. Barker also used hypnosis and relaxation techniques. Until today they hadn't yielded results, but this time, something clicked, and another small door opened in her brain. Once she'd been able to visualize where she was on that Friday afternoon, the images had come, rolling out like a strip of film.

"And?"

"I should have been smarter. I mean, it just sounds ridiculous now that we know."

"Hindsight," Lynn said, "is a motherfucking bitch." She fiddled with her bracelet, and Ari checked for her own as well.

"Hey, you came closer than anyone else," Jesse said. "It wasn't until I saw her grab a cat off the street that I started wondering." He looked sheepish. "I *started wondering* if she was not the odd yet gentle library assistant we all knew. Talk about being stupid."

"Ari didn't say she was stupid," Lynn said hotly. "She was naïve. Like we *all* were. Anyway, go on," she told Ari.

"So, I went back to the library that day. There was this book I remembered seeing, written by this woman who had been married to a serial killer and hadn't known until he got caught trying to kill his fifteenth victim. And I wanted to check it out, see if I could get some insight into how a murderer would hide their true self even from those closest to them. I wrote down some notes and Miss Byroade started asking me a bunch of questions." Ari shook her head. "I told her that I suspected there was a psychopath living in Dempsey Hollow, because of the butchered pets."

"What did she say?"

"She was so sympathetic. I think she put her arm around me." Ari shuddered. "I hate the thought of her hands on me."

"She's dead, Ari. She can't touch us now."

"That's right, Ari. We won," Jesse said fiercely.

"She said she was sure I was right. I left, and a little while later, she pulled up beside me in her car. And then she told me she'd just seen Sourmash with a dog. She thought she'd discovered another killing zone, a fresh one. I think she actually used that word. She was shaking with what I thought was outrage, but now I think it was excitement." Ari swallowed hard. "And so I said I'd go with her to check it out and catch Sourmash in the act." She felt the beginning of a bad headache coming on, something that had continued to plague her since her time in the well.

"And what about Stroud?" said Lynn, scooting closer and propping Ari's shoulder with her own. Ari leaned into her, comforted by her warmth and solidity.

"He was in her car. He was pretty much passed out. She had brandy and I drank some just to settle my nerves. I was so set on us catching up to Sourmash that I didn't really think about him. He was mumbling and laughing, just saying stupid shit about how high he was. She said she was giving him a ride home. I trusted her—" Her voice choked off.

Taking a deep breath, Ari continued. "Once we got to the cabin I followed Miss Byroade into the woods. Stroud got out too and went into the cabin. He could hardly walk." They exchanged glances, and Ari knew they were all thinking the same thing: Stroud had gone into the cabin and Miss Byroade had killed him there.

"I should have done something. I noticed she was watching you. Like, all the time," Jesse told them. "With this intense, hungry gleam in her eyes." He ducked his head, and then looked at Lynn and back at Ari with an almost sorrowful expression.

"I started tailing her and then following you, but it was nothing specific, just a bunch of suspicions." He thumped the table, making the coffee mugs rattle. "When I ran into you in the maze, I'd just watched her bury a plastic bag out there. I dug it up. Two dead kittens."

"Were they . . . ?" Ari couldn't help but ask. *Flayed* was the word that had sprung to her mind.

"No, just dead. Really dead." Jesse swallowed audibly. "I should have said something to somebody."

"No one would have believed you," Lynn said, fussing with a scab on her lip.

"I wouldn't even have believed you," Ari said, handing her some lip balm. For a moment Lynn looked at it as if she wasn't sure what it was.

"And then, that day—" He paused. Lynn gave an almost imperceptible nod. *That day* would always only mean one day for all three of them. "After you pulled the fire alarm, Ari, I saw her at the school. She was there. And I followed her out to the house. I was so stupid. I just figured I was going to be able to deal with whatever happened."

"When she changed," Ari said, giving voice to the memory that still visited her in nightmares, "it was like watching a wolf go from lying in the grass all lazy and sleepy to ripping open a deer."

Lynn's face whitened. She'd been looking out the window and her eyes went wide and blank. She let out a shuddering breath. "I need to tell you." She paused and Ari interlocked her fingers with Lynn's. "It was the same for me. I was on my way to meet you, Ari, after getting that text-to-voice message . . ." She gulped. "Of course, it *wasn't from you.*" She took another deep breath and continued. "I was going to the bookstore to pick you up the new Mary Russell mystery as a peace offering, and she drove by, stopped and offered me a lift. She said she was on her way to the bookstore too. We were chatting, and she pulled over behind a gas station. And then she went quiet . . . and her face transformed." Her hand went to her throat. "She got her hands around my neck so fast, I passed out before I even knew what was happening."

"Hey, at least she didn't hit you with a lead pipe. I feel like the dead guy from *Clue*," Jesse said. His tone grew serious. "There was nothing human in her. Nothing."

Frances had put a Vince Guaraldi CD on—Ari always imagined Schroeder from the *Peanuts* cartoon bent over his tiny toy piano while the rest of them gathered around Charlie Brown's pathetic tree. She felt tears burn at the back of her throat. Once upon a time her world had been all about presents and comic strips and Linus with his smelly old blanket that transformed from a thing of comfort into a weapon.

Her mother bustled in from the back room, carrying a platter of assorted cupcakes. "I thought you might be hungry," she said in a forced cheerful voice. "There's chocolate ganache, salty caramel and lemon buttercream."

She put them down in the middle of the table and looked at them expectantly. Ari reached for one and then held it in her fingers. It looked huge. Impossible to swallow. She put it down beside her uneaten cinnamon roll.

"Eat them all. Please," Ari's mom said, dropping a gentle kiss on the top of Ari's head. After a moment, she did the same to Lynn, and then to Jesse, before whirling around and disappearing into the back room.

"Moms," Jesse said wryly, but he looked pleased. "My grandmother's been making me the full roast beef dinner every night. I think I'll puke if I see another fluffy mound of mashed potatoes."

Ari pushed her cupcake around. "Fixing the world with butter and sugar."

"Mine's let me choose dinner and a movie every day this week," Lynn said. "The L.H. just about imploded from the injustice of it. And the Shits are staging a full rebellion."

"Mark probably thinks you just did it for attention," Ari said, cursing herself when the shadow fell over Lynn's face again. "I'm sorry. I shouldn't have said that."

"It's okay," Lynn said. "You're totally right. I think he's working out how to get kidnapped and held for ransom." This time the smile stayed in place for a few seconds.

"She was twenty-four," Jesse said abruptly. "Not that much older than we are."

Just like that the atmosphere became dark and oppressive, as if every lightbulb had blown at the same time. Lynn grabbed Ari's hand.

For a moment they all stared at each other, eyes flicking away and then back again. Ari saw some of the wariness they had in common. A knowledge, an alertness that most people were lucky enough to escape. She thought she'd learn how to handle it, but worried about Lynn and hated seeing the traces of fear, the sadness sketched on her face.

Jesse cleared his throat and pulled his hat down lower over his forehead. Ari couldn't help notice that he'd spooned about half a canister of sugar into his coffee and now he couldn't stop stirring it.

Under her cast, her arm itched. She groaned and wriggled and Lynn let go of her hand to pass her a spoon. Ari tried to poke the end in to scratch it, but she couldn't reach the spot.

Lynn found the words that were juddering around inside Ari's head. The thought she woke up to and went to bed with. "Is she dead? Are we sure?"

"The police found a black glove," said Jesse.

"And?" Ari couldn't help but ask.

"I saw her go under."

Ari hadn't seen anything. She'd been drowning.

"While you were calling the cops, we watched the river to see if she'd surface," Jesse said. "And they sent divers in and they dragged it."

"She was so strong. It was as if insanity made her stronger," Ari said.

"She was crazy but she wasn't invincible. Like us." Jesse's voice drifted away, and an uneasy expression crossed his face. "She drowned," he said finally. Emphatically.

Ari wondered who he was trying to convince.

"The creek cuts into a ravine for a few hundred yards," Lynn said. "They think her . . . body probably got trapped in there. Underground."

Ari shuddered. It must have been a horrible way to die.

Miss Byroade had tried to kill all of them, but still Ari couldn't really equate that woman with the one she'd thought she'd known. Known and liked. Then she thought about how the librarian's face had transformed into a mask of rigid, emotionless control. It just didn't seem that a river and some rocks could extinguish that kind of energy.

"I survived it," she said.

"Because we pulled you out." Jesse shook his head. "No way to get divers into the ravine, but no sign of her anywhere else."

Ari wished with her whole being that she could believe it.

"It's been three weeks. They set up road blocks. And alerts. She's dead."

But the question that kept circulating through her brain and waking her in the middle of the night was *what if she isn't?* She could have survived too. She could be out there, disappearing and then appearing somewhere else, as someone else. Ari tried to remember what the librarian's face had looked like in repose. It was blurred, no features distinct, except for those weird, unfocused eyes. It was easy to imagine that people would barely register her; that she could slip off one mask and put on another, look younger or older at will. Ari felt a chill slip up her spine. She was the perfect predator. She had evolved.

"What do you think, sweetie?" she asked Lynn, who had her head down, staring at her untouched food.

Ari had shredded her cupcake without even noticing. She swept the sticky crumbs up into a pile, wiped her fingers on a napkin. She pushed the platter toward Jesse, who had already eaten two and now helped himself to a third. At least her mother's feelings wouldn't be hurt.

"I think she's dead," Lynn said finally. "What I want to know is"—she looked up, her face crumpled and tear-streaked—"why she did that to me."

Ari felt her heart break. There were no words. Time was what was needed. That was what Dr. Barker had told her, and what she was sure Lynn's and Jesse's therapists had said as well. Time for things to balance themselves out again. For life to regain some semblance of normality. Ari wasn't even sure she knew what normal was anymore. What had happened was too raw, too recent, too overwhelming.

"It wasn't you. She was insane. She was psychotic. It could have been anyone. Random," Jesse said.

No motive. That was one of the things that made serial killers so hard to catch. They killed for the thrill of it, Ari thought.

"She selected me," Lynn said, shaking her head. "She had a plan. You know it." She turned to look at Ari. "She chose you too. Out of everyone out there, Miss Byroade picked us both, Ari. What does that mean?"

It was a question without an answer, but still it hung heavy in the air between them. Without realizing it, they all drew closer together.

"I forgot to tell you," Jesse said, raising his head. "The police have her sketchbook."

Ari shuddered. She didn't think she'd ever forget those drawings. They were like a window into Miss Byroade's mind. A diary of what she'd done and what she planned to do. Her grand design.

Not Byroade, she thought, *Rose Columbine Maddox.* That was her real name. Three names, like all the famous serial killers.

CHAPTER THIRTY-NINE

I bitterly regret the loss of my sketch diary. The police will pore over my words and art and they will understand nothing. They will vilify me.

Two things give me comfort.

I have always been good at making myself useful, at ingratiating myself. Every small town and big city needs volunteers for the soup kitchen or the library or the school cafeteria. I will find my place again. After all, I have my boning knife with me.

Everything else I need—my tableaux-to-be, all the beautiful details, their faces, their scents and mannerisms, my experiences—still live and evolve, imprinted in my cerebral cortex where memories are preserved.

Even Ari's phone number.

ACKNOWLEDGMENTS

Thanking people always makes me feel like I'm Sleeping Beauty's parents—sure to forget to invite someone crucial to the party—but here goes:

My fierce agent Ali McDonald at The Rights Factory for going above and beyond in all things always, and for enervating drinks in airport bars, and Diane Terrana for her incredibly valuable and incisive editorial input.

Editors extraordinaire Lynne Missen and Peter Phillips, and everyone at Penguin Random House Canada, as well as Linda Pruessen, copy editor, and Sarah Howden, proofreader.

Amazing writer friends who gave much-needed critical feedback and/or talked me down from the ledge: Alison Gaylin, my critique partner E.M. Alexander, Kat Kruger, Elisabeth Bailey, Charles de Lint and Lynn McCarron.

For unending love, support and punctuation, my beta readers Susan Treggiari and Silvia Rajagopalan.

And Charise Isis, Nancy Wilson, Charity Valk, Madeleine Kendall, Kelly Jane Barker and Lisa Doucet—because YOU! And me without you equals not fun.

Thanks to Doug Kearney for the website and human answers to all my cyber questions.

Much love to Deb Lavin, Denirée Isabel and Miss Sara J.

Also Darrin White who let me interrogate him for hours about butchering animals with humanity.

Thanks and accolades to indie booksellers everywhere, specifically (since I co-own it) Lexicon Books in Lunenburg, Nova Scotia, and my delightful partners in books and wine, Anne-Marie Sheppard and Alice Burdick. Eternal respect and love to the libraries, librarians and library assistants of the world.

My kids, Milo and Lucy, who are the reason for everything I do.

And you, Dear Reader.